HE'S YOUR EX FOR A REASON

BRIANN DANAE

He's Your Ex For A Reason

By BriAnn Danae

PROLOGUE

Prologue
SUMMER 2016

-

SHANAE

Sniffling sounds came from the passenger seat of Isaiah's Lexus, and he released a heavy sigh. He knew Shanae's sniffles, mumbled curse words, and sucks of her teeth weren't because she was sad. No. Shanae was highly pissed off and surely wasn't about to repeat herself.

Not tonight.

Not tomorrow.

Not anymore.

"It ain't what you think," he voiced lowly, and Shanae sucked her teeth again in annoyance.

"It's not what I think?" she hissed. "You all of a sudden know what I think now? Were you thinking about me when you gave that girl my money for an abortion?"

Seething with anger, Shanae tried with all her might not to go upside Isaiah's head. She wasn't a violent lover.

She wasn't violent at all, honestly. That wasn't how they got down. All the love she had for Isaiah was pure, from the heart, and consumed her entire being.

For so long now, he was all she knew. The only person she wanted to give herself and love to. Be the person he needed during any time of the day or night. But, things had changed; drastically. Shanae no longer wanted to participate in the games he played, hear the lies that coaxed her ears or suffer from the tugs on her heart and character anymore. She was done for good this time.

"I ain't give that girl no damn money for anything. Why you listening to that dumb shit anyway? You don't trust me?"

Turning in his seat some, Isaiah stared Shanae in her dark brown eyes. They were filled with hurt, but more than anything, disappointment. Not in him, but with herself. This wasn't the first time he cheated and had done some sneaky shit behind her back, but on everything she loved, including him, it'd be the last.

"So, what happened to the money I gave you? You told me you were supposed to re-up with it, and now you claim you're broke. Just... make it make sense."

Isaiah could only shake his head. He'd forgotten all about telling her he needed the money to re-up. That wasn't a complete lie, but not the complete truth either. Shanae's nerves grew worse as she waited for an answer.

She always seemed to be waiting on an answer from him, or an explanation. Simply put, she was tired.

"You know what..." she began and Isaiah cut her off.

"Look, a'ight," he breathed heavily. "I did make her get an abortion."

Shanae swallowed hard. "With my money? The money I gave you as my boyfriend who was in need of help?"

She just wanted to make sense of it all.

When Isaiah nodded and mumbled a yeah under his breath, Shanae reached back and slapped him across the face so quickly, he never saw it coming. Tears flooding her eyes, Shanae clenched her jaw and shook her head.

"I'm done. This relationship is clearly not something you want anymore and hasn't been for a while. I hope she was worth it."

Groaning, Isaiah reached for her, but she was already climbing out of his car. "Shanae! Come on, man."

Shanae slammed the passenger door and rushed inside her 2-bedroom apartment before he could come after her. Locking the door, she inhaled a deep breath and let the tears leak from her eyes. For months, she'd been praying and asking God to remove anyone and anything that didn't belong in her life anymore. And, like only He could, He gave her the sign. Another one.

Before Shanae would ignore them, and she was

guessing that this was the cause of her disobedience. Isaiah had hurt and embarrassed her before, but nothing of this magnitude. Not only had he cheated, but he'd lied to her, gotten another woman pregnant, and used her damn money for her to get an abortion. His actions disgusted Shanae to no end, and after years of tolerating the disrespect, she was finally taking back what was rightfully hers; her dignity.

KALI

Hours later across town, Shanae's cousin Kali, was dealing with problems of her own. After lying in bed with her boyfriend for hours wide awake, Kali had finally decided to leave while he was sleeping. Their relationship was toxic and draining the life out of her. A life she used to enjoy living.

Kali had put up with the bullshit even though she knew she shouldn't have, but for a purpose. Mentally, she had prepared herself to leave. Physically, it had taken some time but now was her breaking point. Not bothering to pack any of her belongings she had at his place, Kali booked it to her sister's house and was there in less than fifteen minutes.

At three in the morning, Kamilla opened the door for her younger sister and sighed. She loved her more than anything in this world, but something had to give. Instead of lecturing her, they sat on the couch and Kali vented. She'd been bottling her emotions and depression in for so long, releasing her pain to someone she knew would never judge her lifted a much-needed weight off her body.

"So, what you plan on doing now?" Kamilla questioned.

"About what, Erik? I can't be with him anymore. He's... he's so fucking toxic Milla, it's sickening. I tried telling him I just wanted to be friends and he spazzed out on me."

"Did he put his hands on you?"

Kamilla's voice was stern and face angry. Had Erik's punk ass laid one finger on Kali, she was calling their brother, Kross, up. Forget what time of the morning it was, Erik was going to get touched. Shaking her head in a hurry, Kali lied. Erik had choke slammed her after she tried explaining to him that their relationship just wasn't it for her anymore. That was only his second time being physically abusive to her, but the mental and verbal abuse had been going on for much longer.

He was her first love, and over the years had become very narcissistic. Every single issue within their relationship somehow was Kali's fault. All blame would be placed on her if they argued and he'd somehow become the victim in it all.

Erik had gotten his act together and started treating her right, but Kali was already disconnected. The love she once had for him had faded. As she laid there in bed with him after crying, she thought back to the times within their relationship when she should've ended things. When she had a thousand reasons to leave. Before, Erik thought just because he had apologized and was changing *now*, that everything was sweet. It wasn't. Kali just wanted her old self back, but it was too late.

"No. Please don't go running your mouth to Kross. He has nothing to do with this," Kali pleaded.

"Yeah, well he will if I find out—"

BOOM! BOOM! BOOM!

Kamilla and Kali both jumped, holding their chests as obnoxiously ear-piercing knocks came to her front door. Kali's heart rate skyrocketed, knowing it could only be one person knocking on her sister's door like the damn police at this time of the morning.

"Kali! I know your ass is in there!" Erik shouted, pissing Kamilla off.

She lived in a nice townhome with neighbors who did not play that loud, disruptive shit. Especially at three in the morning. Hopping up from her loveseat, Kamilla went to open the door, but Kali stopped her.

"No! Wait. Don't open it. I don't want to see him right now."

"Well, you need to do something. He's not about to keep banging on my door like he's lost his damn mind."

The thing was, Erik had. Waking up to an empty side of his bed and no call or text from Kali, Erik was losing his patience with what he considered her petty behavior.

"Erik, please just go away! You're doing too much right now."

"Nah. I ain't doing enough. How the fuck you gon' dip out after telling me you're pregnant? What type of shit you on, Kali?"

Blinking back tears, Kali looked down at the pregnancy test in her hand. It was now wrapped in a paper towel but concealing it did nothing to change the positive results. Earlier that evening, Erik caught her taking the test, and that's when she told him that they could co-parent and just be friends. He still choked her. Kali knew then that if he'd put his hands on her while she was carrying his child, he'd do anything to hurt her.

"I just want peace, Erik. Why can't you understand that?" she damn near cried.

Erik was silent for a moment. "It's another nigga, huh? That baby you carrying belongs to somebody else, and that's why you trying me? You lucky I can't get to you. On my mama, I'd break your fucking neck," he seethed.

"See how you talk to me!" Kali screamed. "It's not about another man. It's about me and my unborn child.

8

About my sanity and safety. I'm too young to be dealing with this shit!"

"Okay," Kamilla spoke calmly. "That's enough. Erik, you need to get from in front of my crib."

"Ain't no breakin' up with me, Kali. If that baby is mine, we stuck for life baby girl," he chuckled arrogantly, making chills cover Kali's frame.

She wasn't scared of Erik. She was simply fed up with him as a person... the person he'd become. It was just her luck when she was ready to end things, she popped up pregnant. Getting an abortion wasn't an option. Though their situation wasn't ideal, Kali knew the consequences of having unprotected sex. She knew if she was grown enough to take dick, she would have to be grown enough to take care of a child. There was no other option in her book.

Walking back over to the couch after hearing Erik's car burn rubber out of the complex, Kali placed a hand on her flat belly. She wasn't sure how far along she was yet but would soon find out. Though her life seemed to be in shambles right now, she knew it'd be back on track soon. Her decision to keep her child wasn't one she needed convincing on.

Leaving Erik was a tough decision, though. Not for the safety and health of her child, but for her. She'd been with Erik since she was sixteen years old, and after five years walking away wasn't how she thought they'd end. Kali just wanted him to do right by her, but tonight proved he wouldn't. Regardless of how many times she knew he was going to beg, plead his case, and try to make her the bad person in the situation, Kali was done. Sometimes you have to make decisions that will hurt your heart but heal your soul. She was willing to place her own needs on hold for her child's; no matter how heartbroken she felt at the moment.

LAYLA

Letting her eyes roam the guy in front of her, Layla pulled the thin, cotton dress she was wearing over her head. Comfortable in her rich, russet reddish-brown skin, she laid back on his bed and caressed her pierced C-cup boobs. She was ready to get their fuck session over with. To Layla, that's all this was with Rodney. That's what all the men she sexed and left on read were to her. A sure way to satisfy her sexual needs with no expectations of them, and no explanation from her.

"Damn," Rodney groaned as she stroked his dick. "Your hands so fuckin' soft."

It was long, thick, and pretty; just how Layla liked them. Ripping the gold wrapper open with her teeth, Layla sheathed his member and flipped over on the bed. Now on all fours, Rodney was given the perfect view of her sickening arch, slim waist, glistening pussy lips, and her need for him. Rubbing his hand back and forth against her folds, Layla exhaled as her mouth watered.

When Rodney's warm mouth covered her before his tongue massaged her clit, Layla knew damn well she wasn't regretting her decision now. At first, she'd tried talking herself out of fucking Rodney, but it was no use. This was who she was and what she did. Though he was an associate of her boyfriend, Liam, Layla felt no remorse as she threw her pussy back into his eager mouth.

"I knew that pussy tasted good," Rodney exclaimed, lightly smacking her ass.

"I bet you did," was Layla's reply.

Grabbing his member from behind, she stroked it a few times and aligned him at her opening. Pushing her hand away, Rodney struggled a bit fitting inside her, but when he did...

"Goddamn, girl," he huffed in utter disbelief.

Layla exhaled softly and arched her back. The dick was good, but she'd never liked giving a man the satisfaction of verbally saying it. If she was wet and hadn't kicked him out, he could be content in knowing the dick wasn't trash without her voicing it.

Stroke for stroke, Rodney put it down on Layla as if she belonged to him. As if she wasn't his boy's girl. Was he in the wrong? Hell yeah, but Layla was dead wrong. Her promiscuous ways had always seemed to get the best of her, even when they shouldn't have. She was trying to fill a void not even Liam could, and for that, she was remorseful. He didn't deserve to get cheated on, but she had warned him.

Layla specifically told him she wasn't the girl to fall in love with, but Liam didn't take heed. Her warnings of not being able to give all of herself to him, commit, and change who he thought wasn't the real her, weren't enough. Layla didn't maliciously cheat; she'd curved the pressure of it for months... until she couldn't. Her appetite for chasing a new, exhilarating rush, outweighed the need to be in a healthy relationship.

Tightening the hold on her waist, Rodney pumped into her with force before releasing into the condom. With his eyes sealed shut, he tried to control his breathing and get himself together, but Layla gave him no time for that. Pushing him back some, Rodney withdrew from her soaking entrance and licked his lips at her small, but plump ass.

"Damn, no cuddling?" he joked, and Layla cracked a light smile.

"Absolutely not. I need to be making my way home."

Just as she climbed from the bed, her phone's ringtone resounded loudly throughout Rodney's bedroom. Slipping her dress over her head, Layla answered Liam's call and placed him on speaker. There was no need to hide who it was; they'd already betrayed him. Rodney shook his head when he heard Liam's voice.

"You have fun tonight?" was Liam's question.

Layla frowned. "Um, sure. Why'd you ask that?"

"Shit, you had to have kicked it hard for you not to be at home. I been parked outside your crib and calling your phone for like two hours."

Purposely, Layla placed her phone on Do Not Disturb for an allotted amount of time while she was with Rodney. Liam's call came through at perfect timing; sort of.

"I'm on my way there now."

Liam chuckled. "Where Rodney at?"

Layla stilled at his question. Slowly, her head turned toward Rodney, and her hazel colored eyes squinted in his direction.

"Who?"

"Ah, come on Lay. Don't play dumb now. I know you over that nigga's house. You fucked that nigga, man?"

Liam was hurt. She could hear it all in his tone. Layla's question was, how did he know? Never wanting to be considered a liar, Layla answered one of his questions. The first one.

"He's standing right here."

A long breath escaped Liam's mouth. He was pissed,

but more hurt than anything. The fact that he'd practically set this entire ordeal up and it backfired had him looking a fool. To save face, he threw every warning Layla gave him in her face.

"I knew it. I knew you was a fucking hoe, and I loved your ass. Ask that nigga how he wants me to send his money."

Layla had been called worse, but to hear him mention money had her seeing red. "Money? What the hell are you talking about?" She swiveled her neck and directed her next question to Rodney. "He owes you money for what?"

Rodney sucked his teeth. "Man look, Layla," he began, and she knew he was about to speak some complete bullshit. "Liam paid me to see if you'd let me fuck, to see if you would cheat on him. I already got half of it, but I don't even want the other half, ma."

Layla's stomach dropped to the soles of her pedicured feet. An ache she'd never felt before resided in the crevices of her chest as her breathing became choppy. With blurred vision, she blinked back tears as her entire body grew hot. She'd been disrespected before, for being her honest self, but this? No, this was on a level she'd never thought Liam would go. They had been good up until now.

When Rodney first approached her being mad

friendly, she brushed it off. Men were like that sometimes. But, when his advances started to actually pique her interests, and he went out of his way to treat her kindly, she thought maybe there could be a real friendship between them. Layla messed it up wanted to sample the dick. Had she known all along that was the reason for Rodney pursuing her, she would've been fucked him and got it over with.

The fact that Liam had actually paid another man to see if he could have sex with his girlfriend crushed Layla. She'd been faithful to Liam, turning down more guys than she ever had, and was all about him. To know he didn't have faith in her or trust her hurt... bad. So bad that Layla's hurt morphed into anger within a blink of her watery eyes.

"Did you get your answer?" Layla spoke into the phone. Her tone even and damn near condescending.

"What? To see if you were a hoe like I thought?" Liam chuckled. "Yep."

"Good because I never wanted to be in a relationship with you anyway. Niggas like you deserve to get cheated on by girls who fuck their homeboys. I was faithful to you, Liam. Never once had I stepped out on you, and though I thought about it, you didn't deserve that. I guess tonight was meant to be, huh? With my hoe ass," she snickered, and Liam's jaw flexed in pure anger.

"I should've listened to my moms, cuz. You a foul ass bitch, dawg."

"Takes one to know one. You played yourself. And, if you were wondering, the dick and head was just as bomb as I knew it would be. Fuck you, and I hope the thoughts of me fucking your friend piss you off forever. Stupid mothafucka," she spat, hanging up in his face.

Going to her settings, Layla blocked Liam's number, slipped her checkerboard Vans on her feet, and grabbed her purse. Rodney stood there, unsure of what to say or do. He was ultimately the reason why Layla was now single and would possibly be colder than a bitch toward men now.

"Aye, Layla. I ain't mean for—"

"Yes, you did," she cut him off. "But I get it. You wanted to sample what's in between my legs and not feel bad about it because you were doing your boy a favor. I get it. If anything, you should've kept it real from jump. Probably would've let you fuck way before now," she shrugged, and Rodney scratched his head perplexed at her words.

He'd never in life met or witnessed a female who owned her shit like Layla just had. Men were dogs by nature, but her? Layla was a different breed; one he respected and wanted to get to know even more now. That was Liam's issue to begin with and why they were here now. Liam was trying to change who she was, and he almost had, but Layla was just... stuck in her ways. Rodney didn't want to take the other half of his pay. It didn't mean a damn thing to him now.

"Um, a'ight," he mumbled, confused by her reply and the situation. "Let me walk you to the door."

Layla giggled and waved him off while securing her long locs in a ponytail. "No need. Save that gentleman shit for the next female you get paid to fuck. I don't need or want the pleasantries."

With that, Layla walked out of Rodney's bedroom and out of his apartment. Taking slow strides to her car, her thoughts immediately went back to the conversation with Liam. *Had he been trying to catch me slipping?* She thought, climbing inside her Jeep. If that was the case, Layla couldn't understand why of all the men, she fell for Rodney. He wasn't anything special, honestly.

"I just don't understand. I wasn't even messing around on him," she grumbled, feeling disappointed in herself more than anything now.

"Now, I'm single because I fucked one guy," she chuckled, wiping the warm tear that rolled down her cheek. "Coulda been hoeing way before this if that was the case."

Layla wasn't a hoe, though. She'd only opened her legs for a handful of men in her twenty-four years of living, but she did entertain them. Get their hopes up and then bruise their egos when they realized she wasn't as easy of a catch as they assumed. Liam was different though... or so she thought. The one man she thought she had something good with, even with her slip up, had proved her wrong.

Layla didn't know why tonight had gone down the way it did, but she knew there was a reason. There was always a reason to the madness, and now Liam was forever going to be the ex-boyfriend who was the cause of the way she was treating men from now on. They weren't going to be given any chances of a real relationship with her.

"I guess relationships with people aren't my thing," she chuckled but was okay with that. It had been that way her entire life now, so what was the use in change, especially when it hurt this bad?

1

Present Day
SUMMER 2019

Bent over in her kitchen with her hands grasping the granite countertop, Shanae moaned loudly and winded her hips. After ignoring his calls and texts all day, she'd finally given in and let him come over. She couldn't remember dick, his specifically, feeling this damn good.

The grip he had on her waist loosened some before his hand slid into her thick, curly afro. Snapping her head around, Shanae glared at him.

"You know not to touch my hair," she hissed before moaning as he smirked and stroked deeper. "Mooove."

"Make me," he spoke lowly.

Clenching her muscles around his dick, his hand glided down her back. It was covered in a thin layer of perspiration. Gripping her love handles, his strokes became deeper, harder, more purposeful. Shanae had already come twice and was glad he had finally reached his peak.

"Damn," he groaned. "I missed this pussy."

Shanae rolled her eyes and went to reply, but the sound of her front door being unlocked halted her harsh words. Standing up, she snatched her shorts over her behind, tugged her tank top down and pushed the guy toward her pantry closet.

"Man," he chuckled stumbling over his shorts while trying to pull them up. "Whatchu doing?"

"Go in there," Shanae hissed quietly. "I don't want her to see you over here."

"Hell, nah. I ain't hiding out in no closet."

The front door opened and Shanae groaned. "Isaiah, please. Come on."

Sucking his teeth, Isaiah let her shove him into the

closet and close the door behind her. Walking out of the kitchen, Shanae picked up the can of air freshener, spraying some in the air while faking like she had been cleaning up, rather than getting her back blown out. When her mama rounded the corner with grocery bags in her hand, Shanae smiled.

"Hey, Mama. I didn't know you'd be here so soon."

"I told you three o'clock. Don't tell me you forgot," Sharee sighed at her daughter and looked over her attire. "That's why you're still in the same clothes you had on when I talked to you on FaceTime."

"Ma, I was cleaning up. I didn't realize it was this late."

"Mhm," Sharee hummed, walking toward the fridge. "Who's truck is that outside?"

"Huh?"

"If you can huh, you can hear."

Snickering, Shanae shrugged her shoulders. "I don't know. Probably the maintenance man. They've been coming by changing people's air filters."

"In that nice truck? They must get paid real nice around here. Let me tell your cousin he needs to apply," Sharee said and reached for the handle of the pantry to put Shanae's cereal away.

"Wait!" Shanae screeched, causing her mother to turn around. Calming down, Shanae giggled nervously. "I mean, don't put the box up. I'm going to make me a bowl."

Curiously, Sharee stared at her daughter. "What's wrong with you? You high?"

Shanae busted out laughing, and her laughter wasn't the only one that could be heard. Her eyes widened at the sound of Isaiah's manly laugh. Looking back toward the pantry, Sharee tooted her lips out and pulled the door open. Inside, Isaiah had a goofy grin on his face.

"How you doin' Ms. Sharee?"

"I'm fine. I would ask you what you're doing in here, but I'm going to mind my business. You know your ass is too big to be trying to hide somewhere."

Chuckling, Isaiah walked out of the cramped pantry and brushed a hand down his head. "You right. Was just abiding by your daughter's rules."

"I don't know why. Y'all are grown. How's that little girl of yours?"

Shanae sucked her teeth. "Ma."

"What? I'm just making conversation."

Isaiah looked Shanae's way and frowned before shaking his head. "She's good. Getting big."

"I bet she is. They grow so fast. Well, let me get out of here and give y'all some privacy." She left out but stopped when she passed the dining room table and picked something up. "By the way, if y'all were trying to hide, this condom wrapper was a sure giveaway. Glad you're wrapping it up though, honey. I'm not quite ready for grandkids yet."

Palming her forehead, embarrassment flushed Shanae's face as her mother tossed the gold wrapper in the trash and walked out her apartment. In such a rush to get a quickie in, Shanae had forgotten all about the wrapper.

"Ugh," she groaned. "That was so embarrassing."

"You know yo' mama be getting dicked down," Isaiah said. "Ain't nothing embarrassing but you acting like you had an issue with her asking about Jazlynn."

Rolling her eyes, Shanae tried walking by him to place the cereal in her pantry, but he grabbed her arm. They had a stare off for a few seconds before Isaiah let her arm go.

"You a trip, man."

"What? I didn't even say anything."

"You ain't need to. It's written all over your face. Got this stank ass attitude 'cause she brought my daughter up."

Sighing, Shanae leaned against the counter and faced him. "What, you wanna argue with me now? I just don't feel it's necessary for her to be asking about her like that. She's your child, not mine."

Isaiah drew his head back and shook it. "You on some disrespectful shit, for real. Only reason she brought her up is 'cause you probably be mentioning shit to her. Yo' ass claim you hate people in our business but stay running your mouth."

"That's my mama, Isaiah."

"Don't matter. One minute you all in love with a nigga again, the next you pissed 'cause of our past. Make yo' mind up, man."

Now he has an attitude. Shanae thought and rolled her eyes. Not bothering to answer him, she walked out of the kitchen and to her bedroom. Of course, Isaiah followed behind her. She wasn't trying to argue with him today, especially about his daughter. The topic alone still made her sick thinking about it.

It'd been three years since that conversation in his car, and Shanae found out he cheated. Three years of learning to love him less, keep him at a distance, and focus on her. Somehow, within that time, she kept him at arm's length for only so long before he was right back in her space. Her head, heart, and bed space.

She'd tried to let him go. Let the love they shared dwindle and chuck it up as a mistake and bad judgment on his end, but nothing had changed. They'd only aged, and while Isaiah seemed to be creating a life without her, Shanae kept trying to hold on and include him in hers. Again, after what should've been a lesson learned, here she was taking the course again. That sign she'd asked

God for clearly wasn't the one she was looking for. It couldn't have been.

Isaiah watched intently as Shanae moved around her room, gathering an outfit. She and her mother had plans for the evening, and sitting here arguing with him wasn't on the schedule.

"You gon' keep staring at me, or you have something you need to say?" Shanae questioned as she looked at him through her mirror.

"You changed man," he muttered as if he were disappointed.

"That's just like a nigga to break your heart and then tell you you've changed. Did you expect me to stay the same?"

"Might as well have. You still fucking with me, ain't you?"

"And, that can quickly come to an end. All we do is fuck Isaiah. Let's get that out there now."

Arrogantly, Isaiah stroked his beard. Plenty of nights Shanae had grabbed him by that beard and kissed his dark lips to hush him up. That was one of the many attributes of his handsomeness that Shanae loved. No matter how good looking he was though, it couldn't make up for the ugly things he did to her. That's what Shanae couldn't get over.

"You stay saying that, but your feelings are involved. I

know you Shanae. Ain't no need to front with me. What you ain't gon' do is keep bringing up my daughter like she's a problem. If you can't accept her anymore, then we don't have shit to discuss straight up."

"I just don't get how she ended up pregnant right after you made her get an abortion. Did she not get one? Just tell me the truth. I won't get mad."

"Why you wanna talk about this shit, man? I'm 'bout to leave," Isaiah said, standing up from her bed.

"Why can't you just tell the fucking truth?"

Shanae's voice quaked in anger and disgust. For so long he'd stuck to the story of Natisha getting pregnant months after she'd broken up with him, but Shanae felt like that was a lie. The timing of their break up and the birth of his daughter Jazlynn wasn't adding up. Tucking his hands in the pockets of his shorts, Isaiah eyed her with sincerity.

He loved Shanae in his own kind of way. What he considered to be the love she accepted from him. The only kind he seemed to offer up. They just weren't meant to be, and she was in a way forcing what they used to have on him every chance she got.

Accepting the small amount of time, attention, and affection he did give her sufficed her needs. Shanae, for some reason, didn't mind coming second to everyone he put before her. She was back settling worse than when they were in a relationship just for that smidgen of comfort she was so accustomed to. It was sad, but she didn't know how to shake it. After taking three years to find herself and a man who cherished just being in her presence, Shanae was still settling for the bullshit.

"Tell you the truth for what? It ain't like it's going to change anything. You ain't going nowhere. I got a daughter, she ain't going anywhere, and if that's so hard for you to accept then I guess this is where we can end things... again."

Shanae's throat ached. The familiar feeling of being hurt by his truthful words always crushed her tough girl resolve. As bad as she wanted to tell him okay and let him walk out, she couldn't. The words to formulate a full sentence to utter wouldn't align in her brain.

In a sense, Isaiah was her security blanket. That's what she saw him as because as long as she wasn't offering another man her time, energy, and love, he couldn't break her heart too. Isaiah was a dangerous yet safe zone for Shanae, and she hated it. Hated herself for not being able to shake him and whatever the hell they called themselves doing.

"I didn't say I never accepted her, I'm just still hurt behind it all. But, whatever. It's fine."

"You sure 'cause you know Jazlynn loves you too," he said, walking up on her.

She's two nigga. Damn baby doesn't even know me. She thought but kept her comments to herself. "Mhm. Positive."

"Good," he said, kissing her lips and pulling her into him.

Shanae's thick, 5'5" frame fell into his as he hugged her tightly. His words and actions were always on different pages. Rubbing his hands down her back and stopping at her ass, Isaiah gripped it like he knew she loved and kissed on her neck.

"You know I love your little ass. You gotta move on from the past, ma. We starting fresh from here on out."

Wrapping her arms around him, Shanae rolled her eyes and melted into his embrace at once. "I love you too."

Pulling back, Isaiah looked down at her with a smirk and kissed her full lips again. "You better. Call me later and have fun with ya moms."

"I will. Be safe in them streets. You know they don't love nobody but themselves."

That's why Isaiah loved her. Why he abused her loving, he had no answer. "I'm always safe, baby. These niggas know not to play with me."

Shanae had heard him tell her that plenty of times. Regardless of how he'd hurt her, she always prayed over his safety. His daughter hadn't asked to be on this Earth, and that's all she thought about whenever he was out being reckless.

Hopping in the shower, Shanae chastised herself for once again accepting the bare minimum from Isaiah. She was a damn good woman, and he knew it. Using the love she had for him against her. Though she felt played, and for a good reason, Isaiah had really played himself. He may not see it now, but he'd feel it later. That's just how the universe worked.

While quickly brushing her teeth, Shanae rushed around her room trying to find her other sandal when Sharee walked in. Admiring her daughter from the door, Sharee grinned. She was the spitting image of her. Shanae's warm umber colored skin was smooth, blemish-free, and had a natural highlight. Her natural 4a/b hair was a mixture of black and light browns, fluffy and fit her round face.

"You look pretty," Sharee commented as Shanae picked out her large 'fro.

Smiling, she blew her a kiss through the mirror. "Thanks, Ma. I get it from you."

"You know it. That's why I don't understand why you settle for a guy like Isaiah. Instead of cherishing you like a gem, he doesn't. And, you let him. Why? You don't have to settle for him and none of his baby mama drama Shanae."

Sighing heavily, Shanae applied her lip gloss. Adding a second coat, she snatched her phone off the charger. "I'm not settling, Ma. Isaiah and I are comfortable with what we have going on. As long as I'm happy, you don't need to worry. I forgave him."

"But are you happy, though? You can forgive him without giving him access to you and your heart. Forgiveness takes more than just brushing issues under the rug, and acting like it never happened."

Shanae knew the heartbreak happened; that's something she'd never forget. Those restless nights crying her eyes out looking for a sign as to why. That was her main question. Was it something she'd done? Had he been ready to leave before then, what? A fear of never finding a love better than what they shared settled over her for a while and this is how she was right back at square one. The fear of losing herself again to a man who cheated and mistreated her. What was the point in that when she could just stick to the no-good nigga she already had?

"You need to forgive yourself. There are men out there who will never ever put you or your feelings to the side to appease their own. You're a beautiful, young, black woman and do not need to be spending your twenties on a man you have to tuck away in your pantry because you're embarrassed by him. That's not love, baby."

Shanae nodded and swallowed the lump in her throat.

"Everyone plays the fool sometimes, Ma. I guess I'm just going through another phase."

She wanted to make it work with him but knew it never would. What they used to have is nothing like what they have now. Shanae was lying to herself while Isaiah continued to feed her the same lies. Until she was completely fed up with him and his mediocre loving, Shanae would continue to miss out on what life truly had to offer.

"I hope this phase ends soon; I truly do. Let's hurry so we don't miss our movie," Sharee told her.

Taking one last glance in the mirror, Shanae followed her mama out of the apartment. She too hoped this phase ended soon. Isaiah was still draining the life out of her, leaving her empty. Even if another man did come along and swoop her off her feet, she'd have nothing to offer him because she'd given all her love to a nigga who had no clue what to do with it besides abuse it.

2

Holding her cell phone between her shoulder and ear, Kali headed down the hall to her son's bedroom. Wiping the sweat from her brow, she huffed and adjusted her damp tank top. She'd been cleaning her apartment from top to bottom all day and lost track of time.

"You don't need to send much. Just a few outfits," Ms. Rhonda, Erik's mama, said into the phone.

That's all I was sending anyway, Kali thought preparing her son's overnight bag. "Okay. How far did Erik say he was again? I shouldn't be long."

"About ten minutes away."

"Okay. Well, let me get my baby's stuff together. Can you send me some pictures?"

On the other end of the phone, Ms. Rhonda grinned. Khyri was her first grandson, and she treated him as such. She was thankful Kali didn't show her ass and act a way with her like her other son's baby mother's did. They each had daughters by one of her oldest sons Elijah and drove her crazy.

"You know I will. We'll call you later."

Telling her okay, Kali hung up and sat her phone on the TV stand. Her music began to blast over her speaker in the kitchen. *Love, Thought You Had My Back*, by Keyshia Cole was just the song to get Kali in her feelings.

"I loved you for your ways, but your ways hurt me bad boy. Hurt me so bad why you wanna see me sad boy? I'm tired of crying over you, but I miss you so much I don't know what to do," Kali sang, feeling every single word Keyshia sang.

Getting over her first love, her first everything, was tough. Tougher than Kali thought it'd be. From the beginning, she knew a guy like Erik wasn't any good for her. He was a self-proclaimed bad boy; the type who didn't settle down with any female. Kali didn't know how or what she did to him, but Erik had turned his player card in for her... for as long as she could hold her breath.

When they met, Kali was twenty-years-old. At five years older than her, Kali surely thought Erik was the mature man her mama said would come into her life. Before Erik, she'd dealt with young niggas who didn't want anything more than to have sex with her. Kali wasn't going for it, not until she met Erik. Easy on the eyes, with his caramel skin tone, 6'1" frame, dope boy attire, and charming words, he immediately captured Kali's young mind.

Manipulation at its best was played by Erik until he really fell in love. He approached Kali thinking she was a good girl and green to the type of games he was attempting to run on her. Green Kali was not. Her brother, Kross, had laced her with the game but somewhere in between giving her heart and virginity to Erik, Kali had fumbled.

Getting pregnant and being in a verbally/mentally abusive relationship was not in her plans. Kali didn't regret having Khyri at all; he was her pride and joy. Had she not been so conflicted with her emotions back then, she would've left Erik before she got stuck with him for life. Regardless of when Khyri turned eighteen, Kali knew Erik would be in both of their lives until one of them left this Earth.

Stuffing the last pull-up in Khyri's Ninja Turtle backpack, three knocks resounded at her front door. At two and a half, Kali was so sick of buying diapers it wasn't funny. The minute Khyri started tugging at his diapers, she began potty training. That in itself was a daily struggle, but he was getting the hang of it. Strutting to the door, Kali tugged her shorts down over her ass and pulled her door open.

"Took you long enough," Erik grumbled. "What up?"

"Not a thing. Here you go," Kali rushed, holding the backpack out to him.

With his face frowned up, Erik pushed her hand away and stepped inside her apartment. Behind him, Kali had no choice but to close the door. It was hot as hell, the beginning of summer, and her air was on full blast. Inhaling a deep breath, she released it slowly before turning around. Erik was staring directly at her.

"I ain't welcomed in yo' crib no more?" he asked, a smirk dancing in the corners of his mouth.

"You in here ain't you?"

"Here you go with that smart mouth shit."

Kali waved him off dismissively and placed the backpack on the couch. "Whatever. What you want, Erik?"

Kali was going to have to repeat her question. Erik's eyes were glued to her toned legs, slim thick frame, and her ass as it jiggled with each step away from him. It was a struggle for her to gain weight and make it stick until she got pregnant. This wasn't the first time Erik had noticed her curvy frame, but it'd been a minute for sure. Those little shorts she was wearing had his dick hardening, and he knew if he had any chances of sliding between her legs, he'd have to play nice. Kali had slipped up once and let him hit while in her feelings, so he was definitely trying his luck today.

Following her into the kitchen, Erik leaned against the counter as she washed the dishes. "I'm just checking on you. Can I do that, baby mama?"

Kali cut her eyes at him. "Can you bring my baby's shoes back this time?"

"Fuck is you talkin' 'bout?"

"Every time I send some nice shoes with you or yo mama, either they don't come back, or one is missing. Same with his clothes. No one is funding for that but me, so I'd appreciate it if y'all send it back with him."

All thoughts of playing nice with her went out the window. "What you mean ain't nobody funding for his clothes and shoes? Like I don't drop bread to you every other week. My mama buys him shit all the time. You better gon' with that bullshit."

"Nah, nigga. You better gon'. You drop bread for daycare and toss a little extra cash here and there. I work hard for every single dollar I bring in this house, and there's nothing wrong with me wanting you to bring

Khyri's stuff back to where it belongs. It's simple, honestly."

Erik stood back watching her rant and had the right mind to go upside her head. As pretty as she was, her mouth was reckless. That was the shit Erik couldn't stand. He had definitely judged a book by its cover. Kali's bright fawn skin, full pink lips, soft facial features, and faint voice gave off the impression that she couldn't take it there. But, she most definitely could. Especially when it came to anything concerning Khyri.

"Aye, man," Erik chuckled in a pissed off tone. "Don't piss me off with that bullshit you talking. Trying to talk bad like I'm some deadbeat ass nigga."

"No one said any of that. Just have the same respect for the things I buy him, the same way you do for the things you buy him," Kali said rinsing the last bowl.

Turning around, she momentarily forgot what she was about to do next. Erik may have worked her nerves like no other, but he was fine. Too damn fine for his own good. Rocking a gray Nike jogger shorts set, black Nike shoes, and a fresh cut showing his impeccable fade, Kali shook the sexual thoughts of him out of her head. Remembering what task she was doing next, she tried bypassing him in the kitchen, but Erik pulled her to him. Jerking away Kali put some space between them.

"Boy," she chuckled, nervous jitters swarming her belly. "What? Don't be grabbing on me."

"Lemme' ask you something."

"You just did."

Erik's facial expression turned serious. "Who you been fucking with?"

"What?" Kali questioned, brows pinched in confusion. "Where did that come from?"

"Just answer the question, man. You been messing around with another nigga?"

Kali knew where this conversation was headed, and she did not want any parts. She knew he'd only asked her that because he was probably getting some bullshit info from his cousin Bobbi. A few months before Erik met Kali, Bobbi's boyfriend, Murda, was trying to holler at her. Kali had turned his advances down not even knowing he was in a relationship, but Bobbi didn't care. She saw her man all in another bitch's face, and since then she'd had it out for her. To this day, Murda still had a thing for young Kali, and Bobbi hated her for it.

"What does me messing with someone have to do with you?" she asked, crossing her arms over her chest.

"Everything!" he boomed, making Kali flinch, stumbling into the counter some.

"Okay," she spoke evenly. "I think it's time for you to go. You're doing too much."

As she walked away from him, Erik's nose flared. Kali not answering his question had him hot, but her walking away from him had him about to blow a gasket. It was a blatant sign of disrespect in his book.

"Nah," he grumbled, reaching out and grabbing her by the back of her neck with force. "I ain't doing enough seem like."

"E-Erik. Get the hell off of me!"

Shoving her into the couch, Erik held her down by her neck. "What nigga you got around my son, huh? You think some other nigga about to play stepdaddy to mine? You got me fucked up."

In the position he had her in, Kali couldn't swing her arms, but she damn sure could use her feet. Lifting her right foot, she kicked him hard in his shin, making him loosen the grip he had around her neck. That was all the room Kali needed. Swiftly, she turned over and pushed him off of her.

"What the fuck is wrong with you!?" she screamed.

"You! You my mothafuckin' problem. Got some lame ass nigga around my son," Erik huffed, walking up on her.

Kali scrambled to the opposite side of the living room and picked up one of the statues off the table. "On my son, I'll fuck you up in here. Back up," she spat.

"Why you can't answer the question, huh?"

"'Cause it ain't none of your damn business! That's why!"

Erik began walking her way but stopped when the front door opened. Kali was facing the door, so she saw her brother walk in before Erik did. Turning around, Erik couldn't help but frown when he saw Kross.

"What you in here doing all that hollering for?" Kross addressed his sister, peeping the scene.

"'Cause I'm irritated."

Tossing Erik a head nod, Kross plopped down on the couch and grabbed the remote. "You cook?"

"No," Kali replied, putting the heavy statue down. Grabbing Khyri's bag, she held it out for Erik to take.

Smirking, Erik licked his lips and nodded his head up and down a few times. "You got that Kali. We ain't done with this conversation."

"Yeah, whatever."

Walking out the front door, Erik hopped in his Challenger and peeled out of her complex. Rubbing the back of her neck, Kali exhaled and closed her eyes for all of five seconds. Erik had to have been high or out of his damn mind to have put his hands on her. Not wanting to tip Kross off about what had just gone down, Kali got herself together and moseyed toward the couch to sit down.

"Where you coming from?" she questioned.

"The barbershop. What yo' baby daddy want?"

Cracking a smirk, Kross glanced his sister's way. After confiding in Kamilla when she found out she was pregnant, Kross and their father were the last two she wanted to tell. Kali was the baby of the family, and the men in her life treated her as such. Kross spoiled she and Kamilla both, and Kali knew he'd be disappointed in her for getting pregnant at such a young age. Kross was more hurt than anything though.

His disappointment only lasted for about a week, and then he was bugging her every day until Khyri was born. That was his little partner in crime now, and no one could tell him shit about his nephew.

"Stop playing with me," Kali mumbled rolling her eyes.

"What? That's what he is, shit."

"I promise becoming a baby mama was so ghetto. Why couldn't I have waited?"

Kross not knowing if she was serious or not cracked up laughing. The expression on Kali's face said she wasn't joking at all, but he couldn't hold his laughter back.

"Aye," he wheezed, trying to catch his breath. "You funny as hell, man. I ain't gon' lie though. That shit only ghetto 'cause of the nigga you got a kid with."

"Ugh. Tell me about it. Anyway, I know you didn't stop by here just so I could cook you some food?"

Going to Netflix on her TV, Kross nodded his head.

"Yeah I did. Ma or Milla didn't answer the phone, so you were my last resort."

"You lucky I love you," she said, mushing him in the head and standing to her feet. "You need to find you a nice wholesome woman who can cook you meals in the middle of the day. That's where Khyri gets that mess from."

"Nah. I don't want no good girl. I'm addicted to these hoes, sis."

"Clearly. These hoes aren't going anywhere; trust me. You need to go ahead and give Milla and me a niece or nephew," she smiled.

Kross sucked his teeth. "Now you talking crazy. Erik must've knocked you upside the head or something."

Damn near, Kali thought. Had Kross walked through the door a minute sooner, they wouldn't be having this conversation. Kross never had a problem with Erik. As long as he took care of Khyri and respected his sister, everything was all good. Kali kept Kross and her family on a need to know basis. She made the mistake of airing some of their business out one time, and some of them still hold it over her head. The only person she confided in on a regular was Shanae.

"Whatever. What you want to eat?"

"It don't matter. Cook up whatever's in there," Kross replied, getting comfortable on the couch.

43

Pulling food out of the fridge and freezer, Kali began to prep for some Philly cheesesteak sliders and homemade fries. She had no plans on cooking since she'd just cleaned up, but for Kross, she'd make an exception. Plus, it was Friday, and she had nothing better to do since Khyri was with his daddy for the weekend.

Tomorrow though? Kali was heading downtown to do something she should've done years ago. Why it had taken her so long to try to put what they had behind her, she wasn't quite sure yet. Today confirmed that though. Regardless of the love she used to have for Erik, it just wasn't there anymore, and she wasn't going to pretend like it was to pacify his feelings. All Erik was at this point, and moving forward was Khyri's dad.

B iting down on her bottom lip and balling her hands into fists, Kali exhaled a deep breath. The shading when getting a tattoo was the worst part for her. Especially in the spot her tattoo artist was working on. What once used to be Erik's name tattooed right underneath her right breast, big as hell, was now a beautiful sunflower arrangement. The vibrant yellow popped gorgeously against her skin tone, and Kali couldn't wait until it healed completely.

"A'ight. We're all done," her artist Juelz said. "Let me grab the mirror so you can see it and then I'll wrap it up for you."

Wincing as she sat up some, Shanae gave her cousin a smile. "It looks good. Makes me want to get one."

"You should," Juelz chirped. She had over twenty tattoos and wanted more. She just had to figure out where to get them at.

"If I decide to, I'll be sure to come to you," Shanae told her.

"Oooh! I love it."

Kali maneuvered her body side to side and smiled. She was so glad to finally be putting her and Erik's past behind her. On a whim one night, they both went and got each other's names tatted. At the time, Kali thought it was the most romantic thing for them to do, and now thinking back, it was one of the dumbest decisions she'd made.

"I'm glad you like it," Juelz smiled.

Putting some ointment on the tattoo, Juelz made sure Kali was good to go before they headed toward the front of the shop. Her light steps glided across the checkerboard tile as her eyes roamed the walls of the hall. Scattered across them were various pictures of different celebrities and other artists, lyrics from rap and R&B songs, and Kali's favorite; mirrors. As she stopped to fix her eyelash in a gold triangular framed one, the sound of her name being called halted her movements.

Turning on her feet, Kali glanced into the room across from her and grinned. Damn near blushed, honestly. "Hey."

"What up, schoolgirl."

Playfully, Kali rolled her eyes and stepped further inside. "Here you go with that mess. What're you getting done?"

"My niece's names. They've been begging me to put their names on me, so shit. You know how that go," he grinned, exposing his gold bottom row of teeth, before licking his lips.

Kali wanted to agree with him, but she had momentarily lost her train of thought. Rondo's warm brown skin, full silky brows, and chiseled jawline held her captive. She'd caught herself staring at him plenty of times in class, admiring his handsomeness, but there was something about him barely clothed and off of campus that had her seeing him in a different light.

"You got some new ink?"

"What'd you say?" she asked, as he snapped her out of her lustful daydream.

Rondo smirked, already knowing she was checking him out. "Your tat, ma. What'd you get done?"

"Oh," Kali chirped. "Some sunflowers and birds. You know... something girly."

"That's what's up. You'll have to show it to me once it heals."

Kali hoped he hadn't heard her swallow the lump that formed in her throat. "It's not necessarily in a place that's easy to show off."

Rondo's piercing dark eyes trailed her frame, and he gave her an easy grin. "Shit. Even better then. It'll be for my eyes only."

"Whatever. Let me get out of here. Will you be in class Tuesday?"

"You gon' be there?"

Kali chuckled. "Now, you know I'm always there."

"That's all I needed to hear then. I'll be there."

"Mhm, I hear you. I'll see you on Tuesday, sir."

Rondo gave her a head nod. "Fasho. You be good, schoolgirl."

Shaking her head, Kali walked out of the room and headed to the front. Juelz had already taken her next customer back, so all Kali had to do was pay the receptionist.

"How was everything?" the receptionist asked nicely.

"Great as always. Whoever runs this place does an amazing job. Much better than the previous owners," Kali spoke truthfully.

"That's good to hear. Mhazi, the boss, loves to make our customers and clients happy."

After paying, Kali and Shanae left out the building. The sun in California was not letting up one bit. It was so hot, Kali was thinking about cutting her hair. As much as she knew she'd regret it later, she didn't care about it at the moment.

"It's too damn hot out here," she huffed, hitting the unlock button on her key fob.

"Who was that guy you were speaking to?" Shanae asked.

The grin on her face couldn't be hidden even if she tried. "Rondo. We have a summer course together."

"He's kind of cute."

"Kind of? Girl, that nigga is fine. Ole hood ass. He's just the type I need to stay away from, for real."

Kali wanted to believe she'd learned her lesson with Erik, but there was just something about a bad boy that she couldn't shake. She didn't know if it was because she'd grown up around them all or what, but Rondo was just her type. He was the perfect combination of an educated, hood gentleman that she craved.

"Maybe not. I saw how you were looking at him," Shanae smirked, giving her cousin the side-eye. "He can't be any worse than Erik."

"Oh, chile. No nigga is worse than him. I can guarantee that."

Shanae snickered but stopped when she thought about her current predicament with Isaiah. "Isaiah may have him beat. Did I tell you he got mad at me for not letting his daughter stay at my house while he ran an errand?"

The last part of her sentence was spoken with air quotations from her fingers. It seemed since their conversation about accepting his daughter or not, Isaiah had grown a much bigger pair of balls. Ones Shanae had to let him know needed to shrink some. It was one thing to accept Jazlynn, but to be a damn babysitter? Oh, no. Shanae wasn't built for that.

"You lying?" Kali gasped softly, looking her way.

"I promise. It took everything in me to tell him no, but I'm glad I did. Like, damn. You already had a baby on me, and now you want me to watch her? What type of time do these niggas be on?"

"Bullshit o'clock. I would've cursed him out something serious. He got his nerves. Where was his baby mama at?"

Shanae rolled her eyes and shrugged. "Probably at work. You know we work together."

"Oh, nah. See," Kali chuckled. "I'd be fired."

"She hasn't said anything to me yet."

"And she better not. I don't give a fuck about coming up there and whooping her ass. You're too young and too pretty to be this stressed about Isaiah's ass. One day, these niggas are going to realize they lost the best thing to happen to them, but by then it'll be too late."

"Honestly?" Shanae sighed. "It already is."

Kali couldn't help but agree. Covering Erik's name up today was proof of that.

3

"And you know it's crazy because I once used to love. I loved a man so deep I could've drowned. There was no life jacket to save me, and praise me for the efforts I'd put in. I was just... getting swam over and pulled under into the tide. Lost in what I believed was good for me. But do we really know what the fuck is good for us?"

The crowd laughed and snapped, encouraging Layla to continue. She was in her zone now.

"I mean, what the fuck is good for me? And, who is he to make any calls on where we should be? I wanted to do nothing but lay, nakedly, exposed sinfully, to the way my body craved his. The scent of him and sound of his timbre as he whispered in my ear, stroked me deeply, erupting inside me. Giving me a high not even my edible could take me... and then he'd make me remember why I wasn't built for this shit. Cause hurt people, hurt people. And I was the hurt person who gave a fair warning of who I was and what I couldn't be. But, he didn't listen. So, we laid, nakedly, painfully, exchanging energies with one another even though they were sinfully... delicious."

Layla paused and exhaled softly.

"So, yeah. I used to love. I used to love this nigga so deep that when he cut me, the wound was so intense I did end up drowning. And no one was there to save me. Not even myself."

A standing ovation is what Layla received when her set was done. She hadn't rehearsed one bit before coming on stage, and the crowd loved it. *Mic Check* was the place to be on any given weekend, and for Layla, this was new for her. She only ever performed on Tuesdays or Thursdays. Something in her spirit led her to perform on a Saturday, and she wasn't regretting it at all.

Smiling and taking in the audience, Layla told them thank you and walked off stage. She felt like she was floating thanks to the crowd's crazy energy and the edible she'd taken. It was a small peach ring, but it had her smacked like shit. Giggling to herself, she headed to the bar to grab a bottle of water.

"You expect someone to follow up after you just killed it like that?"

Turning to her left, locs swaying against her back,

Layla eyed Q. He was a well-known poet/singer that performed at *Mic Check*. Layla had been getting flirtatious vibes from him since they met over three months ago and she was tired of the meaningless conversations between them. Q was everything Layla would have wanted in a man, physically, if she were ready to settle down.

Three years closer to thirty, Layla knew exactly what she wanted. Q's sensual voice is what turned her on to begin with. His poems were explicit, sprinkled with a dab of love, and finished off with what Layla considered to be a panty-wetting performance. Had she ever worn any. Inhaling his scent, Layla made up her mind right there on the spot that she was going to sit on his face, sample the dick, and make it home before the sun touched the horizon.

"I would suppose so. That was light work."

Q smirked. "Cocky."

"Confident. Was there something you needed from me?"

Without a hitch, Q openly thanked the man above for Layla. In his eyes, her body was a masterpiece. Perfection if he could consider it that. Her hips were sharp, stomach flat in her red tube top, and small but plump ass poking in her long skirt. What attracted him most was her daring eyes, septum nose piercing, and long locs.

"What if what I need from you, you aren't willing to offer?"

"Closed mouths don't get fed, now do they?" Layla replied, not bothering to answer his question.

Stepping closer into her space, Q wrapped a hand around her slim waist. "In that case, would you like to come back to my place?"

Though she knew she was going to say yes, Layla decided to give him a hard time. Smirking, she removed his hand from around her waist.

"Actually, I don't think that's a good idea."

Q's entire face masked a look of confusion. Damn near hurt by her decline. "Oh. A'ight. I'm trying to get fed, and you want to starve a nigga, huh?"

"The longer you wait, the better it'll taste," she smirked, walking away from him and to the bar.

Watching her walk away was almost better than seeing her coming. Shaking his head, Q took a swig of his water. He'd been sipping Hennessey all night and had to drive home. If he had any intentions on getting Layla back to his place, he needed to at least make it there.

At the bar, Layla ordered a basket of honey glazed wings and a side of celery with ranch. Turning in her seat, she watched a young girl who couldn't have been any older than twenty rap over a sick beat. Bobbing her head, she caught the lustful gaze of Q who was ducked off in the corner. Blowing him a kiss, Q playfully caught it.

"Have I waited long enough?"

That was Q's question to Layla as she stood in front of him in his bedroom. The bar was closing in an hour, but the two made their exit before then. Back at Q's place, Layla seductively tossed her locs into a bun, stripped from her skirt, exposing her bare flesh, and removed her tube top. Stepping closer in between Q's legs, she softly shoved him back onto the bed and straddled his face.

"I don't know, but let's find out," was her reply.

The first swipe of his tongue against her slick folds had Layla buckling at the knees. She should've known a nigga who could sing like Tank and Vedo, could definitely eat some pussy. Straight devour it.

Gripping her thighs, Q licked on her clit as if he hadn't eaten a thing all day. The taste of her was so satisfying, throaty moans escaped him as he brought the first orgasm out of Layla.

"Sshhit," she hissed, body quaking. "Fuck. Just like that."

Reaching behind her, Layla tugged his boxers down and began to stroke his dick. His thickness had her a little apprehensive, but the constant flickering of his tongue eased her worries. She was leaking, and Q wasn't letting a drop of her essence go to waste. Smacking her ass, he slurped on her clit, causing Layla to come again.

"Oh, hell yeah," she moaned, rotating her hips.

"I knew this pussy was good. Damn, girl," Q huffed, guiding Layla off his face. His very drenched face.

Layla tried not to roll her eyes at his statement. For as long as she'd been having sex, majority of the guys she had sex with always claimed they knew her pussy was good. At first, she didn't know whether or not to take it as a compliment or an insult. As if they'd been waiting to sample it. Either way, Layla never delved on it for long. What were facts was that they were right.

Reaching for the condom on the dresser, Q opened it and rolled it over his erection. A satisfied moan left her lips as she slowly slid onto him. Finding her groove, she fucked him like she'd wanted to for three months. Q was trying to make love, wanting her to slow down, and kissing on her neck, but Layla wasn't having it. Hopping on her feet, she put some distance between them.

Staring up at her, Q softly smacked her ass. "You better ride this dick."

"Oh, I am."

Layla smirked and flexed her muscles around him. Q's eyes closed and his grip on her waist tightened. She was putting it on him like he was fresh out of jail. No more than twenty minutes later, Q was releasing in the condom and Layla was trembling from her third, no fourth, hell whatever orgasm she was on.

Huffing, she climbed from atop Q and licked her lips. "Damn, it's late."

Looking at the time on her phone, Layla hated that she had to drive home but staying the night was not happening. Ever. No matter how late it was, sleeping in a man's bed wasn't an option.

"It is. You might as well stay the night," Q offered, slipping the condom off and sliding his boxers on.

"No. That's okay. I'ma use your bathroom then head home."

Layla ambled to his attached bathroom, peed, washed her hands, and walked back out. As she slipped her clothes on Q watched in bewilderment. It was damn near four in the morning, and Layla was dead set on going home. Realizing he didn't know her at all, Q's first assumption was that she was trying to get back home to someone.

"Layla, you single?"

"It's a little too late to be asking that don't you think?"

She could never just answer a question. Q shook his head.

"You got to be the way you leaving up out of here. I'll sleep on the couch. You don't need to be driving this late."

Layla sighed. "Quentin, I'm fine. Trust me. I'll text you when I make it home."

Knowing there was no changing her mind, Q stood from the bed and walked her to the door. At it, he tried placing a kiss on her lips. Chuckling, Layla turned her head, letting his lips land on her jawline. Kissing was way too intimate in her book.

"Damn. I can't kiss you? My lips were just all over you."

"That's a little too much for me."

Q shrugged. "Yeah, a'ight Ms. Layla. You have a good night and let me know when you make it home."

Heading down the steps of his building, Layla spotted her car, hopped in and headed home. She'd left before the sun had come up as promised, and she couldn't wait to shower and get some sleep. Thankfully, she was off work this weekend, so sleeping in didn't sound too bad. It took her all of twenty minutes to get home, and she yawned for what seemed like ten of them.

Driving until she came to her building, Layla sucked her teeth in frustration. At four in the damn morning, the last thing she wanted to be doing was knocking on her neighbors' doors to see who had parked in her spot; but she would. As much money as she paid in rent, someone was going to get woke the fuck up tonight.

Cutting her car off and snatching her keys from the ignition, Layla got out and locked her doors. The apartment complex she lived in was one she didn't see herself moving from anytime soon. At least not until she was ready to take on the responsibility of maintaining a home. Her neighbors were polite, the dogs didn't do a bunch of barking, and no one ever parked in her designated parking spot... until now.

Having a good idea of what cars belonged to whom, she tried figuring out who's company the car belonged to. She didn't have to wonder for long though. Hearing the sound of footsteps coming down the stairs, Layla eyed the thickly shaped woman walking in front of her neighbor. Layla had to hold in her chuckle. The girl looked thoroughly fucked, as so did she.

"Is this your car?" Layla asked her.

"Yes. Is there something wrong?"

"Just the fact that it's four in the morning and you're in my spot. Next time, please let your guests know to park where they're supposed to."

Her statement was for Brody; her fine ass neighbor. Well, not quite her neighbor since he lived three doors down, but he still counted as one. Even in the dark, his handsome features stood out. Bronzed mahogany skin, a set of white teeth that made Layla roll her tongue over hers they were so perfect, and a low-cut fade with short sponge twists. His towering, stocky frame was covered in basketball shorts and a white wife-beater.

Perfect dick appointment attire, Layla thought. Q had tossed on the same type of outfit when he walked her to the door.

Smirking at her little attitude, Brody said, "You got it."

Hopping back in her car, Layla backed up some so the girl could pull out. When she did, Layla whipped into her spot, grabbed her purse, and climbed out. Brody was still standing by the steps as she made her way to her apartment.

"What up?" Brody greeted, checking out her outfit. The beads around her waist had him intrigued.

"Not a thing Brody," Layla gently replied. She was not in the mood to hold a conversation.

He chuckled lightly as they climbed the steps. Making their way to the second floor, Brody kept talking as if he hadn't just climbed out some pussy. Whether he did or not, small talk from Layla was always a plus in his book. She'd always kept it short and sweet with him. Layla was never rude, she just didn't understand the weird sensations she felt in her belly whenever he approached her. It was strange for Layla, and mostly because it wasn't the lustful feeling she'd get with other men.

"You stay giving me the cold shoulder, woman."

"Did you not just walk a girl to her car after dicking her down?" Layla pressed, turning around to face him. "And, you would've never known had you been inside before now. Where you coming from?"

Rolling her eyes, Layla turned her back to him and entered the code to her door. "Not that it's any of your business, but a friend's house."

"Maybe we can be friends one day. You know, let a nigga borrow some sugar and shit."

Layla laughed, now standing in her doorway facing him. She didn't have to strain much by looking up at him, but he was still taller than her. At 5'9", she was sure Brody had to stand at a good 6'1" or 6'2". His body was one built like a football player who'd spent hours on the field and in the gym. He had a slight gut, but from the times of seeing him at the gym, Layla knew it was nothing but muscle.

"Sucks for you if you did need sugar, I don't buy it."

Brody tossed his head back. "You sure you black? You telling me you don't own any sugar?"

"I don't know why that's hard to believe."

"Shit, I guess 'cause I ain't ever met a black person who didn't."

"Well, glad I could be your first," she smirked and let out a yawn. "So, was there something else you needed tonight? It's late."

Licking his lips, Brody gave her a smile. One Layla

was sure to have dreams – wet ones – about. "Nah. Just making sure you made it to your door safely is all. Have a good night."

Layla watched him stride confidently to his door before she called his name.

"Yeah?" he questioned.

"You have a good night too."

They both smiled while Brody entered his apartment, and Layla closed the door to hers. It was something about Brody that Layla couldn't place her finger on. He was charming, that was for sure. It was his bachelor ways that had Layla somewhat intrigued and trying to figure out why he always seemed to want to spark up a conversation with her.

Brushing off whatever it was she was feeling, Layla ambled into her bedroom. Flipping on the light, she slipped off her sandals before tossing her clothes and undergarments in the hamper. Just as she walked in her bathroom to shower, her phone rang with an incoming call. Ruffling through her purse, Layla sucked her teeth at the number on the screen. Knowing better than to answer, Layla sent the call to voicemail, and like clockwork two minutes later she received a voicemail notification.

Hovering over the play button, Layla knew whatever message was left, especially at damn near four in the morning was either going to piss her off or have her in her feelings. Whatever the case, she tapped the play button, and her biological mother's voice filled the quiet room.

"Lay. Lay, baby. I know it's late. Shit, maybe it's early, but you gotta forgive me. You know Mama loves you. I was just young, Lay. Going through some shit I shouldn't have been going through. I don't want you to hate me. You can't hate me. I love you. I know it may not feel like it, but I do. If you'd just give me a chance, a real one, I can show you. Can you just give me a call back? Or even text me? Whatever you want me to do to resolve our relationship, I'll do. Just... just don't hate me for my horrible decisions back then. I love you, Layla. Bye."

Her hands were trembling so bad, Layla wasn't sure how she was still holding onto her phone. Tears burned her eyes, dying to be released, but she wouldn't let them fall. Not now at least. Locking her phone, Layla tossed it onto the bed and headed for the shower. She didn't bother to check out herself in the mirror like she normally did. Once the water was perfectly hot, damn near scalding, she climbed inside.

A gut-wrenching cry from her soul emitted from her frame, as she let her tears escape her. Inside the shower, away from anyone who could possibly see or hear her, Layla broke down. On the outside looking in, she had it all together. The brown skin beauty, with gorgeous locs, a killer smile, unapparelled rhymes, and mellow personality, seemed to be doing just fine.

On the inside, past the exterior, Layla was merely a shell of the woman she wanted to be. Her promiscuous ways over the years were how she coped. The attention was gratifying to a certain extent, and that's when poetry became her outlet. When neither could provide the escape she desperately needed, Layla felt trapped. Like now.

She owned her promiscuous ways but didn't internally accept them. There was an intense loneliness in her life and desire to be accepted, but Layla acted as if she didn't want to be. Not because of how Liam played her, though his deceitfulness played a role. It was because of her mother, Tatum. Getting attached to anyone and opening up all for them to leave her high and dry was why Layla was so closed off.

She'd yearned for an intimate relationship, even a simple friendship with men and women, but the fear of being abandoned always won the battle. Resting her head against the cool tile of her shower, Layla let the water flow over her body, draining the last of her tears and the night's sins away. She knew the first step to healing was forgiveness, but how could she do that if she couldn't forgive herself first?

"I'm going to need a new set of lashes done," Layla grumbled, wiping the sweat from her forehead and eyelids.

Glancing her way, Amelia, her cousin who was more like a sister honestly, grimaced at the sight of Layla practically dripping in sweat.

"How do you sweat like that? Geez."

Layla shrugged and chugged down her bottle of water as Amelia pulled out of the parking lot. The two had just come from the gym burning off some calories, and the stress Layla seemed to be under. The phone call from her mom a few nights ago was still on her mind, and sadly, Layla was still annoyed by it. Not because she had called, but because she knew there was a reason behind the call.

It'd been a few months since Tatum had reached out to her daughter and the only reason why she hadn't was because of Layla's attitude toward her. She was cold-blooded, and in her eyes for good reason. For so long Layla wanted an explanation as to why she was abandoned. After not receiving an answer she felt was suitable to ease the heartaches she endured, Layla stopped caring; to a certain extent. Tatum hid her pregnancy for as long as possible, and it wasn't until her seven-month mark when a family member spotted her out.

They were excited for her, but Tatum hadn't felt that excitement since she found out she was pregnant. Knowing she couldn't love or care for Layla the way a child should be loved and cared for, Tatum did what she thought was best. Instead of going through the process of searching for an agency for adoption and spending money she knew she didn't have, Tatum securely wrapped Layla up in a blanket, placed her inside her car seat with a warm bottle and dropped her off in front of a fire station.

When Amelia's mother Missy, Tatum's sister, finally ran into her, of course, she asked about the baby. It'd been over six months since she'd given birth and no one in the family had seen her since. It was like she disappeared from the city. Guilt settled when Missy asked what happened to the baby, and Tatum had no choice but to whisper out what she'd done. Stunned by her reply, Missy demanded that she give her any information she could regarding her niece and within a year she had complete guardianship of Layla.

It was no secret that Layla didn't belong to Missy. Her beautiful chocolate skin, lanky frame, and quiet personality was nothing like Missy's kids. When she was of age and began to notice the difference and hear her grandma and family members whispering about her is when Missy told her the truth. Layla had questions of her own even at a young age, and instead of lying to her or having someone bully her about not being Missy's daughter, Missy told her the truth.

Layla had no siblings that she knew of, so the bond she and Amelia shared was one she cherished like no other. She did have a few friends but kept them at arm's length. Many of them were secretly some haters and Layla could honestly do without them. She'd always be quick to cut someone or a situation off before they could cut her off. It was a defense mechanism.

"Wish I had an answer for you," Layla chuckled, replying to a text message.

"Who you texting?"

Taking a quick peek at her screen, Amelia grinned when she saw the name. It wasn't everyday Layla showed genuine interest in someone, so for her to have an actual text thread with someone had Amelia impressed.

Playfully, Layla mushed her head. "Could you mind the business that pays you?"

"Nope. Was that Brody's name that I saw?"

Layla rolled her eyes and huffed. "Yes. He's just asking how my day is going."

"That's so cute. How'd he get your number again?"

"He went out of town and asked me to keep an eye on his place. Why? I don't know."

Amelia giggled. "Did you keep an eye out though?"

"Yeah. I'd look down the hall at his door whenever I

was headed to mine," she answered, making Amelia laugh harder.

"You need to stop giving that man a hard time."

"I'm not giving him a hard anything. He's just my neighbor, who has somehow in his head become my friend."

"Nothing wrong with having a male friend," she said, turning into the parking lot of Queen's Smoothie Shop.

"I didn't say there was. What are you trying to get at Millie?" Layla was over the back and forth with her hints.

"So, what if he wanted to be more than friends. You know. Ask you out on a date or something like that. Would you decline?"

It didn't take Layla a second to think of a reply. "No. I wouldn't decline. Having lunch with a friend is just that; lunch."

"I said as more than a friend, though. Have you seen what Brody looks like, or are you blind?"

Amelia had seen him in passing and even spoke a few times while visiting Layla. He was much buffer than she'd prefer, but still a sight to see. A sight she was sure her cousin gawked over plenty of days.

"I see him more times than I'd like. I'm not looking to be in a relationship, and I'm sure he's not either. The amount of females he has in and out of his crib I'm sure is enough on his plate."

Amelia stared at her for a beat, not believing one word she was saying but wouldn't push her. Layla was good for shutting down and shutting people out, and she'd hate if it were her.

"Okay Lay. Whatever you say. Let's get in here and get us some smoothies girl. I have a lash appointment at two."

Closing the passenger door behind her, Layla stepped inside the shop and her stomach immediately rumbled. There was nothing like a fresh smoothie after an extensive workout. She tried eating more, but her stomach never agreed.

"Hey. Welcome to Queen's. What can I get you ladies today?" one of the workers cheerfully greeted them.

"You know what you getting?" Amelia asked Layla while glancing at the menu. Everything looked good to her.

"Yeah. Can I have a large Green Machine, please?"

"Sure thing. And for you?"

Humming softly, Amelia let her eyes bounce back and forth between two options. Deciding on the latter, she clapped her hands.

"I'll take a large Berry Blast, but more strawberries than blueberries please."

Scribbling their orders down, the worker started their smoothies. The duo stepped off to the side and didn't have to wait long before their order was called. Amelia paid for both of their smoothies, and Layla thanked her cousin while heading toward the door. The person entering the shop made her steps halt abruptly.

"Damn," Liam let out. "What up Layla?"

He couldn't help the lustful thoughts that ran through his mind while letting his eyes take in her beauty. The sports bra, red spandex shorts, and her locs in a bun was the sexiest shit he'd seen all day. Behind him, Rodney couldn't help but ogle as well. He had one sample of her body and was mad as hell that he couldn't get more rounds with her. Even though that was years ago, Layla had that effect on men; especially the two standing wide-eyed in front of her.

"Liam," she said dryly.

"I haven't seen you in a minute," Rodney spoke.

"That's a good thing. Y'all have a good one."

She tried bypassing them and was almost clear of having to hold a lengthier conversation when Liam decided to follow them outside. For weeks his treacherous ways and disloyalty ate at Layla's self-esteem. She couldn't understand why he had played her the way he did and for no reason. Once she left Rodney's house that night, Layla didn't bother forking information out of Liam about his motives for the pussy ass stunt he pulled. Layla figured if it were supposed to happen, then it just had to happen.

"Yo, Layla. Wait up. Lemme holla at you," Liam called out, doing a slight jog to catch up to her.

Turning to face him, Layla gave him the meanest mug she could muster up. Had she been on some real disrespectful shit, she would've spat in his face.

"We don't have a damn thing to discuss."

"I can't ask how you been?" Liam frowned.

"You mean after you set your homeboy in there up to fuck me? Is that what you want to know?" she asked with a smile. "Well, I've been just fine. It seems niggas are actually into hoes these days, so I guess you did me a favor back then. Your girl has been out here hoeing since. Just living my best life and shit."

Liam was confused and taken aback by her reply. Scratching at his head, he gave her a head nod. "I mean, I guess that's what's up. You changed your number on me."

Layla laughed so loud, Amelia couldn't help but snicker along with her. "Please don't tell me you tried calling me."

"Yeah. I thought I could at least apologize and let you know that I was tripping. I should've never done that shit. That was foul."

"Indeed, it was. The fact that you do that type of shit

when you're "tripping" let me know everything I needed to know then and now."

"So, um, yeah. I mean, do you think we could start over? I miss you."

Layla stared at him as if he'd lost his damn mind. "You're not serious right now. I just know you didn't let that dumb shit come out of your mouth."

Liam scratched at the back of his neck, feeling embarrassed. He thought she'd jump all over the opportunity to be with him again. When he didn't answer, Layla laughed and shook her head.

"That's the funniest shit I've heard in a while. Let me tell you this though Liam, and I hope you keep it in mind the next time you want to approach me. Whenever you miss me, remember you had me and did some fuckboy shit to ruin it all. Clearly, I wasn't enough then, and trust me, love, I'm way too much for you now. I'd have you ready to end it all."

Smiling, Layla looked him over, shook her head, and walked away. She couldn't believe he had the audacity to approach her on some 'let's get back together' bullshit. It'd be a cold day in hell before she ever let him in her life again.

4

Placing her head in the palm of her hand, Shanae sighed in frustration. She'd been on the line with this particular customer for damn near forty-five minutes, and as thoroughly as she explained the issue, he was still giving her a hard time.

"Hello! Are you listening to me?"

Clicking the headset off of mute, Shanae answered. "Yes, sir. I can hear you perfectly. Would you still like to speak to a manager or have I resolved your issue today?"

"No, you haven't resolved my goddamn issue. I just want my money back, and you can't do that. This damn company is incompetent, and it'll be the last dime I ever spend with you greedy son of bitches!" the man belted, making Shanae crack a smile.

"As the policy stated, there are no refunds after thirty days, sir. It's written in fine print."

"Fuck you, and that policy!"

When she saw he'd hung up, Shanae sighed in relief and hurriedly placed her work system in lunch break mode. Swiveling her chair after locking her screen, she faced her close friend and co-worker, Bia.

"He finally let you off the phone?" Bia giggled.

"Girl, yes. I don't understand why people don't read the terms and conditions. I mean, it's in bold print. Whatever though. I'm super hungry. What'd you bring for lunch?"

They stepped to the time clock and punched out for lunch. Working at a telemarketing call center part-time while going to school full-time was starting to be so annoying to Shanae. Thankfully, she had one semester of school left, and she was praying she landed her dream job as an editor for this blog site she loved. She'd been taking some freelance and paid jobs and couldn't wait to put her all into them.

"Just a shrimp salad and a smoothie. You know Mitch, and I are going out the country in a few weeks. He has us on this healthy eating mess," Bia rolled her eyes and fake gagged.

"Well, you look good. Your waist is getting smaller."

"Thank you, girl. Yours is too. What you been doing?"

Shanae waved her off as they made it inside the café. "Not eating healthy or working out that's for sure. Probably just from stress."

"Stressing for what? Please don't tell me over Isaiah's ass still."

"More like again," Shanae scoffed. "Him and his issues, plus the ones with his child's mother are making me crazy. Like, I hate that I still feel the need to deal with him, but I feel kind of empty when I don't."

"Maybe that's a good thing. You need a real man who can fill that void. Or hell, no man for a while. Isaiah hasn't gotten his shit together yet, and probably never will."

Though Shanae hated to hear it, it was the truth. She couldn't even argue with Bia on that one.

"Doesn't his baby mama work here still?"

Shanae nodded her head as and the microwave stopped and took her food out. "Yeah. In another department."

"What are the freaking odds of that," Bia laughed. "Her ass better not be stalking you."

"With the way she behaves, I wouldn't put it past her."

The duo found a table near the middle of the lunchroom and continued their conversation. Shanae met Bia her first week of classes her sophomore year, and the two had been tight since. Bia was an intern at the time and took Shanae under her wing as a mentor, turned friend. That was how she got put on at the call center. They were offering a hefty bonus for summertime employees and with Shanae out of classes for the summer, the extra funds were much needed.

"When do y'all leave for your trip?" Shanae asked, taking a spoonful of rice into her mouth.

"The week of the fourth of July. I cannot wait. I need a break, with some strong drinks, nasty sex, and amazing scenery."

Shanae laughed, but she felt her wholeheartedly. Hell, she needed a vacation as well but didn't see one happening anytime soon.

"You and me both. Un, un," Shanae grumbled under her breath. "What is she walking over here for?"

"Who?"

Before she could answer Bia's question, Natisha, Isaiah's baby mama was walking up to their table. Though she didn't too much care for the girl, Shanae couldn't front Natisha was pretty. Her dark skin was smooth, and her weave never looked out of place. Sadly, she and Isaiah's daughter looked exactly like him. *She must have hated that nigga's guts when she was pregnant,* Shanae thought.

"Jazlynn wears a 4t in clothes and a size 4 in shoes," Natisha rattled off.

Shanae hesitated, blinking with bafflement before saying, "What?"

"My daughter. You know, the one Isaiah and I created? She wears a 4t and size 4 in shoes since you want to be her step mama so bad."

Though she didn't mean to, Shanae laughed. "Girl, please get the hell away from my table. If I do decide to buy your daughter some clothes, I damn sure don't need your approval."

"As if I were ever giving it to you. I know Isaiah was at your crib the other day. It's a shame that you can't move on and let him be happy with his family. What y'all had is done; sorry if he's telling you otherwise."

Shanae shuddered with humiliation as Natisha called herself trying to check her. Knowing what she was saying was far from the truth, Shanae did what only she knew would shut her ass right on up. If Isaiah wanted to be happy with his family, she'd gladly let him, if he told her that. Since he hadn't, Shanae was about to burst her bubble really quick.

Picking up her phone, she didn't have to scroll far to Isaiah's name in her call log. He'd called her that morning on FaceTime on her way to work. Smirking, she tapped his name and held the phone up to her face with a grin.

"Now, I hate I had to do this, but I'm sorry he's telling

you otherwise," Shanae spoke just as Isaiah answered the phone.

"What's up, bae. You on break?" his deep voice still made her weak.

"Yeah on lunch with Bia and we have some company."

Panning the camera in Natisha's direction, Isaiah sucked his teeth.

"Man, don't call me with that bullshit," he fussed.

"I'm not. I'm just showing her that if you were done with me, you wouldn't have answered this phone call. Am I holding you hostage Isaiah?"

Natisha stood with her hand propped on her hip, waiting for his ass to say some sideways shit. She'd never jeopardize losing her job, but she'd definitely see Isaiah later on to check him. Seeing as though she wasn't getting anywhere with Shanae.

"Nah, man. Quit listening to her. Natisha, leave her alone, man. What we got going on ain't got shit to do with Shanae," he huffed.

"What y'all got going on?" Shanae squeaked, realizing calling him was probably a bad idea.

"Yeah, you heard him. Ask that nigga where he just came from this morning. That's right; my place that he pays rent at. Where he lays his big ass head at on *most* nights. I don't have a reason to lie, sweetie."

"Man, shut yo' ass up. I was over there to see Jazzy. Shanae, don't fall for that shit."

Natisha giggled. "Yeah, okay Isaiah. Your daughter was sleep at eleven at night, but I'll let you tell her whatever. Like I said, it's a shame you can't move on when clearly all he's doing is stringing you along. But, that's on you, girl. You know niggas don't ever stop messing with the mother of their child. Just thought I'd let you know."

With a satisfied smirk on her face, Natisha switched off toward her locker. Isaiah could try to front all he wanted to, but she and he both knew what the deal was. Shanae now knew the reason he had been ducking and dodging her calls all night. This wasn't the first time, but now she had confirmation of where he'd been at.

Giving him a hostile glare, all Isaiah did was run a hand down his head. "What you looking like that for? You mad now?"

"Why wouldn't I be? I swear you're so full of shit."

Shanae was furious at her vulnerability to him. He'd called that morning like everything was good, and Shanae didn't put up a fuss. His explanation for not answering her calls was that he was sleep. It wasn't unlikely, but now that she had the truth, Shanae wondered how much longer she was going to tolerate the disrespect. The inconsideration for her love for him. The number of times she'd given him the benefit of the doubt because she wanted to trust him. Isaiah wanted to work on building her trust in him again. And just like she thought, he'd lost it quicker than it was given.

"I ain't tell you because I wasn't on shit. I did fall asleep, so I ain't lie," he tried to reassure her, but it wasn't working. Not this time.

"Whatever. If that's where you want to be, by all means, please go right ahead. I'm not forcing you to be anywhere you don't want to be."

Isaiah's nostrils flared in annoyance. Natisha was being messy and mad 'cause he hadn't laid the pipe to her after she sucked his dick. He wasn't going to tell Shanae that and was happy as hell Natisha hadn't mentioned it. For once, Isaiah was trying to do right, but trying wasn't good enough.

"Here you go with that dumb shit. I love your ass, girl. Quit listening to what she saying. Anything that concerns me and you, is between me and you, a'ight?"

"Mhm," Shanae mumbled. "I hear you. The more chances I give you to get your shit together, the more I wonder why I do. You ain't ever gon' change."

Shanae's throat ached with the familiar feeling of tears being next. Saddened by his actions she was not. In fact, she was honestly used to them. Nothing Isaiah did or said could surprise her besides getting his shit together. Shanae was more upset at herself for consistently playing the fool for him. What she needed to realize was that you can't teach an old dog new tricks.

"The shit I can't change is the reason you love a nigga and know you got my heart."

"Tell me anything, Isaiah. Look, I gotta go. I'll talk to you later."

Before he could say some more bullshit that had her rolling her eyes, Shanae hung up. Knowing he'd be sending her a text trying to plead his case, Shanae quickly blocked his number. She seemed to be doing that every other week, but she swore it was good for her sanity. Sometimes, even if for a few days, going without talking to Isaiah was healthy. The type of energy she needed. Not this negative, baby mama drama, bullshit he had dragged her into. Going back to eating her food, Shanae paused when she felt an intense stare from Bia.

"What Bia? Say what you got to say."

"I already did. You're too young for all that drama. You have no ties to Isaiah and a real nigga would never in life put you in a position for his baby mama to be walking up on you trying to check shit."

"Mitch has a baby mama, too, if I'm not mistaken."

"Yeah, and she knows her place. As do I in his life. We aren't enemies, but we sure as hell aren't friends either. There's just certain shit that Natisha shouldn't do. But then again, you and Isaiah aren't in a relationship, so I guess she feels she has some type of superiority over you," Bia shrugged not really knowing why Shanae was playing herself.

"Whatever the case, you're my girl, I love you ,and I want what's best for you always. That situation right there? It's messy as hell, and you're letting it drain you. You should not be worried about any man's baby mama at twenty-two, let alone having drama about it with an ex. That nigga is your ex for a reason; remember that and stop cutting yourself short."

Taking in every word Bia said, Shanae could only nod her head and blink back tears. She didn't know what it was going to take for her to break free from this hold Isaiah had on her, but she hoped God showed her another sign.

As bad as she just wanted to walk away, her heart was too invested. At this point, physically hurting herself by walking away would be ten times better than Isaiah doing it again. Shanae needed to choose her battles wisely.

"I don't know why we came in here on a Saturday," Kali groaned as she looked around the busy nail salon. It was black-owned and surely supported by their own.

The weekend had finally rolled around, and Shanae

was all for a little self-care. She'd been working all week and getting her nails and toes done always relaxed her. Their next stop would be the mall for some retail therapy. Now that, Kali was cool with. She stayed spending a bag on her and Khyri. Him more than her honestly.

"Because I need a fill and your toes are looking a little crusty," Shanae snickered.

"Girl," Kali laughed. "I can't even deny that. Good thing we're up next though."

Just as she spoke those magic words, the duo was escorted to two chairs near the middle of the salon. Slipping off her sandals, Shanae climbed into the chair as, Lu, the nail tech adjusted the water for her.

"Hey, Lu. How've you been?"

"Good girl. Just working. What color you getting today?"

Picking the hot pink gel polish up from her lap, Shanae handed it to her. "Going with something different this time. Same for my nails. What color you getting?"

Kali held up her white gel polish. "You know what they say about white polish."

Shanae's brows furrowed. "Um, no. What do they say?"

"Toes white, so you know this pussy tight. Ah!" Sticking her tongue out, Kali did a jig in her seat making Shanae and Lu chuckle while shaking their heads.

"I don't know how those two correlate but do your thing, girl."

"I got it from Summer Walker."

Shanae grinned. "I love her."

"Me too. I need her to drop some new music."

Falling into an easy conversation, the cousins relaxed and caught up on what each other had been up to. Shanae's mother and Kali's dad were siblings. At just two years apart, the two had been thick as thieves since before they could walk.

When Kali first found out she was pregnant with Khyri, Shanae was super excited for her cousin. Yes, she was young, but she had major support. Their family stepped in and helped wherever she slacked, and for that she'd always be grateful. Erik's family was cool too, but Kali was the first girl grandchild to have a baby, so the extra special treatment she received was a given.

Taking a sip of her water, Shanae cleared her throat. "Do you regret having Khyri?"

Kali frowned and hurriedly shook her head no. "Absolutely not."

"I mean, not keeping him but with Erik is what I meant."

"Some days, yes. He's a great dad; I'll never downplay that. Khyri loves that man so much," she chuckled and shook her head. "It's just this hold he thinks he has on me is annoying. Like, damn nigga. I'm much more than your baby mama. I'm trying to be someone's fine ass wife."

"Sometimes I wonder if Isaiah and I would've worked out had I given him a child."

Lu glanced upward but didn't say anything.

"I know you don't think a baby can keep a man anywhere?" Kali questioned, hoping like hell that wasn't Shanae's logic.

"It keeps him in between Natisha's legs," Shanae scoffed with an attitude.

"Stop. Stop that shit right now."

Kali hated how much power Isaiah had over Shanae. It was a mind thing. He'd had Shanae thinking she wasn't enough, when actuality, she was too much. Way much more than he could handle. Natisha didn't threaten his ego like Shanae did. Deep down he knew how much of a gem she was. So instead of handling her with care, he went for the watered-down version of Shanae. The woman who didn't challenge him to be a better man. Hell, a better human being.

Men like Isaiah were the worst type. He enjoyed the idea of keeping a weaker woman around after dealing with Shanae. His true inadequacy whenever in Shanae's presence always made him reevaluate himself; he wasn't shit simply put. What Shanae needed to come to terms with was knowing her worth and loving herself. Isaiah was merely a weak man constantly selling her nightmares disguised as love.

"I'm just saying."

"*And* I'm just saying to stop trying to compare yourself to that hoe. Fuck her, straight up. Let her have his ass. I pray to God every night and day that Erik finds a woman to love his crazy ass so he can leave me alone."

Snickering, Shanae shook her head. "You'd be okay with that?"

"I'd pay a bitch to keep him away from me. I'm beyond okay with that."

"I guess I'm just not there yet. Not completely anyway. Some days I am, and I'll block his number and be good. The next, I'm laid up with his ass and questioning how we went wrong."

"Trust me, I understand. Wait until you're completely over him. Girl, that feeling is like no other in the world. You won't give a flying fuck about anything he says or does because it'll no longer affect you."

Shanae sighed, wondering what that would feel like. Her thoughts immediately went to never speaking to him again, and pain funneled into her chest.

"We'll see."

Kali chuckled, and Shanae gave her a puzzled look. "You know the definition of insanity?"

"Being mentally ill, right?"

"Yeah, and doing the same thing expecting something to be different. Boss up on that nigga, show him you can live without him. You're going to keep forgiving him because you love him until you hate his ass. And we're related, so I know that'll be a scary sight."

Shanae didn't want to chuckle, but Kali was telling no lies. The thoughts that ran through Shanae's mind some nights scared her. The only reason she hadn't followed through on most of them was because of love. But shit, was love really enough?

Their spa day had come to an end, and they were now roaming the mall. Kali had a few bags in her hand and was trying to figure out she was going to hold them and eat her pretzel from Auntie Annie's.

"All that bread goes to your ass," Shanae snickered as she stood off to the side. She wanted some real food, and the only thing a pretzel was going to do was annoy her.

"I'm trying to get thick like you. Let me hold some titties, girl," Kali giggled, making the young man behind the counter blush.

"I could lose a few pounds."

"Nah, baby. You look perfect in my eyes."

The gruff, orotund voice from behind Shanae had her swiveling on her heels. His cologne greeted her before his voice could register in her brain. She came eyes to chest, a very defined chest, with a man she was quite familiar with. Looking upward, she grinned and playfully hit him.

"Perfect, huh? What's up stranger," she grinned as he pulled her into a hug.

Oh, my Lord. This nigga smells heavenly. Shanae's toes tingled and nipples hardened against his chest. When they parted ways, she hoped he hadn't felt them through the thin tank top she was wearing.

"Yeah," he licked his lips and grinned. "Perfect. And I could be saying the same thing. What up Kali?"

"Hey, Levi. Long-time no see."

"Right. You up and moved then popped back up like a damn celebrity," Shanae giggled. "How's life been treating you?"

"Better than I ever expected it to, especially coming from here. But shit, I'm blessed."

Yes, the hell you are, Shanae marveled. She let her eyes take in all 6'3" of Levi's tall, rich cinnamon colored complexion. Starting at his fresh out the box Pumas, legs covered in distressed black denim shorts, a white V-neck fitting like a second skin against impeccable abs. Abs Shanae was sure he didn't have before.

Levi's beard was thick and shiny, lips full and kissable, and had a crisp line that lead to neatly twisted locs that were braided down his back. His skin was so smooth looking, Shanae wanted to ask him his facial routine. His eyes were what intrigued Shanae the most. They always had. His golden honey orbs were gentle and held a hint of sincerity Shanae never saw in most men's eyes.

"I heard that," she replied, after salivating for a moment. "How's your grandmother doing?"

Levi smiled wide. "Still busy like she doesn't have a bad knee," he chuckled. "Good though. You should stop by and see her."

Shanae's grandmother, Mrs. Cheryl, and Levi's grandmother, Ms. Gene, used to stay across the street from one another. When they were growing up, all the kids on the block were either at Ms. Gene's house, or Mrs. Cheryl's. It'd been a while since Shanae visited her old neighborhood. When her grandmother was killed by a burglary gone wrong, visiting the home didn't seem right without her presence. Her PaPa wasn't even the same man, and she couldn't blame him. Losing the love of his life had shattered his heart to pieces. Though it happened six years ago, the memories were still fresh.

Levi's departure, unbeknownst to Shanae, was because of that night. The jack boys had been coming to rob him and gotten the houses mixed up. When Levi caught wind of it, he taught them a lesson but felt guilty as ever. He loved Mrs. Cheryl just as much as his own grandmother. The gang life had sucked Levi in at a young age and retaliation was all he knew. After getting at the niggas who killed Mrs. Cheryl, the streets were damn near bleeding every night. Between Shanae's family and his crew, any nigga not affiliated with them was getting touched.

To put his grandmother at ease after two years of banging heavy, Levi moved out to LA with his aunt. Out there he was on a different wave. His cousins were down there making legit money, and Levi wanted in. Not at first, though. It took some time to get him out of that gang mentality and realize there was more to life than that. Don't confuse him with a lame though. He was still very much affiliated, respected and would check whoever about his.

Now, at the age of twenty-six, and a birthday approaching in November, he was co-owner of a bar called *Shottas*. It was originally his cousin Arsenio's who had given it to Levi's brother Lamar, and now he helped run the place. Not for long, though. Lamar was going to have to start looking for more help because Levi was currently in the process of opening his own.

"Yeah," Shanae agreed as they stepped to the side. "I'll have to do that."

"Don't you and your brother own that bar right off the beach?" Kali asked.

Nodding, Levi scratched his beard. "Yeah. That's our spot. Working on securing another in Emeryville."

"That's what's up," Shanae beamed, genuinely happy for him. "I'm happy for you."

"'Preciate it. When y'all get some time, y'all should slide through. Drinks on me."

Kali tooted her lips out, just as her phone rang. "Oh, we were coming through anyway. Y'all better have some good food too."

Stepping away from them, she answered Erik's call, knowing it was Khyri. Shanae grinned not knowing what else to say. Levi was staring at her so fiercely, he was making her nervous.

"What?" she asked, running a hand over her thick brow.

"You still pretty as hell."

Waving him off, Shanae blushed and thanked him. "When'd you move back?"

"Couple of months ago. Been keeping busy and out the way for real."

"That's a good thing. Not much has changed since you left."

Levi's eyes did a sweep of her short, stacked figure and subconsciously licked his lips. "Nah. Things have definitely changed. You aren't that fifteen-year-old, braced-face girl anymore that's for sure."

Boldly, with an air of confidence Shanae didn't know she had, she stared right back at him. "And you aren't that nineteen-year-old who thought he was my daddy," she said playfully rolling her eyes.

"Somebody needed to tame your little ass."

"And you see how that worked out," she smirked, loving the flutters in her stomach from their flirtatious behavior.

Levi wanted to make a comment on her situation with Isaiah, but he left it alone. For now. He'd recently became friends with her on Facebook and saw all her statuses about him. He had to remind himself how young she was at just twenty-two, but on the real her age shouldn't have been the reason Isaiah was doing her wrong. Levi wasn't trying to get into all that though. What he did want to do was keep in contact with her, personally. Not through no social media app.

"Gon' put yo' number in here for me," he said smoothly, handing her his cell phone.

"Why is this phone so big? I'd drop this all the time."

"My hands too big for anything smaller."

Shanae looked up from his phone screen, smirked, and shook her head. *I bet something else is still big too.* They'd never had sex, but Levi was the first person to teach her how to kiss. He was so patient with her, while Shanae was naïve as hell to how he could have turned her out. Thinking back on that night in his granny's crib, she smiled.

"You two better not be up all night either," Ms. Gene spoke flicking the kitchen light off.

"Yes, ma'am," Shanae replied. "Goodnight."

"Goodnight, baby."

As soon as Shanae heard her bedroom door close, she was fussing at Levi. She'd wanted to go to the skating rink where everyone was at, but he insisted on staying in the crib that night.

"You better not have picked a boring movie either," she fussed, hitting him with a pillow. "I could have been at the rink with my friends."

"Them hoes ain't your friends, girl," Levi chuckled but was serious. "Plus, I got a weird feeling that some shit gon' pop off and you don't need to be nowhere around it."

"With your boys?" she questioned.

Levi faced her. "Yeah, but that ain't something you need to worry about. What you need to do is share this cover with a nigga."

Tugging it over his lap some, Levi pressed play on Last House On The Left and got comfortable. Not even thirty minutes into the movie, Shanae was flinching and covering her eyes. She didn't know why she let him pick the movie, knowing she was not a fan of anything scary.

"I feel like something bad is about to happen," she whispered, biting her thumb nail.

Levi glanced her way. "It's supposed to. They in this creepy ass crib."

"Oh my God," Shanae breathed, scooting closer to him. "I'm scared."

"Man, watch out."

Jokingly, Levi pushed her away, and she clung to his arm instead. When what she thought was a scary scene didn't happen, Shanae relaxed some and curled her feet underneath her. Being this close to him made her already erratic heart pace faster. They'd always been cool and Levi showed her love, but Shanae felt something different this time around. Maybe the crush she had on him wasn't as made up in her head as she liked it to be.

"What you wash your hair with?" Levi asked randomly.

Shanae giggled. "Um, shampoo."

"I mean what kind. It smells hella good."

She hadn't realized he was inhaling her until his hand slid into her head. With a handful of her curly mane between his fingers, Levi gripped it tightly and tugged her head back some. His aggression caught Shanae off guard and turned her on all in one breath. Loosening his grip, Levi massaged her scalp. The intimate act hadn't surprised her as much as the aggressive one. He always seemed to *display a calmer, more controlled side with Shanae. Even when the boys in their hood used to tease her because she was chunkier than the rest of the girls.*

Levi would playfully pinch her cheeks and ask her if she wanted him to beat them up. That always got a smile out of her. There was no smile on her face right now though. Levi's hand was now massaging her neck ever so gently and Shanae was losing her mind.

"Levi," she called out in a whisper, looking up at him.

His hand slid from the side of her neck to her jaw and caressed it. "Yeah?"

"Wh-What're you doing?"

"What it look like I'm doing?" he questioned, now rubbing his thumb across her bottom lip.

Shanae gulped. The pit of her stomach was hollow as hell. "Why're you touching me like this?"

Leaning down, Levi placed gentle kisses against her shoulder, before smoothly moving to her neck. His hand was back in her hair, and Shanae moaned as he massaged her scalp.

"I can't touch you? This soft ass skin," he groaned, kissing down her chest. "It needs to be touched."

Wanting to test if her lips were just as soft, Levi ventured upward. Removing his hand from her head, Shanae's eyes popped open.

"Wha-Why'd you stop."

"You gon' stop playin' wit' me?"

Shanae didn't know what he was talking about, but she nodded her head yes anyway. She blinked her eyes slowly, as her chest rose and fell at a quickened pace.

"A'ight then. C'mere," he mumbled as if she weren't close enough.

Levi's kiss to her lips wasn't rushed. He'd been wanting to taste her lips all day and now that she'd given him the privilege, he was going to take his time and savor the moment. Shanae squeezed her eyes shut, not knowing what to do, but she didn't need to know. Skillfully, Levi sucked on her bottom lip, before deepening the kiss. A leader in his own right, Shanae mimicked his moves and did the same while he slipped his tongue in her mouth.

Breathless and needing somewhere to place her hands, Shanae moved them onto his lap while damn near trying to suck his face off. The hint of weed she tasted on his lips turned her on even more. Just when Levi gripped her waist with one hand, causing him to shift under the cover, Shanae's eyes popped open. He knew she felt his dick bulging through his shorts; it was written all over her flushed face.

Pulling away, Shanae licked her lips and pulled them into her mouth before saying, "Was that your, um, you know?"

"My dick?" Levi bluntly answered.

"Uh, yeah. Why is it that... I don't know, big?"

"The mothafucka ain't supposed to be small Shanae."

The two stared at one another before cracking up laughing. Shanae because she was freaking out on the inside after feeling his damn anaconda of a penis. Levi because Shanae was so innocent and had she been another broad tonguing him down like that, Levi would've put the pipe to her ass in a heartbeat. She wasn't just some broad though. And, for that reason alone Levi stood from the couch.

Watching him adjust his third leg, Shanae swallowed the extra saliva in her mouth before making eye contact with him. "Where you going? Did I do something wrong?"

"Nah. But I'ma do something wrong if I keep sitting here."

"Well, where you going? You can't leave me down here," she practically whined. Levi looked down at his crotch, and Shanae followed his gaze. "Oh," she gasped before giggling.

"Oh is right. I'll be right back."

"You're going to jack off?"

"Aye, man," Levi laughed. "Chill out. It's either that or have you stroke this mothafucka for me, with yo' scary ass."

That got her quiet real quick. "Whatever. Handle your business so we can finish watching this movie."

Shaking her head at the memory, Shanae typed her

name then her number in his contacts before handing him the phone back. Levi knew she wouldn't flake and give him the wrong number, so he didn't bother calling it.

"You locked in now. Don't be calling me no stranger when I ring your line."

"*If* you ring my line. You know how niggas are. Get ya number just to claim they got it."

"That's them lames you been fucking with. I ain't that."

Whether she needed a reminder or not, Levi was going to give it to her. His matter-of-fact tone made Shanae cream the panties she was wearing; again. Clearing her throat, she tugged on one of the curly tendrils hanging near her shoulder. Wash-N-Go's had been her thing since summer hit and surprisingly, her shrinkage hadn't been doing her dirty.

"Girl, I'm so sick of this nigga," Kali spat, breaking the tension between them.

"What's wrong?"

"I'll tell you when we get in the car. Levi, it was good running into you. I'm sure we'll link up soon."

Levi gave her a one-sided hug. "Most def. Can I get some love too or you gon' leave a nigga hanging?"

Shanae playfully rolled her eyes and willingly opened her arms to hug him. His frame engulfed her, and her eyes fluttered as his hands wrapped around her waist. His potent cologne would be stuck to her attire and in her head as he whispered in her ear. So close to her ear, Shanae shuddered when he spoke.

"When I call you better answer for me."

It wasn't a demand, just a simple reminder that he'd be calling. Even if it was a demand, Shanae didn't mind at all. That was one phone call she was looking forward to answering.

5

_____

W alking into Erik mama's house, Kali hoisted Khyri up higher on her hip. He was laid out asleep on her shoulder and was almost bigger than her. Laying him on the couch, she slipped his shoes off before placing a few pillows on the ground. Khyri was a wild sleeper just like his daddy.

She and Shanae's weekend had been cut short thanks to a nasty ear infection Khyri got. Erik couldn't figure out was wrong with him. He was normally outgoing, running around with the rest of his cousins, but Saturday was a rough one. He wouldn't eat, had been crying at the top of his lungs, and sleep was the last thing on his mind.

Kali didn't care that her day had to end because he was sick; it was Erik's annoying banter that pissed her off. Instead of calling and updating her on what was wrong with Khyri, he'd called and pressed her for answers about who she was getting cute for. As if her being a mother was supposed to stop her from feeling fine for herself.

After taking him to urgent care, the antibiotics he was prescribed cleared up the infection in no time. It was now Thursday evening, and Kali had to be on campus in less than forty-five minutes for class. Thankfully, Ms. Rhonda's house wasn't far from the university. Parking was what took up most of her time. Even in the summer there seemed to be no parking close to the hall her class was in.

"Hey Ms. Rhonda," Kali spoke.

"Hey Kali. Look at my big boy. Daycare be wearing him out, huh?"

Kali giggled and shook her head no. "Hardly. I bet if we were going home, he'd be wide awake. It's the heat. It be taking my baby out."

"Him and me both. You see I haven't gone anywhere today."

Ms. Rhonda was in her late forties but still looked closer to thirty. Erik had inherited her caramel complexion and her eyes, but everything else came from his dad. The short honey blonde bob on Ms. Rhonda gave her an even younger appeal, making Kali smile and compliment her.

"I love your cut."

"Thank you. My hair is too thick for it to be trying to

grow out, especially in the thick of the summer. No ma'am," she chuckled, taking a seat. "How've you been?"

"Good actually. Just taking these classes, ready to graduate."

"That's good. I'm glad you didn't let having a baby stop you from pursuing an education."

"I have an amazing support system, so thank you."

Ms. Rhonda waved her off. "You don't have to thank me, Kali. Just keep being a damn good mother. Hopefully, Erik gets his shit together and doesn't miss another opportunity with you."

Kali had mad respect for Ms. Rhonda. She didn't want to laugh in her face and let her know that Erik's chances with rekindling anything with her were ultra-slim to none. Unfortunately, his ship had sailed. Kali couldn't even imagine being in any type of relationship with Erik besides the one they were in now. Co-parenting had its days, but it worked for them. Well, for her at least. She didn't give a fuck what Erik wanted to work out.

Chuckling, Kali shook her head. "Honestly, Ms. Rhonda, there aren't any other opportunities. As long as he's in Khyri's life and does his part as his father, I'm perfectly fine with us not being together."

Ms. Rhonda smiled. "Well, okay, then. I guess I'll stop trying to play meditator and matchmaker."

"I don't know why you were in the first place," Bobbi, Erik's cousin, said walking in the living room.

Kali glanced her way and couldn't help but chuckle. The girl looked a hot mess. The wig she was rocking looked like a damn Sunday's best hat, the shorts she had on were sure to give her a yeast infection, and she had the nerve to have on a swim top she knew wasn't her size. Kali didn't even want to get on the plastic heels that were sticking to her sweaty feet.

"Where in the hell are you coming from dressed like that?" Ms. Rhonda frowned.

"The pool. It's nice out."

"It ain't that damn nice. Go put some clothes on. Only woman walking around my house damn near naked is me."

Chuckling, Kali shook her head. "I'll see you when I get out of class."

"Is something funny?" Bobbi hissed in Kali's direction.

"Yeah. You."

Not giving her any more attention than that, Kali strutted past her and out the front door. When she stepped outside, Murda, Bobbi's boyfriend, was dumping the guts of a Backwood in the grass. Kali rolled her eyes and walked right by his bum ass.

"Damn. You can't speak?" he asked standing up.

"Sure can't."

Murda smirked. "Ion't know why Erik still be chasing behind your stuck-up ass."

"Oh, you know," Kali sassed, flipping her curly hair over her shoulder. "The same reason your bitch doesn't like me. 'Cause you wish you were the one chasing behind me instead. Have a good one."

Hopping in her car, Kali backed out of the driveway and made it to her campus in fifteen minutes. To her surprise, there was a parking spot directly in front of her building. Grabbing her backpack from the backseat, she climbed out and locked her doors. Not realizing it until it was too late, Kali let her eyes roam the parking lot for Rondo's red Benz.

When she didn't see it, she headed inside. Taking the steps to the third floor, Kali was out of breath by the time she walked into class. Even with a two-year-old at home, she was out of shape like crazy. The smallest amount of exercise had her panting. Taking her seat against the wall, she pulled out her folder and notebook, prepared for the 3-hour lecture.

Scribbling the date and course in one corner of her notebook, she looked up when Rondo came walking smoothly through the door. Just like every other time he came to class, Rondo was dressed fresh as hell. His style of dress made Kali wonder if he had a personal stylist. Biting at the corner of her lip, she drank his six-foot even, brown frame in with utter appreciation.

The Amiri jean shorts, white *All$In* tee, and Yeezy 500's had her mind racing. Even the way he reached into his backpack and veins flexed in his hand had Kali fixated. In her eyes, he was perfection and his barber had to be as well. The precision in his shape up and 360 waves deserved an award. A standing ovation.

This nigga is so damn fine. After dating Erik, who she considered a light skin male, Kali was starting to see darker complexion men in another light. With Erik's light bright ass not in her view anymore, she hadn't fully realized what she was missing out on. Not to say that they were more attractive; she'd just grown a level of appreciation for their fine asses.

"What up class skipper," he joked.

"Oh, whatever. That was my first time missing. My son was sick."

"Damn, that's all bad. He good now though, right?"

Kali nodded. "Yes. Had an ear infection. Where you coming from? I didn't see your car in the lot."

The cocky smirk on his face made Kali's lower lips pulsate. "You was checking for a nigga, huh?"

She kissed her teeth. "Please. Just seeing if you were going to be here like you said you would. I need the notes from Tuesday if you have them."

Rondo glanced at her for a beat. "Nah. You can't get em'."

"What? Why not?"

"If I give 'em to you, you gotta do something for me," he said making Kali toot her lips out.

Crossing her arms she said, "Now, see. Niggas always want something."

"Shit, you the one asking for *my* notes. You want something from me, girl."

Kali laughed and pushed him in the arm. "Whatever. I only want yours because you have nice handwriting and take good notes."

"Man, fuck all that," Rondo dismissed. "Let me take you out. I think that's an even exchange."

"Take me out?" she enunciated slowly.

"Yeah. Why you acting slow?"

Tossing her head back with laughter, Rondo took pleasure in her squeaky tone, high cheekbones, and slender neck. He envisioned himself kissing her there, making her moan and giggle his name, telling him to stop but really wanting him to go further. Kali wasn't the typical woman he'd normally go after.

Looks-wise, Rondo loved all women of all shapes and sizes. Not color though. He'd vowed to never mess with a white chick. A few of his homeboys did, but they weren't his speed. In his eyes, there was nothing or no one more beautiful than a black woman.

Containing her laughter, Kali shook her head. "I'm not; you just caught me off guard for a second. So," she said clearing her throat. "In exchange for your notes, you want to take me out?"

"Shit, on the real you could get these notes for free. It ain't like you need 'em but you seem like the type who needs a little incentive."

Kali's face frowned up. "And what type would that be?"

Just as Rondo went to tell her, their professor walked through the door. Briefcase in hand, glasses damn near stuck to his face, and pants a wee bit too high, he was the type of professor Rondo would have joked on back in high school and got put out of class. College was a different playing field, though. The professors didn't care if you participated, never showed up, and failed altogether; they were already paid.

"This serious ass dude man," Rondo chuckled making the guy next to him do the same.

Kali pinched his arm. "What's my type?" She whispered near his ear.

Rondo faced forward with a smirk on his face. He didn't know her type per se, but he liked seeing her all flustered, ready to go in on his ass.

"Ugh," she fussed. "Remember that."

"Sshh," Rondo hushed her, making other students glance their way. "I'm trying to pay attention, girl."

Unable to hold the frown on her face, Kali grinned and pulled out her PowerPoint notes for the evening's lecture. He'd email them out the week prior and it was up to the students to print them off and have them ready for class. Thankfully, Kali had a printer at home and was able to get caught up on some, but their professor was known to give away all the juicy details during the lecture.

Two and a half hours into his lecture, their professor had made it through every slide, talked their ear off and let them know what they could expect on their test.

"Since we only have one test left of this summer course, I hope you all come well prepared to pass. They make up seventy-five percent of your grade."

"We will be," a student replied.

"Shit, speak for yourself," Rondo mumbled.

"That's what I like to hear. Since we're done a little early today, I'll let you guys go. Have a good weekend, and don't forget to check blackboard for test notes."

The class thanked him and began gathering their belongings. Kali was one second away from falling asleep and she couldn't be anymore happier to be getting let out early. Thirty minutes or not; it didn't happen often. Neatly stacking her papers into her orange folder that was labeled with the class on the top, she yawned, stood to her feet and stuffed it inside her backpack. Rondo was already standing waiting for her.

"You ready sleepyhead?" Rondo questioned.

"Yeah. I'm hella tired today."

"I see. Let me run to the restroom right quick and we can bounce."

Kali nodded and pulled her phone from her purse. Going to her text messages, she opened up a video of Khyri from Ms. Rhonda. He was jumping around on the couch, singing and dancing along to one of his favorite cartoons. Kali's face stretched into a smile that only a mother's love for her child could bring. Khyri was her entire world and her motivation on the days she wanted to give up and say fuck this degree. She knew she couldn't though. He was looking up to and depending on her.

"Damn, who got you smiling like that? I need to hit them up for some advice," Rondo said, walking back over to her.

"My son. He's getting so big and just into all types of shit. They weren't lying about those terrible two's."

"Aye, wait until he hits three. They turn into some damn monsters. Like a switch or something was activated," he laughed but was serious as hell.

As they walked down the steps, Kali realized she'd never asked him if he had kids of his own. She was always gloating and showing off Khyri because he seemed interested.

"You have any kids?"

"Nah. Not yet. Just a handful of nieces, nephews, and cousins."

"You want any?"

One of Rondo's shoulder lifted as he smirked. "It's not something I just sat and thought about no, but I wouldn't mind having a child who looks like me running around here. Shit probably the best feeling in the world, huh?"

Rondo knew Kali was smiling before he turned to face her. To see her so enamored by the mere mention of her child, caused a weird feeling to stir in Rondo's chest. He knew bitches who couldn't give a fuck less about their kids. Hell, some of them were in his family. That's why he was in no rush to have a child, especially with the way women acted these days. It was hard enough finding a woman worthy enough to date; putting a baby up inside one was far from his agenda.

"It is. I didn't even know this kind of love existed until him. He really makes my day," Kali beamed, getting choked up just thinking of how much peace Khyri had brought her in such little time.

"I think I need to meet him. He got a nigga jealous the way he making you smile," he joked, making Kali blush and push him in the arm.

"Whatever. That's my baby. He's supposed to do that. Before I forget," she said turning to face him as they made it to her car. "You were trying to take me out, right?"

"Yeah. I ain't gon' lie to you and act like I'm trying to take you on a study date or no shit like that. I'm trying to see you outside of this school girl element."

Rondo licked his lips and ran a hand down his waves. They were so neatly aligned, Kali wondered how much he tipped his barber for blessing him with such skill. She didn't want to fall under his gaze, but even in the dark those piercing eyes set her skin ablaze. Rubbing the back of her neck, Kali swallowed her nervousness down.

"I'd like that."

The gold and diamonds sparkling underneath the street light, enhancing his already gorgeous smile, damn near took Kali out at the knees. *He better stop smiling at me like that. Shit!* Rondo didn't bother holding back his smile. He was expecting Kali to put up a fight but was glad she hadn't.

"Word? A'ight bet," he chuckled. "I thought you was the type that played hard to get. Make a nigga chase you just for the thrill of it all."

"Who said I wasn't?" She pressed, perfectly arched brow lifting high. "This is a fair exchange or did you forget?"

"Awww, shit. Let me find out you need me to pass this class."

"I'll let you think that," she snickered, loving how easy it was to converse with him. "So, is this the part where we exchange numbers and you text me the details of our date?"

"Nah. I'ma give you the details now and get the number for later."

"Oh," Kali chirped, popping a hand on her hip. "So you had this all planned out?"

"What can I say? I'm a man of determination. Plus, the event my cousin is performing at is this weekend."

"He's a rapper or something?" Kali asked, trying not to let her irritation be detected.

She didn't mind new aged rappers; they were on their grind. It was the ones who knew for a sure fucking fact that they couldn't rap and then expected everyone to support them. In her eyes, they had horrible friends.

"*She's* a poet," he offered and Kali grinned.

"Oooh. I love poetry. Let me find out you on your Love Jones shit. I mean, you ain't as fine as Larenz Tate, but you'll do," she giggled.

"If all I had to do was put on my sexy voice and have my cousin write me up some sensual poetry about being your slave, baby, you should've let me know. Fuck your man, I ain't worried 'bout him."

Kali squealed as he recited Darius' poem, dedicated to Nina. "Oh my gosh," she laughed, blushing like crazy. Her cheeks already a rosy color from smiling so much already. "What am I going to do with you? What your hood ass know about some Love Jones?"

"Hood niggas fall in love too. Am I right?"

Rendered slightly speechless from his unprideful admission, Kali made up in her mind right then that Rondo could take her on a date wherever he damn well pleased. She'd have no objections.

"I'd like to assume so. I guess you'll have to make me a believer."

Rondo's eyes blinked with a hint of determination. He was up for a challenge, especially when it came to a woman who would be well worth the battle. Joking a bit more and exchanging numbers, Kali climbed into her driver's seat, cranked the ignition and let her window down.

"You know what I forgot to ask you?" she said looking up at Rondo.

"Nah. What's that?"

"How old are you. You have this youthfulness to you, but in the same breath could fit right in with a group of thirty-five plus."

"Damn. Thirty-five ain't young?" he laughed.

"No. No. It is. I'm just saying... you know what? Never mind. You'll tell me one day."

"I'm twenty-seven."

Kali gasped. "Shut up! No you are not."

"A'ight. I'm not."

"No, for real. You could *easily* pass for nineteen or twenty. What the hell," she laughed in shock.

"I'm over twenty-one, I just look nineteen," he rapped, hitting her with that old school Messy Marv lyric.

"Okay," Kali sang. "Now you got me ready to play that song."

"Let me know when you make it to the crib."

"Why? So you can call and make sure I'm safe?"

Rondo gave her a blank expression. "Why else?"

Chills covered Kali's arms and exposed legs in the shorts she was wearing. "Oh, um. Okay. Yeah. I'll text you when I get home. I have to pick my son up first."

She found herself explaining to him, not knowing Rondo really appreciated the explanation. Though he didn't need one, he found it amusing as Kali stumbled over her words. He could tell she wasn't used to a real nigga, 'cause that question would've been a no-brainer had she been.

"A'ight," he told her before tapping the hood of her car and stepping back so she could pull off.

On the drive to pick up Khyri, Kali couldn't help but

wonder where this thing between her and Rondo was headed. She wasn't necessarily interested in a relationship but having a male friend and dating one wasn't bad either. Anything was better than putting up with Erik's toxic ass that was for sure.

6

Frustration like no other masked Layla's face. The fact that she hadn't gotten in until damn near four in the morning after a work shift that would break the toughest worker, and having a splitting migraine, her apartment complex should've been the last people to piss her off. Saturday mornings for her were normally spent sleeping in until at least one in the afternoon. But, here it was eight sixteen in the morning, and Layla was inside the office ready to cuss every single person out; all two of them.

"We've called the maintenance men twice and they'll be out as quickly as possible."

"No. That's not going to work for me. As much money as I dish out every month to live here, there's no reason why my air conditioning is not functioning properly. Do you know how hot it is outside?"

One of the leasing agents named Krystal nodded. "I do. And we apologize for the inconvenience, but there's nothing we can do until the maintenance men arrive. Your unit is not the only one with an issue."

"And you guys think that's okay?" Layla scoffed. "My place better be the first one they stop at."

"We'll make sure they do Ms. Love."

"Mhm. Whatever," she grumbled, stomping toward the door.

Just as she grabbed the handle, the door was being opened by Brody. In jogger shorts, a tank top and Gucci flip flops on his feet, he looked like he'd just rolled out of bed as well. Seeing the frown on Layla's face stopped him from ogling her body in the thin, sundress he was sure she was wearing without a bra.

"Good morning neighbor," he spoke.

"It's not a good morning."

Stomping past him, Layla proceeded to head to her apartment. There was no way she was staying there until whomever came to fix her air conditioning. Had she not had a horrible night, she might not have snapped on them the way she had, but it was too late for all that now. Hurriedly, Brody retrieved a package he'd been delivered, and rushed out the office behind Layla. He didn't care if her morning wasn't going well; he was determined to make it better in some way.

"Aye," he huffed, doing a slight jog. Layla's long legs had her striding with ease. "Wait up, girl. You walking like you got somewhere to be."

"And you're rushing behind me like I don't."

Brody shook his head. "You this mean in the morning or all the time?"

Layla stopped midstride and turned around. "I am not mean."

"Shiiit," Brody dragged. "What you call it?"

"I'm a good detector of bullshit and bullshitters. There's a difference."

"A'ight. So what am I? Let me know what type of a nigga I am."

With his head held high, slightly tilted to the left, Brody grinned at her waiting for his examination. The morning sun was hitting his skin just right, causing his already bronze complexion to glow. Layla's eyes were transfixed on his big tattoo-covered arms. *I bet he can pick my ass up with ease. And look at those lips. Damn they're juicy.*

"That's what I thought," Brody smirked, breaking her focus.

"What?"

"You don't have anything on me. Trying to assess what

I have to offer got you looking silly," he joked, not realizing where Layla's thoughts had actually ventured off too.

"Whatever. It's hot, so unless you're trying to offer me some fans to place inside my apartment, I need to get out of this heat."

Brody frowned. "Your air not working?"

"No, and I'm so fucking irritated about it. I'll just have to thug it out I guess."

"You can come to my crib. No need to suffer when you have a friendly neighbor willing to offer up his space," he grinned making Layla shake her head.

"Seriously? Don't play."

"Nah. I'm for real. Grab what you need and meet me over there. I was about to cook breakfast."

"I don't eat meat. Well, not any red meat. I'm pescatarian."

Brody nodded. "A'ight. I can whip you up some salmon cakes. You like açai bowls?"

Layla's mouth watered. "Yes. Let me hurry my ass up."

When she walked the opposite way down the hall, Brody appreciated the view even more. Layla was slim but had an athletic build and a booty that wasn't stiff at all. He was hoping she put on something a little less revealing; something that didn't make her ass cheeks jiggle. Backing away toward his door, Brody bit his bottom lip and thanked his mama for calling to wake him up. Had she not overnighted him some things from out of town, he would've missed this opportunity.

Inside her apartment, Layla fussed and tossed clothes around that weren't even in her way. Working up a sweat by working out was one thing. Going through her drawer, she pulled out a crop top Adidas tee, and a pair of running shorts. Since she was already awake, Layla figured she'd get a quick workout in while they worked on her air conditioning.

Quickly, she hopped in the shower with the temperature set to almost cold and washed up. She'd showered hours prior but waking up sweating and dealing with the California heat guaranteed a two to three shower minimum a day. Twenty minutes later, Layla was rubbing her body down with cocoa butter, getting dressed, tossing her locs in a bun, and slipping on her tennis shoes. Her ceiling fan had provided little comfort while she was getting dressed.

"They better give me something toward my rent next month, too," she mumbled, closing and locking her door.

Three knocks to Brody's door and he was opening it with a handsome grin. "Thought you got lost."

"Had to shower and get my mind right. It smells so good in here," she said, stepping inside.

Taking in the cool air, Layla's eyes danced across his

living room. It smelled just like a man who cleaned up; fresh. The mahogany teakwood scent had Layla inhaling with each swivel of her head. The leather couch, black of course, had barely enough pillows. There were no decorations on the wall, a 65-inch TV was plastered on it though. Layla peeped the game consoles, distinctive smell of weed from the doobie in the ashtray, and how much different Brody's place was than hers. It was homey, but definitely could tell a man resided there.

"You want a tour?" Brody asked.

"I'm sure we have the same amenities."

"Nah. You don't have air," he joked, but Layla didn't crack a smile. "Too soon?"

"Way too soon. Show me to the kitchen joke master. This food better be good."

Leading the way, Layla was somewhat surprised, by how neat everything was. Then, she thought back to what kind of man she presumed Brody to be. A bachelor. The type who had to keep his place in tip-top shape just in case one of his flings stopped by.

"That ain't something you got to worry about. What made you want to become pescatarian?"

"Meat was starting to make me sick. I just wanted to feel better and what better way than to eat cleaner?"

Brody nodded, completely understanding. "Yeah, I

feel you. My trainer got me on this healthy shit, but I can't lie. I see a difference already."

"Your trainer? What do you have a trainer for?"

Brody turned to face her after flipping the salmon cakes. "To keep me motivated. I could easily say I'm going to the gym, but fake at the last minute. My trainer stays on my ass about working out and holding me accountable."

"You should let me train you."

"You," he pointed at Layla, then himself and said, "Train me? Nah. You'd be a distraction."

Layla shrugged. "If you say so. I work out five days a week."

"Damn. For real? I've never asked you, but what do you do for a living? I be seeing you dressed up, with them little beads around your waist, looking all fly and shit."

This man really has me blushing. "Thanks. And, I'm a bartender at *Shottas*."

"That can't be it. I coulda sworn I saw a video of you on Instagram reciting this cold ass poem. You got a twin?"

Layla chuckled and shook her head just as he took the patties out the pan and plated them on a plate covered with a paper towel.

"Not that I know of. I'm sure it was me though. I perform some nights at *Mic Check*. I wasn't aware that I'd gone viral," she mused, pulling her phone out.

"That's a poetry bar or something? Aye, don't laugh. I don't go to that type of shit. Get me hip, ma."

Scrolling through her Instagram posts that she'd been tagged in, Layla's eyes widened. She hadn't checked her page in a few days, thanks to work and needing a disconnect from social media and now she was regretting that she hadn't. Over fifty people had shared a video of her on stage that night she went home with Q. One of her favorite lyricists, Lady London, had even shared it on her IG story.

Filled with nothing but joy, the corners of her lips quirked into a light smile. Loving every post, and leaving a comment on those she could, Layla thanked them all for the love. She was high and in her feelings that night, but clearly the ladies and some men felt where she was coming from.

"They have certain themes on different nights throughout the week. Poetry night is the biggest though. It's good vibes, positive people, and amazing food. What's not to love?" she chuckled.

"I'ma have to check you out one night," Brody said, placing a plate of salmon cakes, eggs and rice in front of her.

"I'm, uh," she began, not really wanting to let him know she was actually performing later that night. Being on stage was her safe haven. It gave her a peace unknown and unmatched. Layla was in her element on stage, blocking out the negativity of the world and in her life. It was one thing for a guy, like Q, to witness her vulnerability. But for Brody? A guy she actually thought about pursuing beyond sexual satisfaction? Layla didn't know if she was ready for that. *I'm already doing a lot by being here, eating breakfast like we're some happy couple. What could it hurt?*

"What was you saying?" Brody asked, sitting their açai bowls down.

"I'm actually performing tonight if you don't have any plans. I know it's last minute so I understand if you can't make it."

"I'll be there. What time?"

Smiling on the inside, a sheer reflection of the one on her face, Layla said, "I go on at nine."

"Bet. I'm starting to learn more and more about your lowkey ass every day," he smirked, before chewing his food.

"Is that a good thing? I guess I'm not lowkey enough."

"Nah. It's perfect for me 'cause I'm lowkey too."

Layla sucked her teeth. "With all the women I see coming in and out of here? You sure I should be eating off this table. I don't know whose ass has been on here."

"No one's yet, but we can change all that in no time."

The stare Brody was giving her Layla would've

normally followed up with one just as intense. Surprisingly, she shied away from him, dropping her head with a grin. Had the plate in front of her not tasted so damn good, she would've taken him up on his offer. There was nothing like releasing a day's stress through an orgasm; she'd bet money on that.

The other reason she continued to eat her food was because Layla wanted to try something out of her norm with Brody. With her sexually driven appetite, the mention of anything sexual would have Layla's undivided attention. Somehow, Brody was keeping that without even having to go that route. Layla had always been so caught up in not wanting to feel forgotten or abandoned, that she used sex as a filler. Brody's conversation and presence alone was making her realize, maybe there was much more to the opposite sex than what was between their legs.

"Yeah," Brody laughed. "Gon' head and eat your food. I ain't even on that with you."

"Really?"

"Yeah. I mean don't get me wrong, you are fine as hell. Got this whole hippy, Black Queen aura about you and shit. Look like you'll fuck my life up with what's in between your legs and in your head, and I'm all for that. But I can tell it's something deeper within that made you that way. Something I don't want to be a just another number for."

Layla swallowed the last of her rice. "So, what do you want to be then? I'm not good with relationships. I tend to go missing some days. My attitude can piss you off so quickly and I'm a workaholic."

"Things that can be overlooked. I'm not asking for your hand in marriage; just trying to be a friend. I don't ever see any friends of yours besides that one chick, she said she's your cousin-sister or some weird shit."

Chuckling, Layla nodded. "Amelia. That's my cousin, but we grew up in the same house so we're really like sisters."

"That's what's up. So I guess my next question is, do you have a man?"

"No."

"A'ight. You said that quick as hell so I believe you."

They laughed and Layla realized she'd been doing that since stepping foot inside his place. It was... refreshing.

Replenishing.

"You have no choice but to believe me. I wouldn't lie about that. So, I have a new friend?" she asked, smiling.

"That you do. Don't go abusing this title either. I know where you live."

Layla tossed her balled up napkin at him. "Oh, whatever."

***

Sipping from the thin black straws in her cup, Layla swayed to smooth sounds of Q's voice. She was sure he was serenading the panties off almost every woman in the building. Luckily for her, she'd already been blessed by his pipe game. Layla smiled at the memory of their sex session before turning to head to the bar.

"One more shot and I'll be good," she thought.

It was going on nine o'clock, and her nerves were getting the best of her. What started off as a shitty morning had did a complete 360 thanks to Brody. If Layla hadn't been clear on his intentions before, he was sure to let them be known before she left his crib that afternoon. Caught up in her head and the possibilities of what they could be, Layla slightly jumped when someone grabbed her arm. Turning around, she smiled at her handsome cousin.

"Hey cousin," she greeted Rondo, who in turn pulled her in for a hug.

"What up LL," he greeted, calling her by the nickname she'd been given by their family. Short for her full name Layla Love. "This my girl Kali, Kali my cool ass cousin Layla."

Kali smiled and stuck her hand out. "Hey. Nice to meet you. Your hair is fly as fuck, girl."

"Thank you. You're his girl or his *girl?*" she enunciated the last one with a syrupy tone that had Rondo shaking his head.

"His classmate from school," Kali cleared up.

"Nah, she ain't my girl yet, but she will be."

Kali blushed as he tossed an arm over her shoulder. "What you drinking on? We need to catch up."

"Just some Henny straight," Layla offered.

Kali gagged, practically feeling the burn in her chest. "Woo! You better than me girl. I can't drink anything straight."

"Well you better prepare yourself for another shot. We can't stand at the bar without taking a shot," Rondo told her and Kali's face scrunched up.

She'd already taken a shot at the door. Upon entering *Mic Check*, each guest was required to take a shot of dark or light, before getting their night started. They adopted the routine from *Shottas*, and that was cool with Levi because his Uncle Sticks owned the place. Plus, he'd only do this on Saturday nights. Kali had Rondo pick their poison, and of course he'd chosen the whiskey for them to toss back. Kali shivered just thinking of how tipsy she was going to be by the end of the night.

"Light or dark?" the bartender yelled out in their direction.

"Dark, please. And we'll take three Dark & Lovelies," Layla told her.

Leaning over Kali whispered, "What're in those?"

"Rum and cherry flavoring."

"Shit," she breathed, fanning herself. "Are you trying to get me drunk girl?"

Layla laughed and slid her shot in front of her, then did the same with Rondo's. "Nope. Just want to make sure you have a good time. Drink up!"

Grabbing the shot glasses the trio brought them together before tapping the counter and tossing them back. Layla took hers like a pro as well as Rondo, while Kali gagged after it went down.

"Don't tell me you can't hang," Rondo whispered in her ear, causing the hairs on the nape of her neck to stand.

Lustfully, she looked up at him and winked. "I can."

"Good. Let's go find us a booth before it gets too packed in here. Lay, you good?"

Layla nodded. "Yeah. Just waiting for my turn on stage. It shouldn't be much longer."

"A'ight. Do your thang. You got this."

She smiled at his encouraging words. Not wanting to

look anxious or antsy, Layla let her eyes do a slow sweep of the crowd. She was sure she'd spot Brody out of everyone, but to no avail he hadn't graced her presence. Not wanting to let his absence put a damper on her jovial mood, Layla straightened her stance and headed toward the back hallway.

Just getting off stage, Q stood near one of the dressing rooms wiping his neck down with a towel. When their eyes connected, he licked his lips and headed her way. He tried focusing on her face, but Layla's body had him distracted.

Rocking a red silk wrap around her chest that was tied at the front, long bellbottom jeans that had her sharp hips protruding, locs high in a bun with the same silk material as a headband, and gold vintage bamboo earrings; Layla was definitely turning heads tonight.

"I saw you up there," she joked, nudging Q with her shoulder, like only a friend would do.

Q was hoping she'd greet him with a hug at least but that was short-lived. "I be trying to do my thing. You going on tonight?"

"Yep. Right after Maya gets off."

"We should link up after the bar closes."

Layla shook her head, and politely moved his arm from around her waist. "Nah. I'll have to take a raincheck.

Haven't gotten much sleep this week. You know how that is."

"If you aren't feeling a nigga, you can say that. You won't hurt my feelings," Q spoke, sounding more hurt than he wanted to let on.

"I'm sure I won't now, but I will in the long run. It was good seeing you tonight."

With those farewell words, Layla pivoted and headed toward the stage. Wiping her sweaty palms along her denim, she inhaled a deep breath and exhaled it even slower. With her eyes closed, she sent a quick prayer and thank you up to the Man above.

"Lord, thank you for my gift. May it be healing words for others in their time of need... and for mine as well. Amen."

"Ladies and gentlemen of *Mic Check*, you already know how special this next poet is. She's fly as hell, doesn't tolerate none of that lame ass game y'all be spitting, and is a masterpiece in her own right. Make some noise for LoveNU!"

Hearing the crowd's applause settled Layla's nerves immediately. Stepping on stage, the bright lights dimmed some as she grabbed the mic. Squinting her eyes, she scanned the crowd unable to find Brody, so she just brushed it off. She had an entire poem in her head but tossed it out last minute when she felt like he'd played her.

"How y'all doing?" she spoke softly, getting some hoots and hollers. "I had something written out for y'all lovely people tonight, but y'all mind if I switch it up a bit?"

"Gon' head girl!"

"Do your thang Love!"

"We love you baby!"

Layla chuckled softly. "I love y'all too."

Clearing her throat she said, "I guess we can title this one, Love for the Unknown."

Snaps of fingers echoed throughout the premises, before it got quiet. Closing her eyes Layla let the ambiance and vibes of the room take her away.

"With ease, he'd entered my mental space, taking up room that no one, no man has ever filled. Not to the brim. You see with him... my cup seemed to runneth over, leak into those wounds I once had. Those wounds I didn't want to be healed because... love. That shit had fucked me over one too many times. It wasn't him or what he could offer, it was me and what I couldn't. Who I couldn't be, things I needed to change. Parts of me that needed to grow... in peace.

But, you see. He wouldn't allow that. Not for me to do it alone anyway. He'd ease my worries, massage my guilt away, stroke my insecurities out of me and place ever so soft kisses on those wounds he hadn't caused. But was it for me or was it for him? Was I so damaged he felt the need to heal me? To save me? Stake claim on a piece of my mind, body and soul so that he could fulfill me to his liking? Bringing me to a peak only he could reach with his words?

Oh, girl. And his attentiveness. You see, I normally like my men a little obsessive. Just how I like my thongs, ladies. Up my ass."

The woman laughed and snapped their fingers, agreeing with her.

"I guess I haven't learned my lesson yet. This thing called love was like a game of chess. And who was I to second guess? Every second in his presence, made me want to turn them into minutes, before hours passed us by and weeks consumed our time. And those months of learning one another slowly grew into years of loving... who we thought they were.

So those wounds weren't healed, couldn't be since I hadn't let him in. I'll admit it, I was afraid of what loving him could bring. The emotions it could provoke, because I'd hate for a bitch to have to go crazy because he was lazy with my love. I needed a caution sign. One that still read slippery when wet. Because those wounds... those fucking wounds had never been sealed and had he drowned in them, I couldn't blame anyone but myself. Shit, do I need help?"

Finishing her set off, Layla scratched her head at the question as the crowd stood to their feet once again. Bashfully, she bowed her head and mumbled thank you's into the mic before the lights came back on. Looking out into the crowd, she peeped Rondo and Kali clapping loudly and she smiled. As if her eyes had a mind of their own, they ventured near the back of the club where Brody was standing.

She couldn't see his eyes clearly, but knew it was him from his tall stature and curly sponged mane that sat atop his head. He was practically towering over everyone in the place. Stepping off stage, Maya, another artist, was first to greet her.

"Damn girl. That was fire," she beamed. "I'm glad I recorded it."

"Thank you. I appreciate that."

Walking out into the crowd, Layla headed straight for Brody. She was surprised to see him, but was happy nonetheless. She didn't break her stride, not even when a female walked up to Brody. The woman placed a hand on Brody broad chest, but it was quickly removed as he glanced down at her with a look of disgust on his face.

"Aye, watch out. I don't fuck with you like that anymore," he spoke evenly, delivering a clear message. But clearly, she didn't get it.

"Oh, so you don't fuck with me now? Since when? I

saw the way you were staring at that weird, brokenhearted chick on stage. That's you now B?"

"Kaniece. Gon' with that bullshit 'fore you get your feelings hurt."

"By who, you?" she scoffed with laughter in her voice.

"Nah. By me. And I'm not brokenhearted, honey. I'm fed up with niggas not acting right. I'm guessing that's what the issue is here? Brody played you and now you miss him?"

Boldly, Layla stepped forward and positioned herself in front of Brody.

"I-uh," the girl stammered.

"No, I get it. You see him out, giving attention to another woman when you thought it belonged to you? It hurts, I know. But, that's just how it goes. You win some, you lose some. Brody is letting you take this L nicely, but if I were you, I'd walked away before it gets real ugly in this bitch. I don't handle disrespect well, and I'd hate for you to take my harsh words as a replacement of these hands. They'll hurt your feelings for real."

Kaniece stood for all of five seconds, assessing the situation and weighing her options. Brody had already been ignoring her calls for the last two weeks and that pissed her off. She'd hate to get embarrassed by Layla, especially with all the love everyone had just shown her. Too surprised by Layla's read to do more than just nod, Kaniece walked away. That was her best bet.

Behind Layla, Brody was so caught off guard he hadn't spoken a word. His hand had wrapped around her waist when she stood in front of him though. Turning around to face him, Layla smiled.

"Hey. You made it."

"Shit, do you need help for real?" Brody questioned, his eyes slightly widened at how quickly she simmered down. He'd never seen no shit like that ever.

Held tilted back, Layla laughed a good laugh in his embrace. "Stop. I was just letting the girl know what she needed to hear."

Pulling her closer to him by the belt-loops in her jeans, Layla wrapped her arms around his neck. His broad chest, wide shoulders, bulging biceps and firm hold on her waist made her melt. Loving how comfortable she seemed to be in his arms, Brody placed a kiss to her neck and damn near wanted to attack she smelled so good.

"Yeah? You gon' tell me what I wanna hear too?"

Layla giggled. "What's that?"

"That you're happy to see me and wore this little top for me."

Giggling some more, Layla shook her head. Brody had her out of her element. To anyone watching their playful banter, they could easily conjure that Brody was the man she spoke on in her poem. She'd been feeling a way around him since forever, but the time they shared in his apartment hours prior awakened something in Layla she didn't want to rest... just yet.

"I'm happy to see you and I think someone is happy to see me too," she whispered closely to his ear, while letting her hand stroke the semi-erection in his jeans. "Mmm, that's all you?"

Brody grabbed her wrist and put some distance between them. Layla frowned not liking his actions. "Aye chill out, a'ight? You killed that shit up there tonight."

"Thanks," she replied dryly. Unenthused by his rejection and praise in one sentence.

"If you got an attitude, I'm 'bout to shake."

Layla shrugged while adjusted her top. "Whatever. Go fuck with them hoes you got. I'm sure that's why you were late in the first place."

Not liking where this was going, Brody practically yanked Layla to him. Possessively, he grasped her waist and held her close as a group of people walked by.

"Good shit tonight Love. I fucks with you," a guy spoke.

"Thank you," she mumbled his way before looking back at Brody.

"You can let me go now," she hissed lowly.

"Shut up. I'll let you go when I want to. I'm not about

to fuck with no hoes if that's what you think. I was late getting here because I overslept. Had you remembered our conversation from earlier, you'd know that I have to be at work at ten-fifteen."

Layla's face softened and her resolve crumbled a bit. "I'm sorry. I just... I don't know."

"You thought I was abandoning you, huh? If I tell you I'm going to do something or be somewhere, you gotta believe that. The last thing a nigga wants to do is hurt you with lies. That's not me, but I'll have to prove that to you."

The noise around them zeroed out as Layla took in every word he said. For him to offer an explanation was priceless in her book. She respected him even more than she already did and learned just that much more about him. Playing with the collar of his denim button-down, Layla exhaled and poked her bottom lip out.

"Forgive me. You did tell me you had to work."

"I know I did so quit all that tough girl shit. Had I left up out of here for real, you would've been standing outside my door waiting when I got off work."

Chuckling, Layla shook her head from side to side as he caressed her hips. "I'm not that crazy. Plus, you only live a couple doors down. I would've just been checking my peephole."

She said that with a shrug and Brody couldn't do shit

but laugh. "Same difference, girl. This a cool little spot though. The energy in here is crazy."

"I know right," Layla beamed. "Let me introduce you to a few people. You have time?"

Checking his watch, Brody nodded his head. "Yeah."

Walking him over to the booth where Rondo and Kali were sitting, she introduced everyone. Rondo stood and slapped hands with Brody, and Kali gave him a quick wave.

"Girl," Kali dragged. "I don't know what nigga hurt you, but baby. He fucked up and lost a gem. You are so freaking talented."

"Thank you, girl. I just be trying to get out what I'm feeling."

"That's the best way cuz. Don't be holding that shit in. Brody, you drinking?"

"Nah. I gotta be at work in a few," he answered.

"Make that money, don't let it make you," Kali sassed, snapping her fingers.

Rondo shook his head and pulled her closer into his side. "Excuse her. She been drinking like a fish. Bae, eat some of these fries."

"Oooh. I'm bae now?" Kali cooed looked up at him. "You so fine Rondo. I might make you my second baby daddy. But you boyfriend material too."

Layla's head fell into her palm. "Yeah, she's good and tipsy. I'm going to walk him outside and I'll be back."

"A'ight," Rondo replied, while Kali kissed along his neck. "You better chill out 'fore you start some shit."

"I like starting shit."

Outside in front of Brody's matte black Dodge Durango SRT, Layla marveled over the tires as if it were her first time seeing them. Her favorite color besides black was red, and the big body vehicle made her want to drive it every time she saw it.

"I'm starting to think you like this mothafucka more than me," Brody chirped, getting her attention.

"Aww, don't be jealous. What time do you get off?"

"A little after eight. You gon' wait up for me?"

"Absolutely not," she said making them both laugh. "Now, what I can do is bring you some lunch. When is that break?"

"Man, you ain't getting up at three o'clock to bring me no food."

Layla cocked her head to the side. "What'd you tell me in there? If I tell you I'm going to do something or be somewhere, you gotta believe that," she said mocking him, tone and all.

Brody chuckled, scratching at the hair on his face. "A'ight. You got me. It's at three-fifteen. Don't be trying to bring me no heavy ass meal that's gon' have me sleepy either."

"I won't. Nothing I eat is super heavy anyway. You'll love it."

Brody smirked. "You cooking me a fresh meal at the wee hours of the morning? What did I do to deserve such treatment?"

"You showed up. That means more to me than you know."

Feeling all the emotions in her eyelids, Layla blinked rapidly to keep her tears at bay. So many times people, including her mother, had made promises but broke them. They never showed up for her when she needed them but Layla kept hoping they would. She tried not letting those who let her down be the reason other people in her life suffered, but it was hard. So damn hard.

Thankfully, the window of opportunity had been left open just for Brody. He was a man of his word so far, and for that Layla was going to show him nothing but love from here on out. He at least deserved that if anything.

R ondo was willing to risk it all... but only if she were down.

The sexual tension inside Mic Check had thickened

and surrounded them inside Rondo's Benz. As he cruised the streets heading from the bar, Kali couldn't keep her hands to herself. It'd been a while since she gotten loose and just let her hair down. Rondo didn't seem to mind, and for that she was elated.

"I can't believe how much fun I had tonight," she gushed, leaning over the console, all in his face.

Rondo kept his cool, per usual. "I'm glad you did, love."

"I am too. I like you."

He glanced her way and smirked at her low eyes, lazy smile and relaxed posture. She cared not one bit about being all in his personal space as he navigated his vehicle to her crib.

"Yeah? What you like about a nigga, huh? Or that's that liquor talking?"

She giggled some more. "You're just you. Cool as fuck and can make me laugh. Plus you fine. You know how fine you are?"

Rubbing a hand down his cheek, Kali stared at the side of his face with pure lust in her eyes. She wanted nothing more than to end their night with Rondo's head plastered between her legs, and her back arched. It'd been a while; too long if Kali could be honest. When Rondo coolly licked his lips, every nerve in her body shot straight to the inside of her thighs.

"You all in my face," Rondo chuckled.

"So. I can be wherever I want to be," she sassed back, running her hand down his defined chest. "And you smell so good. I want you so bad."

"I got you. Sit back for me so I can concentrate."

Doing as she was told, Kali sat back in her seat but her hand never left his body. It roamed his frame and massaged his muscular arms as he drove. Before she knew it, they were pulling up in front of her place. Before he could place the car in park, Kali was unfastened her seatbelt and climbing into his lap. With the space between them now limited, Rondo had no choice but to feed into her sexual advances. Gripping her little ass in the skirt she was wearing, Kali bit down on her bottom lip.

"Oooh. Your hands fit perfectly on this ass."

Rondo smirked. "You're drunk, ma."

"I'm not," she whined. "I'm a little tipsy, maybe, but I'm giving you full consent to do what you need to do to put this fire between my legs out."

"You burning?" His brow shot in the air, though he was joking.

Kali slapped his chest. "Stop playing with me. Come inside. I know you want to."

Grinding in his lap, Kali felt the effect she had on him and wasn't disappointed at all. The seat of her panties were soaked, leaving little to the imagination of how turned on Rondo had her. The more she grinded on his lap, the hotter her body grew. The drinks she indulged in played a part as well.

"You sure about this? I need a definite answer," he spoke, looking directly in her eyes.

Grabbing his hand, Kali slid it over the seat of her underwear and held it there. She was scorching hot and dripping wet. Rondo closed his eyes and inhaled her sweet essence that coated the air like a car plug-in.

"Hop up," he told her.

Climbing into the passenger seat, Kali took a few seconds to compose herself before opening her door. Cutting his car off, Rondo came around to her side and helped her out. Hitting his locks, he wrapped a hand around her waist as he guided them to the door of her townhome. Hours before he had no intentions of returning, but oh how quickly plans change.

Not a hint of nervousness settled when Kali closed and locked the door behind them. She was well prepared for what was about to go down... so she thought. Walking up behind her, Rondo moved her hair from one side of her neck to the other.

"And, here I thought you were a good girl," he said, letting his lips brush against her neck.

Kali exhaled softly. "I never said that."

"Good, 'cause if you were I was turning your ass out

tonight."

Turning her around, Kali took the lead and pulled his lips toward hers. Nothing was gentle about the need she felt in the pit of her stomach for Rondo. He'd been on her radar since classes began, and though she was a bit apprehensive at first, Kali was glad he'd made the first move. As their tongues danced to a beat of their own, Rondo hoisted Kali up around his waist causing her skirt to rise to her belly.

"Which way?" he mumbled against her lips.

"Up the steps, first door to the left."

Rondo's long legs made it up the steps of her townhome in record speed. Bumping her door open, he wasted no time, tossing Kali's small frame onto the bed. She bounced a few times, giggling..

"Don't be throwing me like that," she fussed with a smile, drinking all six feet of his milk chocolate frame in.

Stripping from his shirt, Rondo tossed it in the chair nearby and stepped to the end of the bed. Grabbing her ankle, he gently yanked Kali in his direction before removing the heels she had on. Next was her skirt. Kali peered up at him as she lay in nothing but a lace thong. She'd removed her shirt while he removed his. The thickness of her petite frame caused a throaty groan to escape Rondo.

Damn she's fine. He thought running his hands up her

thighs that felt like silk. Forcing himself not to rip her panties off like the beast in him wanted to, Rondo removed them with precision. His mouth moistened at the sight of her naked frame. Her breasts had a slight sag thanks to Khyri but were still perky enough to wear no bra on most days. Stomach was flat and decorated with light stretch marks that Rondo couldn't help but run his hands over, appreciating the sacrifice she made with her body for her seed. When his eyes finally adjusted to her treasure, he licked his lips and pulled her closer to the edge.

I gotta taste her.

Lowering himself to the ground, Rondo spread her puffy lips apart, admiring the pinkness of her center. Like a sweet snack after dinner, he dove right in. His thick lips brushed against hers. Kali inhaled sharply at the feeling of his warm lips and she gasped as his warmer tongue caressed her clit.

"Huuu," she breathed.

Hearing the sound of contentment in her small huff, Rondo, without warning, began to eat her savagely. Flickering his tongue back and forth against her swollen flesh, Kali's body thrashed about the bed, making her head swim. Her body was overwhelmed with pleasure and an intense need to release.

"Damn Rondo," she moaned, clasping a hand to the back of his neck.

When he sucked on her pearl, Kali's entire back arched away from her peach colored comforter. "Shit." Skilled in everything he mastered, Rondo took her words as encouragement and slurped on her center like he was dying to get the last corner of a beverage from a cup through a straw.

Loudly.

Unapologetically.

And downright nasty, Rondo satisfied his thirst for Kali. Her stomach caved when one then two of his fingers sank inside her. She was tight. Unusually tight for someone as fine as she was. Rondo didn't think she was out there busting it open for just anyone, but damn. She had his dick even harder now, straining to be set free from its barrier.

"Oh, my," Kali breathed, chest rising and falling as if she couldn't breathe. "Yes, right there."

Cupping her ass in his hands, that fit perfectly like Kali said, Rondo devoured every last drop of her. Rotating her hips, Kali moaned out breathlessly, giving him all of her. Legs trembling, back arched, and hands firmly on his head; Kali came unraveled. The pace of his tongue rapidly flickering and strokes from his fingers had her beat.

"Ro... Rondooo," she groaned loudly.

Kali's stomach sank as her first orgasm flushed over her entire body. Limbs stiffening, she lay there shivering as Rondo placed soft kisses to her center before doing the same to the inside of her thighs. Removing his fingers, his entire hand was drenched.

Licking his fingers like he'd just completed a hearty meal, Rondo smacked his lips. "Knew that pussy was fire. With your pretty ass. Look at you."

Kali blinked a few times before peeling her eyes open. Her bright fawn skin had taken on a reddish hue. Her cheeks were puffed out, and no longer was she tipsy from the drinks; Rondo's head game had made her silly drunk. Grabbing the pillow next to her Kali covered her face and groaned softly as he delivered a smack to her thigh.

"I't know what you hiding for. You wasn't just shy a second ago."

"I'm... whew. I can go straight to sleep," she giggled, removing the pillow.

Unbuckling his jeans, Rondo shook his head and removed them. "Nah. No sleeping with me. Ain't this what you wanted?"

Massaging his length through his boxers, Rondo removed them as well. His dick sprang out, capturing Kali's undivided attention. Unable to respond verbally, Kali simply nodded her head and propped herself on her elbows. Licking her lips, she tweaked her nipples as Rondo gathered juices from her glistening lips and covered his dick with them.

Though he wouldn't mind seeing her pink lips, the ones on her face, wrapped around his dick, he had the carnal desire to delve into her gushy walls first. Her hair was wild and all over her head and Rondo smirked once he saw the passion mark he'd left on her right thigh.

As bad as his smaller head wanted to slide up in her with no rubber, he was sure he'd make do on her joke to becoming her second baby daddy. He wasn't even going to lie to himself. Reaching in his pocket, he retrieved a condom from his wallet and slid it on. Grabbing her ankle, Rondo drug Kali to the end of the bed where she'd scooted away from. Hovering over her, he kissed her poked-out lips and patted her thigh.

"Flip that ass over," he commanded.

Sexily, in a drunk-sex manner, Kali tooted her ass high in the air and peeked over her shoulder. "Like this?"

Rondo smacked her ass cheek, before gripping both. They jiggled in his hands as he nodded with appreciation for their softness. "Yeah, just like that. Don't move."

Unable to help himself, Rondo got another helping of her pussy lips before aligning himself at her entrance. Slowly, he eased inside and quickly pulled out.

"Shit," he grumbled, shaking his head. "This pussy dangerous."

"Hmm?"

Kali had not a clue what was going on behind her.

Attempting to compose himself from busting too soon, Rondo closed his eyes and slid inside. The warmth and tightness that engulfed him, had him gripping her waist so tight. He stroked slowly at first, savoring the way her walls clenched against his dick. When Kali began to throw it back on him, Rondo tossed all thoughts of pacing himself out the window. If he nutted too soon, fuck it. They had all night.

Taking a handful of her hair, Kali whimpered, loving his aggressiveness. He was beating her shit out the frame with no mercy. It'd been a minute since she'd taken dick, but you'd never know. Sex was like riding a bike; once you mastered the technique you'd always remember. With the way Kali was bouncing her ass and fucking Rondo back, he wasn't going to last much longer. The way she was taking all of him boosted Rondo's ego.

"Ooh, this dick feels so good," she cried, lying flat out on the bed.

In that position, Rondo took full advantage. Pulling her legs closed, he stroked her deeply while massaging her cheeks. Kali rolled her hips loving this position even more. Leaning forward, Rondo kissed across her back, licked down her spine and repeated the action. Kali gripped the sheets tightly in her fist. She was on the brink of her third... or was this the fourth, orgasm.

Lifting her body up from the bed, Rondo cradled her

against his chest with her legs in the hook of his arms. Sucking on her neck, he bounced Kali up and down on his dick.

"Aahhh!" she shouted, not giving a single fuck about how loud she was.

"Yeah, that's it. Wet this dick up," Rondo encouraged. "This pussy was made just for me.

Wrapping her arms around his neck, Kali held him tightly in the awkward position as she released all over him. Her entire frame shuddered as he stroked her clit through her orgasm. Behind her lids, Kali was seeing the stars, the moon... *shoot, is that heaven?* Rondo had taken her body on an adventure. To an entirely different stratosphere.

Seeing that he hadn't come yet, Kali squeezed her muscles around him and whispered in his ear. "Mmm. Give me all that dick."

One hand held her up, as the other clasped around the front of her neck. The freakier she talked in his ear, the closer Rondo was to coming undone. Putting his back into it, he thrust deeper inside her, getting a yelp from Kali's trembling lips. She was on the verge of climaxing just by him being inside her.

With a firm grip on her, Rondo's legs locked and balls tightened. His release weakened his stance, causing him to fall back on the bed. Breathing hard, his hand fell lazily from her neck and wrapped around her waist as she sat atop him.

"Goddamn, girl," he groaned when she turned around, him still inside her.

Giggling, Kali hovered over him and pecked his lips. Rondo opened his eyes and shook his head. "Don't tell me you're tired. I can go all night," she told him.

"Get a nigga some water first, please," he huffed out making them both laugh.

Pecking his lips again, Kali climbed from his lap and went to use the restroom before grabbing a robe from the back of her door. She winced with every step to the kitchen but a satisfied smile was on her face. Opening her fridge, she frowned at it being the last battle of cold water she had. Room temperature water just wouldn't do, so they'd have to share. Making it back to her room, Rondo was still laid out but sat up some. Twisting the cap, Kali drank from it first before passing it to him. Sharing that ice water after sex was so damn uplifting; Kali knew Rondo was a keeper.

Having sex on the first night didn't have her feeling a way at all. In fact, had the opportunity presented itself before now, she would've taken it. But, timing was everything and Rondo came through and showed out just in the nick of time.

7

Shanae hated being in her feelings. Especially when there was wine involved. The almost empty bottle stared back at her as she took a sip from her flute. The TV was on but the sound was drowned out by the consistent warnings in her head. The ones she should've listened to before now. The culprit behind her being in her feelings was no one other than Isaiah himself.

Not only had she been blowing his line down and getting ignored, but she'd actually thought after their talk a few days ago he'd change. Or, at least try to. But who was she kidding? This was the same boy who'd played with her heart plenty times before and made no conscious effort to ease any pain he'd caused her. Shanae knew better, and she knew it too.

"I can't stand his ass," she hissed, pouring the

remainder of her wine in the glass and gulping it down. "Ol' stupid ass."

Standing to her feet, Shanae ambled toward the kitchen for more wine but the vibration of her phone caught her attention. Hustling to turn around, she hoped like hell it was Isaiah because she was going to surely give him a piece of her not so sober mind. Picking the phone up, she sucked her teeth as Kali's name flashed across the top. Knowing her cousin wasn't the reason for her attitude, she answered her call.

"Hey Kali."

"Eww. Don't be answering my call like that. Let's start that over," Kali fussed. "Hey cousin! How are you?"

Stepping inside her kitchen, Shanae rolled her eyes. "You're too much in a good mood for me to be talking to you."

"Awww, what's the matter?" Kali asked concerned.

Holding the neck of the wine, Shanae blinked back tears. She was so tired of crying over the same nigga, about the same issues, it wasn't funny. She couldn't help it though, nor turn them off long enough to stop caring. It was a vicious cycle and if anyone knew about that, she was sure Kali did.

Sniffling, she placed her on speaker. "I'm just so fed up with Isaiah. Like, for real Kal. I'm tired. I shouldn't be going through all this bullshit this young. Should I?"

"No. You absolutely should not be. But like I told you before; you'll be done when you're ready to be done. I can give you all the advice in the world, but it won't matter if you're not ready. That nigga be acting up and guess what? You be letting him. You gotta get a backbone and stand up to his ass. It's supposed to be a hot girl summer and you over there about to have a heart as cold as ice."

Shanae snickered at her analogy. "Shut up. No I'm not. I've been drinking too... so, yeah."

"Oh, goodness. Well, look. Enough about that sad shit. I have something to tell you." Kali bopped in her seat she was so hype.

"Ok. I'm listening."

Flopping down on her couch, Shanae turned the TV down that was actually loud as hell now that she wasn't inside her own head.

"I had sex with Rondo," she whispered with a blush coating her cheeks.

"Oooh. It's a hot girl summer for real," Shanae laughed. "When was this that you were busting that thang wide open?"

Kali laughed. Loud. "Giiirl. Over the weekend and let's just say I'm ready to do it all over again after this final in an hour. That nigga's dick was *goodt*."

"With a 't'?" Shanae laughed.

"Yep. And he was just everything. Damn, I been

155

missing out. Trying not to date too soon because of Khyri, but fuck that. Mama gotta have a life too."

The cousins cracked up over the phone. Shanae understood completely though. It wasn't like she and Erik were ever getting back together, so she might as well have some fun.

"I heard that. I'm happy for you. I know he had to comb through them cobwebs."

"Girl, fuck you," Kali laughed. "Oh! I almost forgot. Guess who I ran into at the store earlier?"

"Who? You know you know everyone and their mother's, mother," Shanae yawned.

"Levi."

Time stood still for a second after hearing his name. Placing her glass atop the coaster on her marble and gold table, Shanae crossed her legs. Just the mention of his name had her hot.

"Oh. That's what's up."

"And I-uh. I accidentally gave him your address. But it wasn't out of ill intentions. He said you'd been ignoring him and I know you like him, so I thought he'd reach out to see why," Kali rushed.

Shanae picked her glass back up and took a generous sip before saying, "And you thought telling him where I live was how he could reach out? Kal," she whined.

"I know. I know. I'm sorry. It's not like we don't know

him. Plus, I don't think he'll actually pop up at your place anyway."

"Yeah, well let's hope—"

The buoyant ding-dong from her front door jangled Shanae's nerves, causing her to jump. Looking around the room as if someone else were to get the door, brought her crashing back to consciousness as good as a slap to the face.

"Oh, my gosh," Kali squealed in a whisper. "Is that him?"

"I don't know," Shanae whispered back.

"Go see. And why the hell are we whispering? Want me to stay on the phone?"

Shanae couldn't verbally answer, but a nod was given. On trembling legs, similar to a fawn, she wobbled to the door. With the phone clutched tightly in her hand, she lifted on her tip-toes and jumped back when she saw his face and the doorbell sounded again.

"It's him. I'll call you back," she rushed, hanging up in Kali's face.

Wiping at the corner of her eyes to remove any eye boogers, Shanae cleared her throat and unlocked her door. She about lost her breath at the sight of Levi standing before her.

"My bad. Were you sleeping?" he questioned, deep baritone making Shanae's core quake with need.

Shanae sure wish she would've been. Her dreams had been nothing but him since that day at the mall. At least in her dreams she could hide the silly grin on her face. Not right now though. Donned in a red polo, white shorts, with red and white Retro 3's, Shanae admitted that was her favorite color now. It looked damn good against his sun kissed, cinnamon skin.

"No. I was just chilling. What's up? I'd ask how you got my address, but she already told me."

Levi smirked. "Is that a problem? I could've easily gotten it on my own, had you returned a nigga's texts. You running from me?"

Playfully, Shanae rolled her eyes. "No. If you'd come in, I can somewhat explain. It's hot as hell out here."

Levi crossed the threshold to her apartment and fanned his shirt that was sticking to his back. "Hot as hell and you had me out there ringing the doorbell that long."

"You survived. Want a water?"

"Yeah. Fasho. Nice spot you got. I see you been sipping."

While she grabbed him a bottle of water from the fridge, Levi had no problem making himself right at home. Grabbing the neck of the wine bottle, he read the label before placing it back down.

"It's sweet red, thanks to your grandma," Shanae

smiled. "She stayed leaving a bottle open and I would sneak it all the time."

"And she thought it was me. You look good and tipsy."

Peeping her lazy smile, Levi took a seat on the couch. In that position, he was given a nice view of Shanae's short, thick legs in the shorts she had on. The t-shirt she was rocking a little young, causing her pudge to poke out but he didn't care nothing about that. And let it be known when she tried tugging her shirt down.

Pushing her hand away he said, "Ain't nothing wrong with what you wearing, but if my presence is making you uncomfortable I understand."

"I just wasn't expecting company. These are my lounging clothes."

Levi licked his lips, eyeing the print of her pussy before shaking his head. "I like 'em. Sit down 'fore I do some shit you gon' be regretting."

He didn't have to tell her twice. Shanae took a seat next to him and tucked her feet, before facing him. It felt like old times at Ms. Gene's crib with them just chilled back, relaxing. Twisting the cap on the bottle, Levi took his time drinking from the plastic. His eyes were fixated on Shanae's as the cold liquid entered his body. The motion of his Adam's apple bobbing had her breathing hard. Something so simple as him drinking, was so damn masculine and sexy.

When he was done, draining the contents in seconds, Levi burped lowly and excused himself. Shanae swooned at his mannerisms. Isaiah never said excuse me. Ever.

"Nothing like some cold water straight out the fridge."

"That must be all you drink?" Shanae questioned before the words could process in her brain.

Levi smirked. "Why you say that?"

"Because... your skin. It's so freaking clear. You used to have acne back in the day."

"And that shit was ugly. Had to start taking care of my skin. That's not all I drink though. What about you? You the one still pretty as hell, not a flaw in sight."

Waving him off, Shanae grinned. "Thank you and yeah. Only water and wine. Some juice here and there. The perfect balance if you ask me."

"Sound like my grandma. But, what's up? Tell me why you been ignoring me. I don't like that shit. Now that I'm back in town, we have some unfinished business to handle."

"Oh, do we?" she chuckled, slightly tilting her head.

"Yeah... we do. Now talk, woman. I know that wine got you feeling good. Gon' and gossip to a nigga like you used to do."

Shanae couldn't help but smile. She stayed coming to him about the females in their neighborhood and at school who had a problem with her. Even if they didn't, every day she was either at his grandma's running the day's events down to him or over the phone. She missed those days when the drama and issues back then were nothing. Now, she wasn't so sure about airing her business out.

"It's about another nigga, so I'm sure you wouldn't like to hear that."

"Nah, not anything concerning him; just you. My concern will always be you. You caught up in your feelings that's why you dodging me?"

Shanae's frame practically melted into the cushion. *Lord, what is he doing to me?* Getting comfortable on the couch, she exhaled.

"Yes and no. Yes, because I didn't want to reach out to you knowing I'm still dealing with someone."

"Dealing with or tolerating?" Levi questioned and fidgeted with the drawstring on her shorts. Being honest with herself for once, she gave him the real answer.

"Tolerating. Holding on to some shit I should've been let go of. Always wondering where I stand with him, I guess. Where we stand with each other."

"Having to wonder where you stand with a man, is where you stand. A man, a real one who appreciates you, wouldn't have you questioning your position in his life; it'd be known. He'd let it be known."

Truer words had never been spoken. Shanae grabbed at her chest, feeling the impact of his words hitting her hard. Many of times she'd question Isaiah about what they were doing, if they should even be together, and why couldn't he give her an answer. No answer was the answer and Shanae was starting to realize that.

"Damn," Shanae sighed. "I've never thought about it like that. Look at you coming over here dropping wisdom on me."

"Aye. You know I'ma always keep it a buck. So, what you feeling like now? You ready to see what being treated by a real man is like?"

The stroke of his hand against her thigh, made Shanae cough. His strong, large hand caressed her thigh, causing her breaths to become shallower than they already were.

"Um, I don't know. I don't want to get hurt or make the same mistakes I've made in the past."

Levi's hand stopped moving. "I won't let you."

"H-How do you know that?"

"Because, you were meant for me. Why would I hurt the one thing God placed on this Earth for me? You were mine since the day I saw you skipping class outside of Mr. Wallace's store."

Laughing, Shanae shook her head. "You bought me lunch that day and for the rest of the week."

"Yeah, and you still friend-zoned my ass. Had a nigga breaking bread for damn near a week straight."

The two laughed and some of the tension settled, but

not the intensity of their conversation. Rubbing up and down her leg, Levi put all inhibitions aside and lifted her onto his lap. She was so small situated above him, he couldn't help but have her closer. He needed to feel her energy. Have her in his face. Shanae licked her lips, trying to shake her jittery nerves.

Levi's golden honey eyes were staring into her soul. His gaze was so intense, Shanae dropped her head. She couldn't look at him while sitting on his lap and feeling how she was. Somehow in her mind she was cheating on Isaiah.

"You gave that nigga what belonged to me?" Levi asked, lifting her head so she could look him in the eyes.

Her eyes softened and heart rate quickened. "It was supposed to be yours, but you left."

"I'm here now. Can I still stake claim to it. Write my name with my tongue all over it?"

"Levi," Shanae whined, as his hands slipped in the back of her shorts.

Gripping her ass cheeks, he rocked her back and forth over his growing erection. Kissing along her collarbone, Levi found her spot and stayed there. Torturing Shanae in the worst way, he sucked on her neck and moved his left hand to the center of her panties. They were soaked. Running his hand across the fabric, her nipples hardened and clit blossomed at his touch.

"I missed you," he rasped, pushing them to the side and stroking her slit with the pad of his digits. "You ain't miss a nigga, Pumpkin?"

That nickname, one he'd given her the week they met, made her smile. He claimed she had a pumpkin shaped head, but it fit her body. When a finger slid deep inside her, Shanae gasped and let her head fall onto his shoulder.

"Levi, please," she begged. Not knowing what she was begging for.

His tongue was licking at her neck slowly, savoring the taste of her chocolate skin. While one hand was wrapped around her waist and the other finding its way home, Shanae's eyes rolled in her head at the thickness of his fingers stretching her out. Levi pushed deeper, causing her to drip onto his palm.

"Ahhh, Levi," she moaned into his neck, as his thumb stroked her clit.

Gripping the back of his neck, Shanae rode his fingers and pressed her chest more into his. Her wild, curly mane tickled the side of his face and the pace of his fingers quickened. Levi had always loved her natural hair, whereas Isaiah always wanted for her to "do something with it." The shit annoyed her to no end.

The sound of his name being moaned from her lips, turned him on in a way Levi didn't know could happen. It was just something, no everything, about Shanae that had him wanting to lose control. Wanting to flip her over on the couch and give her exactly what her body needed from him. Instead, he kept his composure and brought her to her peak.

With his free hand now gripping a handful of her curls, Levi skillfully spread her juices over his thumb and massaged her clit in a circular motion. Shanae's eyes popped open and she gasped loudly before smashing her lips into his. Riding the wave of her orgasm, she tongued Levi down with every breath in her. When her thighs tightened around him, and pussy walls contracted around his fingers, Levi held onto her securely. Safely in his arms where she should've been all along.

The way she moaned his name through her release and held him just as tight had Levi wishing he'd never left to begin with. Shanae's eyes fluttered open and she lifted her head. Biting on her bottom lip, she held onto his wrist and grinded a little more while grinning.

"Yeah?" Levi questioned, smacking her ass. "Give me the word and I'll have your little ass bent over this couch."

Giggling, Shanae shook her head. "No. I don't think I'm ready for that."

She looked down and her toes tingled. Levi was packing. Thick and long was the outline of his dick and Shanae just knew what he had between his legs would make her crazy. Pulling his hand from her panties and shorts, Levi nastily licked his fingers. Slowly, twirling his tongue around each digit until they were clean. Shanae watched him in awe; her stomach doing flip flops at the way his tongue moved.

"You're so nasty," she said, hopping up.

"Shit, you taste good then a mothafucka. And that pussy tight so I know you ain't been getting piped down like you deserve," he said standing up. Adjusting his hard-on, Levi chuckled cockily, in only a manner he could. "It's all good though. When you're ready, it'll be well worth the wait."

Swallowing hard, Shanae just blinked. What the hell could she say to that? "Um, yeah. Okay."

He smiled making her do the same in return. "Got you speechless. Where ya bathroom at?"

"Straight ahead, down the hall."

Levi gave her a nod and headed in that direction. Stuck, standing, looking silly with a goofy grin on her face, Shanae did a twirl in the middle of her living room. Rubbing the side of her neck where he gripped it at one point, she sighed in sexual satisfaction. Before she could even enjoy her high, thunderous knocks were pounded against her front door, scaring the shit out of her. Jumping, Shanae fixed her clothes and rushed to the door.

"Shanae! You better open this fucking door, on God!" Isaiah belted from the outside.

"Oh shit."

Shanae's eyes popped out of her head as she rushed to grab her phone. She wanted to kick herself when she saw five missed calls from Isaiah and some threatening text messages. So caught up in all of Levi, she hadn't paid attention to her phone since he arrived.

"Need me to handle that?" Levi questioned calmly, walking back into the living room.

"No. It's my ex. The situation I was telling you about."

"Oh, a'ight. Get the door. I'ma sit right here," he said, nodding toward the couch they were just on.

Knowing there was no way Levi was leaving and Isaiah wasn't either, Shanae had to put on her big girl underwear. Though she was freaking out, a small part of her couldn't wait to see the look on Isaiah's face when he saw another man in her crib. Unlocking the door, she pulled it open.

"Why are you banging on my door like you're crazy?" she asked calmly.

"Man, who the fuck car is this out here? You got a nigga in here?"

When he tried stepping inside, Shanae pushed him back. "That's none of your business. We aren't together. I've been calling you all day and now you want to pop up on some angry shit? Boy, bye."

Smacking her hand away, Isaiah brushed by her and inside the house. The scowl on his face deepened when he saw Levi casually chilling in her crib.

"Aye. Who the fuck is you homeboy? All up in my woman's crib."

Levi looked away from the TV and shook his head. "I ain't nobody bruh. Nobody you need to be worried about or talking crazy too, anyway."

Isaiah tugged his jeans up. "Nah. You somebody my nigga. So what's up. You fucking my girl?"

Disgusted by his behavior, Shanae grabbed ahold of his arm. "Will you stop! Don't come over here disrespecting my company. You need to leave."

"Leave? I ain't going nowhere. You better tell this nigga to leave. And what the fuck you got on? Got yo' fucking belly and ass all out," he spat, roughly grabbing ahold of her arm.

Levi stood up. "You better take yo' hands off her, cuz."

"Cuz? Nigga you know who you talking to? I'll lay your bitch ass out in here."

"Do what you gotta do, but you better take yo' hands off her. I ain't telling you again."

Shanae stood with her body filled with fear of the unknown. She'd seen Levi put plenty of niggas on their ass, and knew he was for sure, or used to be, about the gunplay. When he lifted his shirt, showing the handle of a gun she pushed Isaiah toward the door.

"Please. Don't start fighting in here. Just leave Isaiah. You doing all of this for nothing. We're done."

"Bitch ass nigga, you ain't scaring nobody with that gun. My shit bust just like yours do," Isaiah yelled over Shanae's head.

"Get to bussin' then," Levi chuckled, disrespecting him even more.

"Levi, please," Shanae begged. Her tone much different than the one she was singing earlier.

Isaiah's head jerked back. "Levi? The same nigga who got ran up out of his own hood? You a joke, nigga."

"Nah. I'm the same nigga who had them people crying at your folks' funeral. Now, that's a joke."

Anger like no other overtook Isaiah as he tried rushing back into the house. The sound of tires screeching and coming to a halt in front of Shanae's crib made him pull back some. With his eyes now on the vehicle and the driver exiting it, Isaiah loudly sucked his teeth.

"Fuck man!"

"Yeah, fuck is right nigga," Natisha yelled from the parking lot. "I should've known you were coming to this bitch house."

"Bitch?" Shanae said, snaking her neck around Isaiah.

"Yeah. You heard me. Ol' bobble head ass, bitch.

Always trying to break up a happy home. Leave my nigga alone. I don't know how many times I gotta tell you this."

"Hoe, I don't want him," Shanae fussed pushing Isaiah her way. "I keep giving you the nigga and look where he ends up. Right back over here. You need to keep a leash on his dog ass."

"Aye man. What the fuck?" Isaiah groaned, slapping Shanae's hand off him.

"I will, hoe! Got me out here acting a fool. I'm a whole mother. Something you couldn't be."

That blow to Shanae was low and written all over her face. She'd been pregnant with Isaiah's child but was so stressed out, she lost it at six weeks. That was the reason him cheating and getting Natisha pregnant hurt so bad. She felt Isaiah had intentionally wanted to hurt her. For the sake of her womanhood and rental agreement, Shanae was going to let her have that one. Natisha knew it too, so she dug deeper.

"Yeah. That's right. I know all about that baby. While you was giving this nigga money for an abortion," she said moving her fingers like quotations, "he was using that money to make sure our daughter was straight."

Shanae knew the timing of Natisha's pregnancy wasn't right. Her intuition had never failed her. Yes, Isaiah did give Natisha the money for an abortion, that she got, but he knocked her up right after for feeling bad about the decision.

"You know what," Shanae spoke calmly. "I don't even care anymore. I'm so sick of the bullshit with you and this girl. Just leave. I can't even stomach looking at you."

"Baby. Come on. You know I don't love her. She just has my daughter. You my world, Shanae," Isaiah pleaded.

"You don't love me!" Natisha cried, seeing how affectionate Isaiah was with her.

"Natisha, quit man. Get back in your car. You making a scene for no reason," Isaiah told her.

"Nah. I ain't made a scene yet."

When she pulled a gun from behind her and pointed it at him, Shanae jumped out of the way. With his hands up, Isaiah knew he had to deescalate the situation and quick.

"Natisha, you wildin' put the gun up."

"No! I've loved you way before her. Way before she came into the picture and this is how you do me!" she screamed now pointing the gun at Shanae. "This fat bitch! You gon' choose her over us! Me and your daughter!"

Isaiah stepped toward her and she cocked the gun back. "No. Nah, ma. I'm not choosing her. We can leave together right now. Me and you."

"You promise?" Natisha asked, voice and hands trembling. "Just me and you?"

"Yeah, baby. I promise. We can finally be a family."

Shaking her head, Natisha let the tears fall before looking back up at him. "That's what you said before you just left my house. You lied. Why do you keep lying to me? I loved you!"

"I love you too Tish. C'mon baby. Think about this," Isaiah pleaded, peeping the crazed look in her eyes.

"I have," she said, pulling the trigger. The bullet hit Isaiah directly in his heart. The vessel in his body she desperately begged him to give her. "If I can't have you, neither can she."

As Isaiah's body stumbled backward into the doorway of Shanae's crib and collided with the ground, she covered her mouth before the gut-wrenching scream could escape. Gasps, screams, and shouts from neighbors nearby echoed throughout the complex as they watched in a panic at what just took place. Though she didn't too much care for her neighbor's boyfriend, Chrissy her neighbor, called for an ambulance. She'd watched the entire altercation from her window.

"O-Oh, my gosh. She shot him," Shanae whispered, trying to process what she was seeing.

Isaiah choked on his blood as his eyelids grew heavier. His intentions were to come over and break things off with Shanae for good and really try to be the man and father he needed to be. When Shanae didn't answer his calls or texts and he saw Levi's car, all of that went out the window. Looking down at the gun, Natisha's hand quaked as she fell to her knees. The rage in her from having a broken heart, caused her to do the unthinkable. What made it worse was that their daughter, Jazlynn, was in the car the entire time.

"You shot him! I can't believe you shot him!" Shanae cried, trying to help revive Isaiah but it was no use.

"Come on. I got you. Sshh. I got you," Levi cooed, swooping her up against his chest. He didn't care about the blood on her hands. Seeing her hurt, regardless of it being over another man, didn't sit right with him.

Thinking quick, but not quick enough, Natisha jumped up and rushed to her car, but it was too late. Police swarmed the complex with their sirens blaring and blocked her from leaving. Hopping out with their guns drawn, the crowd of onlookers stood watching one of the craziest scenes unfold in front of them.

"Drop your weapon!" a cop yelled.

"I didn't mean to," Natisha cried. "I-I didn't mean to shoot him. Please!"

"Drop your fucking weapon and get on the ground now!"

With her hands in the air, Natisha lowered herself to the ground and not a second later was she being restrained. Total chaos erupted around what was normally a quiet neighborhood. In total disbelief, Shanae cried hard as they checked Isaiah for a pulse. She knew the outcome, but seeing that white sheet over his body, in front of her door, where he'd stepped foot in countless of times had her losing it.

She knew she prayed and asked God to remove any and everything from her life that were no good for her, and Natisha took his life that quickly. Just when Isaiah was trying to do right, all his wrongdoings had caught up to him. Though in a way he nor Shanae would never expect it to happen, he was now out of her life for good.

Coming straight from her final to Shanae's apartment, Kali was not prepared for the gruesome details of what all went down. The yellow tape had just been taken down, and as much blood as possible was washed from the doorway. Still, the eerie feeling of death surrounded her when she walked inside. She'd been by Shanae's side for over an hour and didn't see herself leaving yet.

"I have to move," Shanae mumbled almost inaudibly.

"Let's not think about that right now," her mother Sharee said. "We'll figure all of that out later."

Sharee had no issues with Isaiah, besides the fact that

he'd played with her daughters heart, but she never wished death upon him. Her heart went out to his little girl and his family. Today's tragedy was such a senseless murder and everyone involved was hurting from it.

"Where's Levi?" Shanae asked no one in particular.

"He stepped outside to take a phone call. Want me to get him?" Sharee asked.

All Shanae could do was nod. When Sharee stepped outside, Levi looked her way and told his grandma he'd call her back. The news just aired Isaiah's death and she was the first to call and check on he and Shanae like always.

"She asked for you."

Nodding, Levi stepped inside. Speaking to a few of her family members, he went and sat by Shanae. Leaning into him, Shanae wrapped her arms around him as tears decorated the sleeve of his shirt. Sliding his hand into her hair and massaging her scalp, he pulled her closer and rubbed her back.

"I'm right here. I'm not going anywhere," he told her.

Shanae's hold on him tightened. "Please, don't."

He knew she was vulnerable and emotional as hell right now, but her feelings for him were real. Levi had left Shanae before, and though he'd returned, she couldn't fathom him dipping out on her again. Not after today.

He'd been her rock, standing strong and holding her up while she was grieving.

Today was only the first day of Shanae starting her healing process over. With Isaiah being murdered, she was going to be missing him in a totally different manner. Levi knew this. He knew if she'd been ducking him before, it'd be nothing for her to forget about him while mourning the loss of her ex. Placing a kiss to her temple, Levi hoped like hell she didn't though. It wasn't going to be so easy for him to forget about her now that he'd finally gotten her back.

I t'd been eight days since the murder of Isaiah and for the life of her, Shanae couldn't wrap her mind around it. She couldn't understand how the mother of his child could just kill him in cold blood. Yes, she'd been beyond angry with Isaiah far too many times and '*I could kill this nigga*', spewed from her lips as well. But to actually go through with it? No, she'd never go that far. The saying "Love will make you do some crazy things", had never been truer.

Standing in her bathroom mirror, Shanae stared at the tired reflection of herself. She wasn't herself; hadn't been for eight days. Her entire week had been a blur. Work dragged by, nights were restless, pillowcases covered in tears, and appetite non-existent. Every time she closed her eyes, all she pictured was Natisha pulling the gun, Isaiah collapsing feet away from her and Levi being the one there to console her.

He'd been her saving grace, honestly. He tried not to smother her with texts or phone calls, but Shanae appreciated every one of them. His efforts in making sure she was good put a smile on her face. Levi's unwavering support during one of the most difficult times in her life showed Shanae how much love he really did have for her. It wasn't out of pity.

"You about ready?" Bia asked from the bathroom doorway.

Glancing her way, Shanae nodded. Inhaling a deep breath, she moseyed with ponderous steps toward her bedroom. Grabbing her phone and clutch from her unmade bed, she was ready to go. In her living room, Kali stood from the couch and gave her cousin a hug. A death hadn't hit this close to home for either of them since their grandmother, and Kali was feeling the effects of it as well.

The drive to the church took Bia a good twenty minutes, and when they arrived the pain in Shanae's chest became heavier with each spin of the tires. Licking her lips, she told herself to calm down, but it was of no use. Especially when she stepped out and saw Isaiah's brothers and group of friends heading inside the church. Without words being spoken Isaiah's brothers gave Shanae a strong hug and her tears fell. The stench of weed was oozing from their pores and she knew there'd be much more where that came from after the service. Shanae's hands trembled, mouth watered and eyes stung the closer she got to the sanctuary. Bia was on her left while Kali accompanied her right. She gripped their hands for dear life as they walked down the aisle. Her throat clogged and stomach tumbled at the sight of Isaiah laying in his casket. A mixture of snot and tears drenched her face as she did her best to keep it together. The few people ahead of her in line seemed to be moving much too quickly. This moment was becoming much too real for the young, heart-broken twenty-two-year-old.

"I can't do this," she whispered to herself. "Look at him."

Bia and Kali both wiped at their faces. They didn't know this type of pain, but they felt it. Every inch of Shanae's frame was on fire and aching. The pain... it was damn near unbearable. Giving her strength, her girls held onto her tightly as they approached his casket. Shanae's eyes danced across his frame, assessing what she knew was just a shell of him. Placing the tissue to her face, Shanae cried hard as her hand reached out to touch his bloated cheek.

"I love you," she leaned down and whispered. "Always will."

Turning, she went to hug Isaiah's mother, step-mom, dad, grandma, her favorite aunt of his, his sister and lastly his daughter. With Natisha in jail, and her parents distraught over the entire outcome of her life, Isaiah's mother was more than likely going to get guardianship of Jazlynn. Finding them a seat, the trio sat down as the church continued to fill with mourners. People Shanae hadn't seen in so long were there to pay their respects and she knew had anyone who didn't belong pop up, there'd be a scene made.

Though she hated for such negative thoughts to form at the time, Shanae couldn't help but wonder how many of the women in the crowd were mourning just like her. Slowly, she glanced around the pews and saw more than a few women breaking completely down. Yes, she was his ex, but didn't that mean something more?

"I can't believe this," Bia whispered.

Shanae couldn't answer. She'd been thinking the same thing for the past week. Right now only confirmed that she wasn't dreaming. Close to an hour and a half later, the service was ending and the crowd dispersed into the hall and parking lot. Regardless of being on church grounds, obnoxiously loud rap music was blasting from several cars, weed smoke infiltrated the air, and drinks were being poured up.

"This ain't no time to be sad," Gwoup, Isaiah's younger brother yelled. Standing on the step of his Chevy Tahoe. "This a celebration for bro. On gang!"

"They're seriously doing this on church premises?" Bia asked Kali.

"Mhm. And we'd be showing out if it were one of ours. Let these people grieve the way they want."

Bia quickly faced her. "I wasn't saying it like that. I've just never seen something like this before. I'm sorry."

"My bad, girl," Kali apologized.

"Y'all good?" Shanae questioned, having overheard their conversation but was too busy watching one girl in particular head to where all the boys were at.

"Yeah. Are we going to the repass?" Kali asked.

"I don't know yet. Let's walk over here real quick."

Taking the lead, Shanae strolled over to Gwoup's truck that was surrounded by a bunch of niggas she'd seen plenty. Some who'd actually tried pushing up on her more than a few times when they weren't around Isaiah.

"What up," Gwoup nodded her way. "You coming to the repass?"

"Yeah, I think so. I think we'll go to the burial site first though."

"Yeah... that's the plan. 'Preciate you for coming through for bro. He loved yo' ass for real."

The chuckle that escaped his lips did nothing to ease the disgust in Shanae's heart when ol' girl she peeped minutes ago walked up. Hopping down from his truck, Gwoup greeted her in a hug.

"What's up sis? You and nephew good?"

Blinking back tears, the girl nodded and placed a hand on her ever so present protruding belly. "Yeah. Acting up in here per usual."

"He can feel his pop's presence all through this moth-afucka that's why," Tino, Isaiah's older brother said, making Shanae take a few fumbled steps backward.

Tino, out the corner of his eyes hadn't even peeped Shanae standing there. When he saw the uncomfortable look of hurt on her face, his eyes softened.

"Damn, what up Shanae?" He reached in for a hug and she shook her head no.

"Gw-Gwoup," she struggled to say. "I'll see you around."

"A'ight. Be safe."

Without another word, but a look on her face that none of them would forget, Shanae hightailed it to Bia's car. It wasn't until she climbed in the passenger seat did her face flood with tears. Kali climbed in the backseat slowly, and for once wasn't sure how to console her cousin. Mourning Isaiah's death was one thing; but to find out he had a child on the way as well? Shanae was outdone.

Waiting in the line to pull out of the church Bia had to ask, "Are we going to the burial site?"

"No. I'm going home."

The finality in Shanae's voice was unmatched. All week Isaiah's family had kept in contact with her seeing as though he was killed directly in front of her place, but they couldn't let her know he had a son on the way? Hearing Tino greet her as sis, the same way he used to do her, rubbed her the wrong way and made her realize that she and Isaiah weren't anything but the past. Regardless of the memories shared, time spent, love made, lies told, and way she felt about him, Isaiah's family was just that; his. Their loyalty didn't belong to her at all.

Yes, it was the sad truth but the truth nonetheless. And that was something Shanae was going to have to come to terms with on her own. Finally.

8

"You must want another whooping," Kali said more than asked Khyri.

"Nooo! I want my Daddy."

Kali chuckled. "Oh, you're going to see him in just a few minutes. Back there acting like that."

He'd been acting out all morning and well into the afternoon. At the grocery store Khyri threw a fit, knocking down a row of cans while Kali wasn't looking and got his behind tore up as soon as she got to the car. She didn't need anyone calling DCFS on her inside the store was the only reason she hadn't inside the store. So frustrated, Kali left the basket that was semi-full of groceries right in the aisle.

She and Erik alternated weekends with Khyri, but not every weekend was granted his. Some he'd be too busy, which Kali understood, but she didn't care today. In fact, she gave not one single fuck what he had going on and let that be known the second she called him on FaceTime minutes prior. She needed a break.

Between the new semester starting up, work, checking on Shanae, and just being a damn woman, Kali was tired. Hardly ever did she complain because she loved being a mother, but today was just overwhelming.

"Ma-ma," Khyri whined, sniffling.

"Yes Khyri? You done being a crybaby? Big boys don't do all that."

He pouted. "I am a big boy."

"You sure weren't acting like it," she sighed pulling into her mama's driveway.

Her place or Ms. Rhonda's house were normally their meet up and drop off spots. Erik's place was out the way, but he'd make a stop wherever to get his son. Plus, his job was closer to here. Shutting her car off, Kali unbuckled Khyri and as soon as his feet hit the pavement, he took off toward the porch.

"TeTe!"

Swooping him up, Kamilla kissed all over her nephew's face and tickled his tummy. "Hey baby. You miss me?"

He nodded happily. "Mhm."

"What up hoe," Kali greeted with a smirk.

184

"Ya mama."

"Mama! Kamilla called you a hoe!" Jumping out the way from her sister's swinging hand, Kali laughed. "What you doing over here?"

Kamilla put Khyri down and huffed. "Girl, soaking up her air. My damn PG&E bill so high. I'm disgusted."

"You better get one of them sugar daddy's to pay it. I know they got it."

"Oh, I know they got it too. It's just how do I get it," she said making them laugh while walking in the house. "How long y'all about to be over here?"

"I'm chilling for a minute. Erik supposed to be coming to get him in a few. Why?"

Smirking, Kamilla ran a hand through her short hair. Unlike Kali who had a head full of dark brown, bra-strap length hair, Kamilla had cut hers off years ago. She couldn't fathom the thought of having hair past her ears now, but she rocked the style with ease. Pulled the mature look off effortlessly and loved it.

"Let's hit the streets for a minute. I'm trying to pull up on my boo."

"Say what now?" Kali grinned, just as their mother walked upstairs from the basement with Khyri trailing behind her. "Hey Mama."

"Hey. What y'all doing over here?"

"Dang. We can't just drop by?"

Mrs. Ada Brighton smirked. "My baby can. You and your sister only come by to eat up all the food and suck in all my air."

A pop to her butt was delivered by her husband, making the daughters grin. He kissed her cheek and smiled. "And I'ma let 'em. Kali, what's up daughter? My grandson got you stressed?"

Standing up, Rich pulled his youngest into his embrace and kissed her cheek. "Yes. Just bad for no reason."

"He need to burn off some of that energy. I'ma take to the back yard in a few minutes. What y'all got going on?"

"Nothing. We chilling," Kali answered and Kamilla cleared her throat.

"No, we're actually about to leave in a lil' bit. Gotta make some runs around the city."

The sisters stared one another down before Kali rolled her eyes. "Yeah, I guess I'm riding with her today."

"Don't sound so excited," Ada joked opening a popsicle for Khyri as he tugged his shirt over his head.

"Oooh. I see your belly," Kamilla cooed. "Show TeTe your muscles."

Holding his arms up, Khyri flexed making them all chuckle. Kross, Kali's brother taught him the move and he was forever showing his little guns off when asked. It was the cutest thing ever. Snapping a few pics of him, Kamilla locked her phone back.

"Y'all let him come over here and do whatever he wants," Kali said with a shake of her head, watching him walk around with his shirt off, Nike shorts slightly hanging and his pull-up showing. He'd just gotten his hair cut the day before and was looking so handsome.

"That's what he's supposed to do while he's here. Then we send him right on home," Ada said.

"Right. Daddy, can you wash my car while we're gone?"

Rich looked at her and shook his head. "Nah. I don't think I can do that. Better get your baby daddy to wash it," he joked.

"Daddy!" Kali fussed, smacking her lips. "Now you know."

"Oh, my fault. Y'all not cool like that?"

Kamilla and Ada laughed.

"You are messy," Kamilla told him.

"Hey," Rich said tossing his hands up. "I thought maybe they rekindled an old flame or something."

"Never. I'm so over Erik it's not even funny. Co-parenting is as far as it gets for us."

"And there's nothing wrong with that, honey," Ada defended. "Not every relationship is meant to last and that's okay. We got Khyri out the arrangement and you've matured into a beautiful, accomplished woman right before our eyes.

"Awww Mama," Kali cooed. "Don't start being all emotional. I'm too G for that."

Ada waved her off. "Oh, whatever. I'm just saying."

"Thank you. Y'all helped me become the woman I am today and I'm still learning from you both. Ain't that crazy?" Kali joked.

"You hear your mama?" Ada laughed. "She's being a hater."

While Khyri was away with Rich, Kali and Kamilla snuck out of the house, she knew there was no way he was going to let her leave without him. Checking out her outfit, Kali hoped her sister wasn't trying to pull up on some fine ass niggas. She wasn't looking bummy, but the tan distressed high waist cargo shorts, white camisole and Givenchy slides was her run around attire.

"Who you about to have us all out seeing?" she asked, fastening her seatbelt.

"Can you just sit back and ride? It's been a minute since we kicked it and I don't mind putting you out."

Kali popped the piece of gum she was chewing on and pulled her phone out. "I didn't ask to ride along anyway. I was forced."

Kamilla laughed. "What the hell ever. If you must

know, I'm going to pick some money up from a friend of mine."

"Yeah? This friend got another friend who don't mind giving out money? I want to buy Khyri a whole new wardrobe."

Snickering, Kamilla turned left. "Don't you have a little friend? What's his name again?"

"Rondo. That's my boo," Kali grinned, just as a text from him popped up on her screen.

Rondo: *'Chu got going on?*

Kali: *Riding with my sister. What's up with you? You miss me?*

On the other end of the city, Rondo smirked at her text and licked his lips. He was posted in the hood with his boys and some of his family. A typical laid-back Saturday afternoon for him and he was trying to lay eyes on his lady.

Rondo: *Yeah, I miss your pretty ass. Pull up on me.*

Three gray bubbles danced across his iPhone screen then stopped. Kali wasn't expecting him to say that, but then again, Rondo wasn't very predictable either. She'd learned that from day one of having class with him. After fucking him on the first night, Kali was sure he'd blow her off as just some hoe, but that wasn't the case at all. Rondo stayed consistent like the real one he was. He'd become even more attractive to Kali honestly. Baby girl was just his speed, if not a little more and he was trying to keep up with her.

Biting her bottom lip, Kali glanced Kamilla's way and turned the volume on the radio down some. "He just asked me, well told me to pull up on him."

"Who, Rondo?" Kamilla questioned. "Where he at? We can swoop by there after I pick this money up."

"I don't know. Let me ask him real fast."

Kali: *I can do that. Text me your address.*

Rondo: *I'm in HP.*

Reading the location, Kali poked her full pink lips out. "Oh, girl. He in the hood for real," she giggled.

"Where at?"

"Highland Park, girl. You got your gun on you?"

Kamilla tossed a look her way that said bitch, now you know. "Always. I'm sure I won't have to use it though. That's where I'm picking some money up from."

Peeping the direction her sister was driving, Kali hadn't even noticed they were getting deeper into the hood. They grew up right around the corner from *HP*, about three blocks away in another neighborhood of the city known as *The Grove*. That neighborhood and plenty others did their father hold court in for years before he moved them out and away from the dangers of it all.

No matter where they moved though, Kross, their brother, still ventured to those parts and even convinced his parents to let him go to school at Highland High from middle school through high school. The girls weren't so lucky. Once they graduated from middle school, Ada enrolled them right in a nice private school. Her biggest fear was one of them getting killed over the jealous females or knocked up, which Kali still did. She couldn't stay out the hood to save her life. And clearly neither could Kamilla.

"Let me find out," Kali teased, cutting her eyes Kamilla's way.

"What? You ain't the only one who can have a boo. I wonder if they know each other."

Kali thought the same thing as Kamilla ducked in and out of traffic; whipping her coke white Lexus like a racecar driver. Thanks to Kross teaching her how to drive, she could speed-race, and skillfully maneuver almost any wheel of a vehicle she climbed in.

Twenty minutes later, they were pulling up on the street. It was hard to detect where either of their men were. The entire block was packed with cars, people, and Kali could smell the tasty scent of the grill going through the vents.

"They kicking it over here."

"I know right," Kamilla agreed, pushing her car through the crowd.

"Where you about to park at? Ain't no room up here."

"Yes there is. Watch and see."

Just like she knew would happen, a Range Rover backed out of the driveway Kamilla was about to pull into and honked its horn. She honked back, greeting the driver, before backing into the spot with ease. Checking her mirrors, she grinned when her boo walked up to her side of the car and tapped the window twice with his knuckle. Letting the window down, warm heat swarmed inside the air-conditioned vehicle.

Leaning over, Kamilla was awarded a tasteful scent of his Versace Dylan Blue cologne, before being graced by his handsome face.

"What'chu do, speed here?" he joked, calm tone sending goosebumps down Kamilla's thighs.

"No. You know I don't be speeding," she fibbed, with a light giggle.

"Yeah, tell me anything baby. Step out for me," he instructed and Kamilla hit her locks.

Opening the door for her, Kamilla stood and tugged upward on the elastic of her blush pink tube dress while straightening the bottom. Stepping back, Jyro took in her appearance, liking what he was seeing. From day one, Kamilla's natural beauty reeled him in. Her confidence and cool personality is what kept him on the line.

His hand went to her waist and Kamilla smiled up at him. At 5'9", Kamilla was a stallion while Jyro stood slightly taller than her at 6'3". When she rocked heels, they almost came eye to eye. Slowly, his hand slid lower and he took a handful of her round ass into his grasp. Unlike her sister, Kamilla had ass, hips, and thighs for days. She was three years older than Kali at twenty-seven and thanked God for her high metabolism.

Brushing a thumb over Jyro's thick, almost unibrow, eyebrows she took his appearance in. Kamilla was in love with his fair tawny brown skin that was sprinkled with freckles and his neatly trimmed goatee. He had a head full of wavy coal black hair that he'd let grow out some, natural low hooded brown eyes, full dark lips, a war wound under his eye, and tattoo covered neck. His rough, thugged out look drove Kamilla crazy... and he knew it too.

"You got all these folks staring at me," Kamilla grinned all in his face.

"Let they ass stare. You here for me."

"And some food. You smell good," she complimented.

Feeling flattered, Jyro gave her a half smirk. Kamilla was good for telling him exactly how she felt and he fucked with that. She knew just how to boost a nigga's ego without feeling some type of way.

"Thank you. You ain't got no panties on under this thin ass dress?" he questioned, letting his large hands caress her cheeks. Jyro couldn't help it; she felt so damn good in his embrace.

Bashfully, feeling caught, Kamilla shook head no. "I couldn't wear any with it. Don't start your shit, Jy."

Jyro licked his lips and pecked her cheek. "Oh, I ain't started shit yet. Let's go in the house right quick."

Leaning closer, he grabbed her hand and strategically placed it on his crotch. Kamilla's nipples pebbled at the slight bulge under his denim. Pushing him away, she snickered. She already knew what type of time he was on and she was not trying to be fucking while there was an entire function going on. Plus, Jyro didn't know the definition of a quickie. He'd want to go rounds once he was in the pussy and have a field day in it.

"No. I'm not about to go in there with you."

"Why not?" he asked, showing off his boyish grin. "You don't want a plate?"

Rolling her eyes, Kamilla smirked back. "Whatever. Let me see if my sister wants something."

"That's who with you? She can't speak?" Jyro asked, pulling the driver's door open before she could offer up a reply.

Kali's head popped up from her phone in her hand. She was busy sending Rondo a text message, not thinking about getting out the car at all. There were way too many people on the block.

"You ain't about to sit in this car," Jyro told her.

"Um, nice to meet you too. I'm Kali, Kamilla's sister."

Jyro chuckled at her feisty attitude. "What up. I'm Jy. This my shit so you good to get out."

"I'd be good if it wasn't. That's not why I'm sitting here."

"Let that nigga know, baby," Rondo rasped walking up on the car.

Hearing his voice, Kali's stomach churned in anticipation to see his face. Rarely did she get nervous around a nigga, but Rondo was different. It'd been a minute since she found herself actually liking a guy enough to want him to be in her presence, so this unnerved sensation she had going on was new to her.

"That's you?" Jyro asked Rondo as they slapped hands.

"All day. How you doing?" He asked politely, sticking his hand out for Kamilla to shake. "I'm Rondo."

"Nice to meet you, *finally*. I'm Kamilla."

"Y'all could pass for twins for real. Damn. Wonder what y'all mama look like," he chuckled. "I know she fine as hell."

"Don't make me hurt you," Kali fussed from the passenger seat.

"I'm just fucking with you."

Placing her phone inside her purse, Kali fluffed her

curly mane ready to greet her boo. Pushing the door open, she was greeted by Rondo's bowlegs in his Jordan Jumpman shorts. *This man walks like he's carrying something heavy. That's right, he is,* she laughed to herself. The thought of that monster between his legs had Kali on go mode. Dressed down in a white tee, two gold and diamond medallion chains with pictures of his close friend and cousin in each, a LA fitted on his head and sexy smile on his face showing off the gold in his mouth, Kali was glad she pulled up.

"A woman of her word. I like that," he told her.

"I bet you do. Y'all got it poppin' out here, huh?"

Looking up and down the block, Kali took in what was just a normal Saturday in *HP*. Loud music was blasting, boys and men were shooting hoops, some playing dice near the porch, while most of the women – some claimed and trying to get chose – sat and stood around in the shade. The atmosphere was live and Kali had to admit, she missed this the most about staying in the hood. There was nothing quite like it.

"We doing a lil' something. You eat yet?" Rondo asked.

"You stay trying to feed me. What you saying? I'm too skinny?"

Rondo loved when she sassed off at the mouth. The closer they became, the more vocal Kali got. He appreciated that, 'cause a broad who was scared to speak her mind around him wasn't the type he wanted in his presence. That confident shit was one of the greatest qualities a woman could possess to him.

"Nah, baby," Rondo laughed, licking his lips. "I'm just making sure you good. Can I do that, with your mean ass?"

"I am not mean! Don't say that."

"Yeah, a'ight. Can I get a hug or some, shit? You ain't acting like you miss a nigga."

Without any resolve, Kali stretched her arms upward, wrapping them around his neck. With his hands at her waist, Rondo lowered his head and planted warm kisses against her neck. He knew that was her spot and it was becoming his favorite. The passion marks from their previous session were just clearing up to prove it.

Wiggling, trying to escape him Kali groaned. "Stooop. You know I'm too light for you to be leaving marks all on me. That shit is so tacky, bae."

"Let me suck on something else then," he murmured against her ear, while gripping the cuff of one her soft butt cheeks. They were slightly hanging out of her shorts and he couldn't help but to cop a feel.

Kali's lower lady parts perked up at the request. Sexual, she couldn't get enough of him either. If she wasn't careful, Kali was going to mess around and fall in love. Something she hadn't been in... not the real thing anyway. That shit with Erik was a joke.

"That's why you told me to pull up?"

Rondo lifted from her neck and nodded. "Yeah and no. I wanted to see you and now I'm trying to taste you."

Now that she was really looking at him, with his hat slightly lifted from his face, Kali shook her head. His eyes were red and sitting low as hell.

"You so high right now."

"A lil' bit," he laughed, licking his lips. "What you looking like that for?"

"No reason," she huffed.

"Man," Rondo dragged pulling his hat off and scratching his head. "I know you ain't got no attitude. You coulda stayed where you was at wit' all that."

Kali swirled her neck. "Who you think you talking to? I sure could have taken my ass right home, but where am I? In the hood, with this hot ass sun blazing on me for your ass. Don't get cute."

"It is hot, huh?" he asked, dismissing all that rah-rah shit she was on.

Incredulously, Kali looked him upside the head like he was crazy. Chuckling, she reached for the door handle, but Rondo grabbed ahold of it.

"What you doing? Watch out," he said pulling her away from the door then leaned against it.

"Nah. You watch out. I ain't come over here for this."

"So what you bring ya lil' yellow ass over here for then, huh? You trippin' 'cause I said I wanted to eat your pussy?"

Kali rolled her eyes. "No. But, we can do that anytime. I just wanna spend some time with you outside of class and my bedroom."

Nodding his head, Rondo peeped exactly what this was. He'd piped her down and now she was in her feelings. It wasn't just over the sex though. Her feelings for him had evolved from that fine guy in her class, to Kali wanting to see and be around him more than two times a week. Outside of class, Rondo checked up on her, asked about Khyri, put her up on game about his game plan after graduating and simply kept her in good spirits.

Their connection wasn't forced and Kali loved that. What she didn't like was the gray area they were in and headed toward. Surprisingly, she wanted more and there wasn't anything wrong with that. They'd been kicking it for damn near three months now and Kali figured that was more than enough time to put a label on what they were doing.

"A'ight. Tell me what you want then. What you really want," he told her.

"From you?"

"From us. Speak ya mind, baby. You ain't never been afraid to before."

Kali rolled her eyes. "Whatever. All I'm saying is, if this was a mission to get some pussy, then you shoulda said that. I know we've been kicking it for some months now with no titles on what we're doing, but on the real I think there should be. No, I want there to be. If this isn't going any further than sex, a few dates, and seeing you in class though, then let me know now."

"I guess I ain't make my intentions clear enough," Rondo stated, clearing his throat. "I'm trying to be on some exclusive shit with you and you only. If sex was all I wanted, trust me, you'd know. I'd just be bussin' you down and going about my day. A nigga be laid up over your place studying, taking naps, showers, reporting to you after a long day and all. If that don't tell you I'm interested in something more than what's between your legs, then shit," he chuckled with a shrug. "I'ma have to let it be known a lot clearer."

Pulling her closer to him, Rondo tugged at the end of one of her strands of her. "Fix ya face. Pouting and shit like I don't fuck with you the long way."

Kali smacked his chest. "Mhm. Thank you for the clarification."

"It ain't nothing. Just so we're clear, you already know I ain't with none of that baby daddy drama bullshit. Khyri my lil' homie and I'll always respect you as his mother, but yo' baby daddy better cease that slick talking shit if we gon' be together."

Nodding, Kali hoped while she was agreeing that Erik would not start anything once he found out she was dating someone. He was butt hurt when his snitching ass cousin Bobbi saw her out the movies with a friend. Erik couldn't do right when he had the chance, but now every man who stepped to her wasn't good enough in his eyes. Oh, how the tables turn. Kali was going to make his ass sit right at one of them tables and watch her live her best life... without him. She'd let him hurt her and then she let that hurt go. Him included. There was no starting over fresh anymore.

"So, you gon' let a few words dictate our relationship?" she wanted to know.

"Nah. But a few words can get a nigga's jaw broke and then what? You gotta take Khyri up to the hospital to visit his daddy in ICU 'cause the nigga eating through a straw."

Kali didn't want to laugh, but she couldn't help it. The serious expression on Rondo's face was priceless. He was deadass about knocking Erik out if he came out his mouth on some tough shit. Now, if he wanted to sit down as a man and be made aware of the new man in his son's life, Rondo was all for that. Anything else, Erik could miss him with.

The only reason he'd brought it up was so Kali could know where he stood with it. He was all for them being together and knew drama within their relationship would happen at some point, but Rondo didn't want any outsiders causing it. The bond they were building was one he wanted to keep close-knit.

"Don't say that," she giggled. "I'll talk to him about us. Let him know what it is and go from there."

"A'ight. Can we go eat now? Done talked a nigga to death, made me get in a relationship, and won't even feed me."

Tossing her head back, Kali laughed. "I didn't make you do anything. Don't front like you don't wanna be with me. You see me?" she asked doing a slow twirl while tossing her hair over the opposite shoulder. "Nigga it's an honor."

Rondo smirked. "Yeah, you right. My apologies Ms. Lady. It's an honor to be your man, baby. Now, can you bring your fine ass in this house and fix Daddy a plate."

Kali bit her bottom lip and walked up on him. "I mean, since you said it like that. You still trying to taste something else?"

Playfully, Rondo pushed her away and she gasped. "Nope. Not no more. Come on."

Walking away from her, Kali crossed her arms before laughing and going after him. "Don't be walking off from me. I see we gon' have to get them manners in check."

"I'm one of the most respectful men you'll ever meet. Don't play Ms. Sophia Mitchell like that. She'll whoop my ass if she heard you say that."

Kali beamed when he mentioned his mother. It wasn't the first time she'd heard her name and she was realizing how close the mother-son duo were.

"Maybe an ass whooping is what you need. Help you get your act together," she laughed.

Tossing an arm over her shoulder, Rondo pulled her closer and whispered in her ear, "Nah. You the one need some act right; and I'ma give it to you. Keep on playing wit' me."

Smirking, Kali licked her lips. She was all for whatever he was going to give her. A quick dick down didn't sound too bad now after all. Stepping inside the house, they headed straight to the kitchen to wash their hands and fix plates, but Kali had to use the restroom first. After Rondo told her how to get to it, Kali headed in that direction. She did a quick knock on the door that was ajar. Instead of a reply, it was snatched open, making Kali shuffle backward some.

"Leave me the fuck alone, TJ. You're drunk and tripping," Layla hissed, storming out the bathroom, almost bumping into Kali. "Hey. Kali right?"

"Yes, hey. You good?"

"I'm fine. Niggas don't know how to let the fuck go that's all."

"Bitch, I ain't pressed over you. That pussy done seen better days."

"And so has those raggedy ass Jordan's, dingy Balmain jeans you probably borrowed or stole, and that loose neck ass Gucci tee. You should've been the first to boycott them with your broke ass. You 'bout as pressed as the crease in them shoes. Don't get me started," Layla laughed.

Kali was in stitches. She just read TJ his rights and didn't skip a beat or take a breath. Embarrassed, especially because Kali was right there, TJ tried yoking Layla up but froze up when Rondo stepped into the hallway.

"Y'all good?"

"Yeah, yeah. Layla was just introducing her homegirl. What up Rondo?" TJ stuck his hand out for him to do their normal hood handshake, but Rondo left him hanging. Pride wounded, he pulled his hand back and stuffed into the tight pocket of his jeans.

"Ain't shit up nigga. Watch out so my girl can handle her business. The fuck you even in here for?"

His hand on the small of Kali's back lightly pushed her forward toward the bathroom door.

"Bothering me. I done told him he better leave me

alone 'fore I shoot his looney ass," Layla said meaning every word.

She and TJ had messed around years ago. It was one of the times in Layla's life where she'd reached a low point. One of the lowest of lows. Sex wasn't cutting it for her, and she'd somehow turned to that white girl. Sniffing a little powder up her nose here and there soothed her. It made everything she was feeling, going through, and kept bottled inside irrelevant.

The high she experienced was like no other and put her worries at ease. It wasn't until she passed out at work and was rushed to the hospital did she realize how quickly her life was spiraling out of control. Now, instead of using drugs as an escape, she wrote poetry. Almost every thought she manifested were jotted across a notebook, scrap piece of paper or stored in the notes section of her phone. Yes, her life had been a bit rocky, but Layla wasn't trying to take it and she vowed to never go that far off the deep end again.

TJ glanced her way and clenched his jaw. Anger residing in the pit of his soul. Rejection was a mothafucka. "I'ma catch y'all later," he spoke, bopping off.

Layla rolled her eyes and faced Rondo. "Y'all need to watch him, for real. He's not wrapped too tight."

"Them drugs will do that to you. You straight though? I ain't even see you come in."

"Yeah. You were all boo'd up," she smirked, loving how happy her cousin looked.

Truthfully, Rondo was a good man. She'd never witnessed him dog any females out or have a bunch waiting in the cuts for him. He learned early on that having a ton of bitches with needs was a headache and annoying as hell. Every five minutes one of them needed something, whether that be his time, money, sex, or anything else they could get out of him. Settling down for him was always the game plan. Not everyone was meant to be a player.

"Man, watch out," he dismissed with a slight chuckle. "I'm just chilling."

"You must really like her."

"I do, cuz. The feelings mutual though, so you know how that go. I'm about to be ducked off even more."

At the sink, Kali smirked at his admission while she dabbed her oily nose. Regardless of her skincare regimen, her nose remained oily. Drying her hands on a few paper towels, she opened the door.

"I hear you out her talking about me."

"Good. Hope you heard me say bring yo' ass on so we can eat," Rondo said, letting his dark piercing eyes swallow her frame up. When he took one step her way, Kali jumped out of his reach. Layla smirked and walked back outside to give them some privacy. That look in his eyes was a dead giveaway; he was trying to take her in the bathroom.

"Nope," she giggled swatting his hand. "That was a missed opportunity."

"Come on. Ain't nobody even in here," he whispered in a groaning manner.

"You were just hollering about being hungry. I'm not about to play with you. Let's go."

Rondo stood there for a few seconds watching her walk off from him. Not hearing him behind her, Kali turned around and lifted her brow. Rushing her, Rondo wrapped his arms around her body from behind and humped her.

"You gon' regret this later. Mark my words."

A simple 'mhm' was all Kali replied 'cause she already knew. Rondo was going to tear her ass up later on and she couldn't wait. After making them plates of food, they headed back outside. Kamilla was just polishing off her meal and looking every bit of relaxed in Jyro's lap. Kali swooned when he reached up wiped barbecue sauce from the corner of her mouth and licked it off. *Whew. I see why sis was ready to pull up over here.*

"You like that freaky shit, huh?" Rondo spoke lowly in her ear, making her flinch. She didn't even know he was watching her watch them, but she should've known.

"Hush. I just thought it was cute."

Rondo stared into her eyes. "Not as cute as you."

They held their gaze before busting out laughing. "You laying it on thick for this pussy, huh?"

"Nah. I'ma get that anyway. Give me a few hours and you gon' be singing a different tune. I promise that."

And, his promise was kept. Hours later inside her living room – because he wasn't waiting until the bedroom – Rondo had Kali's ass high in the air while his tongue did laps around her soaking wet slit. She was dripping wet and he wasn't missing a stroke. A ravishing craving for her pink, gushy insides had him rubbing his entire face in it.

"Sssh, oohhh," she whimpered, dropping the arch in her back.

Rondo pushed her back down in place and clasped his hands around her waist. "Nah, don't run," he slurped loudly. "Give me all this sweet pussy."

Sucking her clit between his lips, Kali's toes popped. The friction of her tender nipples rubbing against the carpet as she threw it back on his face had her ready to climax. Rondo wasn't letting up. Not even when she tried reaching behind her to grasp onto his arm. Kali needed something to hold onto. He had her head spinning and spine tingling.

"Ooou, baaabe," she whined. "It's almost there."

Needing a better angle to devour her like he wanted

to, Rondo picked her up with ease and lay back on the carpet. Sitting her directly on his face, he made Kali do a Chinese split on his tongue. Spreading her ass cheeks, he dragged his tongue up the crack, probing her tight hole before venturing back to her waterfall.

"Oh my gooosh," Kali cried, squeezing his thigh so damn tight.

Rondo's tongue lapped at her pussy with lightning speed before alternating between strong sucks and turbo flicks. Kali couldn't breathe. This man was sucking every breath she tried to inhale and all her fluids. She was sure to be dehydrated when he was done. The disgustingly loud slurps, groans while he ate her, and his throbbing dick against his thigh had Kali gone. Her world came spiraling down and tears pooled in her eyes when Rondo suctioned her swollen bud with those juicy lips of his and hit her with a licking, sucking, finger stroking her g-spot combo.

"Aaaah, fuuuuck!" she screamed, squirting all over him.

Eyes rolled to the top of her head; all Kali could hear was white noise. Her stomach muscles locked up and body quaked like a 7.5 earthquake in her city. Holding onto her trembling frame, Rondo gently let his tongue roll back and forth over her glistening folds collecting every drop that belonged to him. Jiggling her cheeks with his hands, he kissed them both before gripping one. Seeing her center pulsate and leak had him ready to slide right in her for *rounds.*

"Mmm, now that's what the fuck I'm talkin' 'bout," he praised.

When Kali sniffled, Rondo sat still for a second before sitting them up. Kali's body was deadweight in his arms. Turning her around on his lap, Kali buried her head in the crook of his neck.

"Bae... you crying?" Her curls bounced as she shook her head no. "Stop lying," he chuckled. "'Chu sniffling for then?"

Lifting up, Kali wiped at her reddened cheeks and licked her lips. "I just feel sad."

Rondo frowned. "Sad about what?"

"Sad for all the girls who will never get to experience that tongue and mouth ever again."

He stared at her for a beat and fell out laughing. Kali's small frame bounced atop his as he laughed his ass off.

"Aye," he wheezed. "I ain't fucking with you."

Wrapping her arms around his neck, Kali whispered against his glossy lips. "Yes you are. And you're about to fuck me good too. I need some act right, remember?"

Smirking, Rondo let her peck his lips before he took control. Grabbing the back of her neck, his tongue slithered inside her mouth giving her a taste of what was now his favorite meal. Pulling away, Kali panted and her eyes glistened with lust, need, and appreciation. *Damn, he knows how to make a woman feel good.*

After three rounds of sex, if she could even consider it that, Kali was out like a light. She was half-sleep in the shower they took and no more than five minutes later was sound asleep. Stepping back inside the room after coming from the kitchen, Rondo took in the moment for what it was. They'd just solidified their relationship and he couldn't be any more grateful for her wanting to settle down with him. He wasn't the best him he could be yet, and he knew that, but with her Rondo knew he could be. He wanted to be. Had to prove to her that all that love she deserved would be given back tenfold fucking with him. It was inevitable.

Grabbing his phone off the dresser, Rondo opened his Instagram app and tapped on the camera icon at the top of the screen. Getting the perfect angle of Kali with her hair wild, skin glowing and mouth slightly opened, he snapped the photo. He didn't even bother putting a filter on it before he typed a caption that read 'My Rider' and uploaded it to his IG story. Kissing her pouty lips, Rondo then hit the lights and climbed in bed beside her. Kali groaned a bit before grabbing his hand and wrapping it around her.

Rondo didn't understand how niggas fagged off on

their women and ran the streets all day. There was no place he found more peace in than with Kali. He was cherishing it for the moment because he knew the universe and how it worked. Something was sure to come along and disturb it.

Sunday Afternoon

R eleasing a heavy sigh, Kali pulled into Ms. Rhonda's driveway and parked her car. The headache she felt coming on was aggravating and she knew there'd be nothing to cure it but sleep. That's all she wanted to do for the remainder of the day after the night she and Rondo had, but time wasn't on her side.

"You made it?" Rondo questioned, voice soothing her nerves over the Bluetooth feature in her car.

"Yeah. Just parked. I'ma call you when I get home."

"A'ight. Don't be trying to explain yourself to that nigga either," he spoke evenly... with authority. The type that made Kali's kitty pulsate and purr.

"You ain't running nothing," she chuckled.

"Yeah we'll see. Hit me back though. Handle your

business, baby."

Telling him okay, Kali disconnected the call and ran a hand over her messy ponytail. Sleep deprived and body aching in places she didn't know could hurt so good; she was not in the mood to deal with Erik's hormonal ass. She'd woken up to dozens of texts and calls from him about the picture Rondo posted on his story, but she couldn't care less. He was her man. If he wanted to snap a picture of her, he could, and he did.

What she wasn't about to do was argue with her child's father about something he had no say in. Her life was just that; hers. Knowing she couldn't sit in the car forever, she started to climb out when the screen door was pushed open by Khyri. Behind him was Erik with a frown so deep, it'd become permanent if he didn't stop.

"Mama!" Khyri shouted, jumping off the steps like only a two-year-old would.

Smiling wide, Kali's heart expanded at the sight of him. "Hi baby! You missed me."

On her hip, Khyri nodded. "Yes. Me and Uncle Maine were playing the game."

"That's nice baby. Can you go in the house and get your stuff together? Have Maine help you," she told him, placing him on the concrete. He took off running in no time. "Be careful!"

She watched him until he was inside the house and

then focused her attention on Erik. He was ready to pop off and she knew it. The crease in his forehead was so deep it looked like it hurt.

"So, that's what you on?" he spat, walking up on her.

"I know you better back up."

"I ain't gotta do shit. You saw my texts and calls, Kali. Don't fucking play with me, man."

Kali crossed her arms over her chest. "Who's playing? I don't have to reply to you. It seems to me like you've forgotten who your child is; I'm not him. Who I spend my time with is none of your business."

"You got that nigga all in your crib, laid up like he paying bills in that bitch. You bet not have his ass around my son," he seethed.

"You're all in mine like you pay bills there. You don't anymore. And, no. He hasn't been at the house while Khyri was there, but he's been around him. Let's not act like you don't have any women around him, Erik. For real."

"That ain't the muthafucking point. You think I'ma let some other nigga play daddy to Khyri? You got me fucked up."

The frown on Kali's face matched his. "What? Who said anything about playing daddy? He's my boyfriend and Khyri is my son. I know you don't think that they won't ever be around one another."

"And you crazy for thinking I'ma let it happen. You can be a hoe all you want; keep my son away from that thot shit."

"A hoe?" she scoffed incredulously.

"Yeah, you heard me. Letting that nigga post you on his shit half naked like some hoe. My son don't need to be around that type of environment. Ain't that nigga gang affiliated?"

"No and if he was? You know what..." she breathed, exhaling a sharp breath. "I'm not about to argue with you about a situation I was going to speak to you about. We're grown, first of all. Secondly, you and I are not together. Won't be ever again, so who I decide to have around my child and in my home is my business until I make it yours. Oddly enough, I was going to let you know today that I'm dating someone. Not to throw it in your face, but to let you know that Khyri *will* be around him and vice versa."

As she spoke her piece, Erik stared at her like she had three heads sitting on her shoulders. He didn't give a fuck what she was talking about.

"You wasting your breath, ma," he chuckled. "You heard what I said."

"And you heard what the fuck I said. You had so much to say earlier, blowing my phone up like having Khyri around him is the real issue. Let's keep it real," Kali sassed, rolling her neck.

"This as real as it's gon' get. He not being around that nigga. So figure it out."

"Nah. The real is that you fumbled what we had, miss it and want that old thang back but you can't. I get it. I'm your child's mother and what we used to have no other woman brings you. You didn't love me the way you should've and now you see another man on his shit, you feel threatened. As if he's going to take your place. But see... that's the thing, there is no place. Not how you want there to be. We're co-parents and that's all we'll ever be."

The finality in her voice pissed Erik off even more. Kali was speaking to him like what they shared wasn't shit. Like he was some gum on the bottom of her shoe. The consistent jabs to his character had him boiling on the inside, but what flipped the crazy switch was those passion marks all over her chest. He didn't know how he had missed them, but that was all he could see now. A flash of some other nigga fucking Kali then tending to Khyri like he was their son instead of his crossed his mind and before he could stop himself, his hand was wrapped around her neck.

"Ugh!" Kali gasped, as she was lifted onto her tip-toes and pressed up against her car.

"You out yo' mind if you think I'm letting my family go that easy. You don't love a nigga no more, huh? Tryna have Khyri calling another nigga daddy?"

Kali clawed at his arms, leaving deep scratches that weren't even phasing Erik. He was out of body and mind as his grip tightened. He no longer saw the love Kali used to have for him in her eyes. He saw a conniving bitch who was trying to play get back for all the times he did her wrong. His assumptions couldn't be any more incorrect.

"What the fuck, E!" Maine shouted, shoving Erik hard as hell. He'd just walked outside with Khyri right by him.

Kali sucked in gulps of air before coughing profusely, with her hands on her knees. Feeling Khyri's small hands on her face, Kali's eyes stung as tears flowed down her cheeks.

"Mama! Mama! You okay?" Khyri asked, small voice trembling in fear.

Snatching him in her embrace, Kali held onto him tightly. It took the power of God himself for her not to breakdown. It was bad enough he witnessed his daddy choking her out.

"What the fuck is you on, bruh!" Maine screamed, punching Erik in the chest.

Standing back away from them, Erik's hardened face dropped when he saw Khyri wiping at Kali's tearstained face. Blinking, he tossed his hands on his head and groaned. The realization of his actions settled in and he felt like shit.

"Damn. Aye, Kali," he said stepping toward her.

Khyri cowered back in fear, hugging Kali's neck tight. Erik's heart broke. Khyri's handsome face was balled up as were his fists, ready to protect his mommy. Kali didn't hate anyone in her life, but that all changed in less than a minute. Still coughing, she rubbed at the part of her neck Khyri wasn't blocking and shook her head from side to side.

Hoarsely, she spoke, "No. Don't come near me. Near us. I can't believe you. You need help!" she cried.

"Look man," he sighed. "I was mad. I ain't mean to put my hands on you like that."

"You never did! That's what you said before!"

Maine looked his brother upside the head and his top lip curled in disgust. "You been putting your hands on her, nigga?" Shoving him, Erik stumbled back some.

"Man, watch out," Erik huffed.

"Nah, bitch. You wanna put yo' hands on sis, fight me nigga. Try to choke me out since you so tough."

Not backing down, Maine punched Erik in the chest again. Sucking his teeth, Erik pulled on his jean shorts and glared his older brother's way.

"I ain't about to fight you, bruh. Khyri out here."

"So nigga. He was out here when you was choking his mama out. Let nephew see you get your ass beat for real."

Though he wasn't as tall or strong as Maine, he wasn't

about to let him keep disrespecting him. Squaring up, the brothers went head up with one another. Maine was about to teach his young, ignorant ass a lesson he'd remember. Swinging, Erik missed landing his shot, but Maine didn't. Not by far. The punch he delivered to Erik's jaw drew blood on contact, causing him to stumble back. He had no time to recover as Maine sent body shots to his ribs, bringing him to his knees.

"Let me find out you putting yo' hands on somebody else nigga. I'ma beat your ass worse," Maine huffed, wiping the sweat from his forehead. It was hot as fuck out there, but a lesson had to be taught.

Walking over to Kali he said, "You good? Let me see yo' neck."

"I'm fine, Maine. Thank you. Your brother has some serious anger problems and until he gets help, I think it's best Khyri doesn't come around him."

Maine hated that it had to come to that, but she had a point. Overhearing what she said, Erik struggled to stand to his feet.

"You can't keep my son away from me," he croaked.

"I can't, but the courts can. I don't want to get them involved, but I can't trust you not to flip out on him when you'll flip out on me in a second. That's scary and I don't want my baby around you."

"Man, I would never put my hands on him. Kind of nigga you take me for?" he scoffed.

"The kind who just put his hands on me in front of him. You're abusive, Erik," Kali cried, saddened for Khyri. He loved his daddy, but Erik needed help.

"I can work on it, ma. Please don't let me stop seeing Khyri. Come on, man,"

His pleading fell upon deaf ears. He could get on his knees and beg and Kali wouldn't change her mind. There'd been way too many reports and deaths in regards to women and children losing their lives at the hands of a lunatic man. It'd never crossed her mind that Erik would harm Khyri in any way, but today's antics didn't settle with her spirit.

Buckling Khyri in his car seat, she kissed his head and cheek while telling him she loved him. Maine reached inside and gave him some dap and a twenty-dollar bill out his pocket, while Erik pathetically stood there. Watching his family pack up and drive away, not knowing when the next time he'd see them, crushed him. While he was so focused on hurting Kali, he didn't realize he was only hurting himself in the long run. If he wanted a relationship with her and Khyri, he was going to have to come correct or sit off to the side while a real man took care of the home that was supposed to be his.

9

What am I doing here? Again. That was the only question Layla could ask herself while sitting uncomfortably on the sofa. She'd read somewhere that therapy was good for healing. That somehow, talking to a stranger about her problems would help solve them... to a certain extent. Layla wasn't sure how true that was, but she was willing to give it a try. In fact, this was her third session so it couldn't have been that bad.

Staring off, gazing at nothing in particular, she wondered what Dr. Rush would ask her next. The ambiance inside of the room was calming, making Layla understand why so many people came to her. It was a safe space; free from judgment. When Dr. Rush flipped a page of her notebook, completing the page, Layla looked her way.

Her eyes were gentle as she stared at Layla, giving her a soft smile. *Well, that's good,* she thought, wringing her hands together anxiously. Placing the notebook along the wooden table, she grabbed her notes and crossed her legs at the knee. Eager to know what'd she thought, Layla sighed heavily.

"So?" she pressed.

"That was different from the others you've let me read."

Okay... and?

"And," Dr. Rush began. "What made it different from the others?"

Her soft, but pensive stare somewhat annoyed Layla. She knew exactly what made it different, but she wanted Layla to pick apart and break down her own words. As if she hadn't been the one to write them. Clearing her throat, Layla scratched at her scalp, reminding herself to schedule an appointment to get her locs touched up. *Maybe I'll get some color this time.*

"I don't know," Layla answered flatly. Unbelieving.

Shifting her gaze toward the window, her eyes cast upon a bird. As it chirped, it sent Layla's mind to a place where she always seemed to go the day of a session. Or any day she felt herself slipping into the dark hole she'd once ventured down.

W hy are these birds so loud? *Squinting her eyes, a young 7-year-old Layla peered up at the window above her head. The sun had settled above the horizon minutes prior and peeped through her cotton candy pink curtains. Yawning, she rolled over and hopped to her feet inside the bed.*

Pulling the curtains back, her eyes searched for the culprit who'd waken her out of her sleep. There was a tree directly outside her window, housing just about every bird who'd marked its territory there. Layla's eyes widened in excitement as a yellow canary flew right to the windowsill.

"Hey," she cooed gently. "Was that you making all that noise?"

As if it knew what she were saying the bird chirped, causing Layla to giggle. Her mind ventured to how it gotten there, where'd it come from, and where it was going. She wondered if it had friends or a family. Somewhere safe to sleep at night and food to survive.

At seven years old, Layla's frame of mind and thoughts were much different than her peers. Things a girl her age wouldn't normally think of, she did.

"It's so free," she murmured.

An ache her youthfulness still hadn't come to terms with settled in her chest. Evidence of tears gathered in her eyes as she jumped from the bed and over to the desk in the corner of her room. Shuffling papers, coloring books, and toys around she spotted the matte pink journal with a rose in the center of it. Grabbing a pen, she rushed back to her bed. Sitting Indian style, Layla turned until she came to a fresh, blank page. Words bounced around in her head, formulating sentences of their own with ease.

Today I saw a bird outside my window.
I wonder where it will go.
Or who it will see.
Was it sweet and kind
Or mean like me?
Does it have friends?
Was it left alone at night?
Did its mother leave it too, knowing that's not right...

Saddened by her own words, Layla slammed the journal closed and tossed it toward the end of her bed. When she looked back up at the window, the bird was gone. A lone tear fell from her eye, and down her cheek.

"I want to be free and fly away too, birdie."

"You don't know or you don't want to share?" Dr. Rush questioned, killing her daydream.

Layla didn't say anything for a moment, trying to let her thoughts manifest into what she was actually feeling. It'd been a task to get them on one accord, but she was learning to do so. The first session, she wanted Dr. Rush to hold a magnifying glass over her and peer into what she knew were her innermost thoughts. Ones she couldn't quite conjure.

She knew why she wrote the poem but didn't know what it meant at the time. *I was a sad seven-year-old.* Chuckling, Layla squared her shoulders and smoothed out the long, thin skirt she was wearing. Bangles on her wrist jangled with each movement, reminding her that she was indeed sitting there in a chair offering up the depths of herself to a stranger.

This shit is crazy.

"I was young and sad," she offered, taking a breath.

"Sad about the bird?"

Layla shrugged and scoffed. "Sure. If that's what you want to think."

"I don't want to think anything. I'd like for *you* to elaborate on your words back then and why you wanted me to see them now. What made you and the bird similar?"

"Nothing. That's the thing."

Her reply made Dr. Rush scribble some notes on her notepad. Layla wondered if she thought this shit was easy for her. This wasn't like when she performed for a crowd of people. That she could do and did well. Letting her words miraculously flow from her lips to the tons of people's ears who soaked up her words is what Layla lived for. She breathed it, could lay her heart on the line when those words were out of her head and off her chest.

This isolation inside a room, though safe and free from likes of a crowd, seemed to be suffocating her. The questions, the untold stories she never mentioned, the way Dr. Rush cared too much about her past life... it all angered and saddened Layla at the same time. Shaking her head, she adjusted in her seat; two seconds away from hopping up and leaving. Paid session or not, Layla would never stay anywhere she felt uncomfortable if she didn't have to.

"Your mother... you never mention her."

"And you see why. She left me," Layla growled.

She could feel Dr. Rush staring at her as her gaze focused back on the window. *Maybe I should just leave. This is too much.* Dr. Rush's scrutiny gaze was poignant in a sense, but that didn't waver Layla's vision. The day was nice and she couldn't wait to go home and get in bed. Inwardly, she chuckled at how depressing that sounded.

"Tell me about your relationship with her."

Dr. Rush's voice was soft and hopeful. She felt they were getting somewhere, but Layla didn't. Her mother was a sore topic; and now she was beating herself up for even letting her read the damn poem. Fed up with the open-ended questions, Layla snapped.

"We don't have one okay? She made her decision and is trying to pay for it now by begging and sending me money, as if that'll fix anything. I don't want her money."

"What is that you want from her?"

"Her love?" Layla flipped, tossing her arms in the air so to say *I don't know.* "Something other than money and long voicemails full of apologies and broken promises."

Her voice quivered out of anger and hurt. Swallowing the lump in her throat, Layla sat for a beat, tapping her foot before standing to her feet. She'd had enough for the day, and before she had a screaming match with herself, she'd rather leave. Dr. Rush sat unfazed yet intrigued by her sudden outburst of emotion. Layla's resentment toward her mother was thickening by the second.

"Look, today was enough. I'll see you next week... maybe."

"Sure. I think today was more than enough and the perfect beginning to your healing, Layla. Not all anger is frowned upon. You just have to find another place to reroute it; it's displaced. Don't let it consume you and who you're becoming."

With her back facing Dr. Rush, Layla let her words settle in her head before pulling the door open and leaving today's session behind her. Heading straight to the parking lot with her head held high, Layla inhaled the California air and exhaled it through her nose.

"I need to get high," she mumbled.

Cranking the air up in her car, she sighed at what today was already becoming. She picked a morning session just so she could sleep in before work, but sleep was the furthest thing from her mind. Especially now that she'd had to discuss her mother. Tatum was trying her best, or what she considered it to be, but that wasn't enough for Layla. Some apologies were only just as good unheard because they never helped alter the way Layla felt about her mother.

After grabbing breakfast from one of her favorite Vegan spots, Layla pulled up to her complex and parked in her designated spot. Glancing to her right, she saw Brody's Durango backed in. The gesture to search for him or a sign of him had become routine and she hadn't even realized it. Pulling her phone out, she thought to text Amelia and see what her cousin had been up to but didn't. Instead, she tapped on Brody's name that was located directly under Amelia's in her text messages.

"I wonder if he's up," she hummed, typing out a message.

Layla: *You awake? I have breakfast.*

S he waited for all of thirty seconds and her stomach lurched at how quickly he replied. Biting her bottom lip as dots danced across the screen, Layla wondered what he was up there typing. Upstairs, Brody grinned at her message.

"Who got you over there smiling and shit?" Jesse, Brody's homeboy questioned nosily.

Lifting his head, the same grin was plastered across his face. "My neighbor. She about to slide through for a minute."

"Need us to leave?" Jesse asked, nodding his head toward the door.

"Nah, nah. You good. She cool people."

Brody: *I'm up. How you know I was hungry?*

Layla: *I'm psychic?* 🤨

Brody: *Somethin' else to add to the list of things that intrigues me about you... come through. The door unlocked.*

R eading over his last message a few times, Layla didn't have to wonder what he meant. Brody didn't sugarcoat shit with Layla. He let it be known he was feeling her but had kept things strictly platonic between them for now. He'd fucked up a good thing in the past and didn't want a repeat with Layla. He could tell that one chance was all he was going to get with her and he was cherishing it.

Feeling all giddy inside, opposite of how she felt thirty minutes prior, Layla climbed out her car with food in hand and took the flights of steps to his door. They'd shared breakfast a few times after that morning her air was out, so this wasn't anything new for them. Her sudden draw to him was, though. She welcomed it; appreciating the solace it brought to her life.

Though he told her the door was unlocked, Layla still knocked before stepping inside. His AC had to be on freeze-out the way it smacked Layla in the face. The temperature in the room wasn't as cold as her icy glare that masked her face when she saw a female sitting crossed-leg on Brody's couch. The grip she had on the paper bag of food tightened, cramping her hand in the process.

"Hi. I'm Monae," the girl spoke, giving an introduction Layla wanted to shove back down her throat.

Without acknowledging her, Layla headed for the kitchen where she heard cabinets opening and closing. Tossing of the food on the counter caught Brody's attention. Turning, he grinned ready to greet her but stopped when he saw the frown on her face.

"What's wrong wit' you?"

"Who is that girl on your couch? You invite me up here after a nightcap with one of your little hoes?" Layla hissed harshly under her breath.

It was Brody's turn to frown... in confusion. "What? That ain't one of my hoes. That's my boy Jesse girlfriend."

"Yeah? Well where the hell is Jesse at then?"

Tossing her hand on her hip, Brody got distracted. She stood before him looking like a melanin goddess with her locs sitting atop her head in a long ponytail, a scarf from one of her many collections tied around her head, and smooth brown skin glowing, brightening up his dimly lit kitchen. The way her lips pouted, hips poked, and need for an answer resided in her eyes, made Brody lick his lips. Stepping closer to her, he grinned at her little attitude and wrapped a hand around her waist, pulling her into his chest.

"He's in the bathroom. Any more questions?"

Layla's whole resolve crumbled. Slightly bowing her head, she mumbled, "Sorry. I just thought you were trying to run game or something."

"Never that," he said lifting her chin upward and quickly kissing her pouty lips. Layla gasped and eyes stretched outward. "We good?"

She nodded. Nerves shot straight to hell. "Um, yeah. Yeah," she pronounced clearer. "We're good."

Brody squeezed her waist and let her go. "Bet. Let's eat then. I'm hungry as hell. What you was out doing?"

Stunned by his actions, Layla stood bereft of words. She was not expecting him to kiss her, nor to go on about it and ask about her day like he hadn't just caused a leak in her underwear. *This man,* she groaned inwardly.

"Meeting with my therapist," she answered honestly. Somewhat surprised by her quick admission.

Brody turned around and gave her a reassuring smile. "Word? Was it a good session?"

"She said it was, but I don't think so. I left early," she shrugged.

"That's a'ight, love. Baby steps. As long as you showed up willingly, that's what counts, right?"

Layla smiled and grabbed the cup of orange juice from him. "Yes, I guess so."

"Nah, I need you to know so next time you stay the whole time."

Playfully, Layla rolled her eyes. "Yes, Brody. It was a good session. Happy?"

He nodded. "Yep," he grinned, just as Jesse and Monae stepped inside the kitchen.

"What's up," Jesse spoke. "Aye, bruh. We about to head out. Good looking on the job info. I appreciate that."

Brody stood and slapped hands with him. "It ain't nothing. Let me introduce you to Layla, who almost knocked me upside my head thinking Monae was a little nightcap."

Layla looked toward Monae. "Sorry, girl. You sitting there just caught me off guard."

"It's fine. I completely understand. Let my man have some random female posted on his couch and I'd be ready to make heads roll too."

"Oh. We're not, that's not my man," Layla giggled, trying to hide the awkwardness of her tone. "Just neighbors."

"I thought you said we was friends, too. Damn," Brody dragged. "I see how it is."

"Don't be like that," Layla told him. "We are friends," she then said to Monae. "Neighbors who somehow became friends because he wouldn't stop bothering me."

Brody laughed a good laugh, making Jesse smirk. His boy was definitely feeling Layla. In all of their five years of friendship, he'd never saw a woman besides his ex from years ago, make him behave the way Layla had him going. Sitting at the table and eating breakfast? No, sir. Brody didn't do that. If Monae had been a fling of his, she'd be gone and out of his apartment before the nine o'clock news aired.

"Y'all hear that? Now, I'm a bother," he feigned hurt, holding a hand over his chest.

"You might be," Monae said in jest. "Y'all would make a cute couple though. Just saying."

Layla broke their gaze and focused on her spinach, mushroom, tomato omelet. Had Monae mentioned anything remotely close about a relationship to her a few months ago, she'd be ready to debate with her about why she was all good in that department. Now, she was just as mute as could be. Her desires had shifted over the months and Brody's fine, attentive, wanting to remain friends ass, was the reason.

When they were done eating, the duo retired to the living room; their normal hang out spot when she came over. While he played the game, Layla laid back across his couch, legs bent at the knees, with a blunt stuffed full of exotic weed in her hand. Blowing the smoke in the air, she smiled as it got her higher than she'd normally like to be. Her preference was an edible all day, but she hadn't copped any from her supplier yet.

"Man, this nigga cheating like hell," Brody groaned.

Layla looked toward the screen and saw there was two minutes left of the game. Leaning forward, she put the blunt out in the ashtray and laid back. Brody didn't smoke, not as much as Layla did, but he'd hit the weed every now and then. Even though weed was legalized, Brody had to cut back on his intake. Layla didn't know it, or maybe she had, but he used to be pushing the line of being overweight. A slight scare in terrible chest pains had him rushed to the hospital one night at work, and from then on Brody got serious about his health.

Though there were no cases on weed, the right kind, ever killing anyone, it made Brody pig out on food due to the munchies. He had no choice but to ease up his daily intake from 3-4 Backwoods a day, to 1-2 a week if that. It was a struggle at first, but once the weight started shedding and he got in the gym, the results of his lifestyle change had him feeling better than he'd felt in a while.

"Yeah! Ol' punk ass," he cheered, winning the game by three points. "I should've bet him."

Layla smiled lazily at his excitement. *Men and their games.* "Brody," she called out.

"What's up, love?" Placing the controller on the table, Brody picked the blunt up out of the ashtray, sparked it and took a few pulls while sitting back. Getting comfortable, he tugged Layla's legs from underneath her and stretched them over his muscular thighs.

"What's on your mind?" he asked, rubbing up and down her exposed shin.

"I think I want to talk to her."

"Talk to who?"

"My m – the lady who abandoned me."

An awkward silence filled the air around them for a moment, until Layla elaborated on her words... thanks to

Dr. Rush's skillful methods to get her to open up. Layla was good with words. Speaking them on a subject that caused pain was the issue. Talking about her problems with Brody seemed to come naturally. He was an amazing listener and an even better reciprocator. The passion and words he spoke into her life, were of the same that Layla gave to him. It was beyond refreshing and needed.

"Never mind," she chuckled. "I'm just high and trippin'."

"Nah," he soothed. "You speaking your mind. Ain't nothing wrong with that. Talk to me."

Layla let the words form and they spilled out a second later. "I just want to ask her why she left me, you know. I was just a baby, needing that love from its mother. The only person who should've loved me more than anything in this world. It just sucks because I have so much anger toward her that, being around her may trigger something inside me I can't come back from. I was just sitting here thinking that maybe, just maybe, if I sat down and spoke with her face to face I'd get the truth. Instead of her blowing up my phone and sending messages through my cousin and other family, we could discuss her evil ways like adults."

She breathed and reached for the blunt. "Let me hit this weed," she said and they chuckled.

Brody scratched at his facial hair, needing a cut

ASAP. "Aye, for real... communication is everything. But it's not the most important thing, honestly. Comprehension is. You can talk yo' head off, but if somebody not understanding where you coming from, talking is pointless. We get so caught up in what we thought people meant, when we could've asked. Or, we assume they meant one thing through a text, when they meant another. You see I stay calling you after you text me. It's convenient yes, but at what cost? I'm sure if you reached out to her on some 'I just want to talk' tip, she'd be willing to. But, shit then again you are kind of intimidating so I could see why she only texts you," he said jokingly.

Layla kicked his leg. "Oh, what the fuck ever. Did I intimidate you when you first saw me?"

"Hell yeah. Kinda question is that? You must not see how you be walking around this mothafucka."

"Now you're doing the most," she pouted sitting up. "I'm nice. I can be less intimidating."

"I'm sure you can, it's just the vibes you give off. Well, used to for me. I think I gotta good feel for who you are now."

She cocked her head slightly to the left. Gazing at his mahogany eyes, scruffy facial hair, wild tapered curls and buff frame, Layla's body eased with a yearning that gathered at the pit of her gut. He was so unproblematic. So relaxed, and didn't cower away from Layla's headstrong personality, yet he was simple just like her. There was nothing and *everything* about Brody that made her want to bare her soul to him.

She couldn't deny her attraction and their vibes any longer. It was sad enough she'd damn near bit his head off for having another woman in his place. She had sat up some nights overanalyzing what they were doing, and she always came to the conclusion that they were getting to know one another. A guy could never hold Layla's interest after she orgasmed, and hardly before then, but Brody was different. She wanted what they were doing to be much different than the route she took with guys she just wanted sex from.

"So, you think you have me pegged?" she asked, jokingly.

"Somewhat. I mean, I could be wrong but I don't think I am. You're not that closed off as you think you are."

Layla broke the intense gaze they were sharing and fiddled with the beads around her waist. That was the other thing holding her back from pursuing something permanent with Brody. She felt exposed but didn't want to feel that way until she was ready to expose herself. He hadn't pegged her yet, because Layla hadn't pegged herself yet. There were layers of herself she hadn't peeled back and discovered yet, so she damn sure didn't want to hear how she was viewed from the only person she didn't mind spending more than thirty minutes around.

"Aye," he said squeezing her thigh. "Don't do that."

"I'm not doing anything."

"You shutting down and me out. I'm just letting you know what I see and feel. If I'm wrong, prove me wrong."

"I'm not in the business of proving anything to anyone who already has an assumption about me. That's on you and has nothing to do with me."

"That's where you're wrong. It has more to do with you than you think."

"Why would I want to persuade someone that I'm not the person they think I am? It makes no sense," she shrugged, getting annoyed with the entire conversation. He was close to blowing her high, honestly.

"Why not is the question? Lemme give you an example. Your boss gives you a table to serve at work with more people than you've handled before. He'd already let it be known that you couldn't fuck this up, because you fumbled with the last big table. You got this second chance to prove to him that you're not a fuck up, you just fucked up that one time. You telling me you gon' give the table to another waitress, let her outshine you and earn that fat ass tip?"

When the corners of his mouth lifted into a grin, Layla smiled and shook her head from side to side.

"Nah. I'ma prove his ass wrong and make my fat ass tip."

They shared a laugh. "Exactly! That's all I'm saying. Just because we assume things, we downplay how much weight giving second chances hold. If we don't take them, who knows what we'll miss out on."

They were quiet for a few, letting the seriousness of their conversation settle. Smoke escaped Brody's lips as he soothingly stroked Layla's thigh. Having her in his presence was just as good for and to him, just as much as it was for her. He told himself this was his second chance. Another opportunity to build with a woman rather than break her down like he'd done his last. Young and dumb decisions caused him to lose his first love, but he was older now and ready and willing to put in the work and effort to never be the cause of another heartbreak... including his own.

"So, I think I'ma text her and ask to meet," Layla said, coming to a conclusion.

"Yeah? You think or you sure?"

Biting the corner of her lip, she pondered for a beat. "I'm sure. This has to be done. Especially if I want what we're building to be something more."

Her admission made Brody smirk. "But I thought... aren't we just... you said," he pointed, "We were just neighbors," he mocked her voice causing Layla to giggle.

"We're friends too, but I can see us being more. I'd like if we could be more."

Leaning her way, Layla was prepared this time when he kissed her lips. Slowly, he savored the feel of them while one hand gently gripped her chin. Pulling away, Brody's lips still hovered against hers as his hand eased down her neck.

"I'd like that too," he murmured, grazing her lips with each word spoken.

Layla smiled and ran her fingertips through his growing beard. "You better. I don't just be wasting my time over here, so make it count."

She didn't have to tell Brody twice, hell not even once. He was going to be sure that every moment they spent together was worthwhile. First, she had to handle the situation with her mother though. A woman holding that type of resentment didn't love or share her love easily and at this point, Brody wasn't taking any more losses. If she won the fight against her own battles and healed, that'd mean he'd win too.

Squinting her eyes underneath the dim light in her old bedroom, Shanae glanced at the digital clock on the nightstand and groaned. She'd only been asleep for a few hours at best but was hoping by the time she did peel her eyes open it'd be morning. Nighttime was the worst for her. The silent stillness of the night was when her thoughts got the best of her and nightmares appeared. It was ironic what a ray of sunshine could bring and she vowed to never take it for granted again.

Two weeks after Isaiah was killed, Shanae spoke with her apartment complex about breaking her lease. There was no way she could live, or at least try to live, a peaceful life where a man she loved took his last breaths. Thankfully, her leasing agreement was up in a month and they waived all fees, making it so she could leave without a hassle. Having had the news and media outlets swarming their place the entire week after the shooting, the owner of the building suggested she move as well. It was beneficial to them both.

Yawning, Shanae squeezed her eyes and stretched her body across the bed. The full-size bed was nothing compared to her queen, but it got the job done. Moving back with her mom wasn't nearly what Shanae thought her life would lead to months ago. Sharee had always expressed to her child that if she ever fell on hard times, her home would always be open to her. At a time like this, Shanae was grateful her mother had enough room to accommodate her. She didn't know how long she planned to be under her roof and she wasn't exactly in a rush to leave either. The familiarity of her childhood home brought a calming to her turbulent soul, and in the same breath gave a reminder that she wasn't a little girl anymore. This was the real world grown folks had warned her about and she was dealing with some very grown up shit. Issues she didn't wish on anyone.

The healing process for her had been ugly. Downright devastating, but with each passing day Shanae found strength to get up and go. The process wasn't relaxing bubble baths while aromatherapy candles illuminated the bathroom. It was restless nights, soul-bearing cries, occasional bouts of depression and much more than Shanae bargained for. Her heart ached and struggled to heal its wounds all in the same.

Shanae found herself having to take accountability for the role she played in she and Isaiah's relationship. It brought upon guilt... for herself. The root of all their issues, ones she'd swept hundreds of times under a tattered rug, triggered emotions she'd finally come to terms with. For her, processing the trauma of his cheating and death caused her to have to relive it, which wasn't easy by far but she knew it'd be worth it. Only time would tell.

"Knock, knock," Sharee called out tapping the bedroom door softly.

It was slightly cracked, so she made her way inside.

Though she hated the circumstances it caused for her daughter to be back under her roof, Sharee was glad. Shanae was her baby. Her only child. She cried for a week straight after she helped her move into her first place. Shanae's determination to prove her independency was the only reason she gave her the green light to move out. If it were up to Sharee, Shanae could've lived with her well into her late twenties. It'd been them two together for all her life; why change up now?

"Hey Ma," Shanae greeted.

"Hey you. You got a good nap in?"

Stretching again, doing one of those stretches that had her damn near falling out the bed, she chuckled. "Yes. I could honestly go back to sleep, but I'ma get up."

"Alright. I know you're probably hungry. There's dinner on the stove."

Sitting up, Shanae gave a soft smile while taking in her mother's beauty. Dressed casually in a pair of capri leggings, a white camisole, fuzzy socks on her feet, soft natural short curls, and glowing chocolate skin; Sharee was aging backwards.

"Why do you always cook so much food? Let me found out you have a male friend," Shanae snickered.

Waving her off, Sharee propped herself against the wall. "Maybe I do."

"Really?" The hope in Shanae's voice made her mother grin and release a chuckle.

Shanae's father hadn't been a permanent fixture in her life in a while. He'd pop in every now and again, every five years or so, to 'check up on them,' but that was it. Sharee could recall days where she begged him to be a father, but more than anything a man of his word. When she first found out she was pregnant, he made every promise to stay by her side and do right by his family. That was until Sharee found out he'd had an entire other family tucked away already.

While he was pacifying Sharee with false love, he was living a double life just three hours away. When Rich, Sharee's brother and Kali's dad, got word of how he'd played his sister, he wanted war. Sharee didn't though. She'd witnessed many of women beg and plead for a man to stay, believing they needed him to survive or make do, when that wasn't the case at all.

Sharee would be lying if she said she was surprised by his actions, but she wasn't. Her father had warned her, her mother too, but she had to test the waters. She had to somehow prove to her family that the man she'd go to bat for damn near every day wasn't out here doing her wrong. A happy, loving home with two parents is what Sharee wanted for Shanae. She'd grown up the same and wanted to continue to be an example for her daughter.

Regardless of how many years they shared, Sharee was a firm believer in not doing something just to save face. Sure, she could've kept on living her life knowing he had another family and continue to be placed on the back burner like she had unconsciously been doing, but at what cost? She had a daughter to raise and settling was not something she ever wanted Shanae to do just because that seemed like the only option readily available to her.

That's why she was so hurt behind the situation with Isaiah and Shanae. Sharee had peeped game from day one with his antics and warned her daughter just as her mother did her, but Shanae had to learn on her own. Loving a man, especially one who didn't reciprocate that same love, was a lesson she had to be taught; not told.

"Yes, really," Sharee smirked. "Can I not have a male friend?"

"Yes, I guess so. As long as he makes you happy and respects you."

"He does. I'll have to let you two meet soon, especially since you'll be here."

Shanae's head dropped some. "I'm sorry, Ma. I'm crowding your space. I'll start looking for a place soon, I just... I just need a little time. Maybe a month?"

Sharee stepped over to the bed and sat down. Grabbing Shanae's hand she made her look up at her. "You take as much time as you need. I am in no rush to get you out of here again. It feels good knowing you're safe under my roof and can come here. What type of mother would I be to leave you hanging?"

Shanae shrugged. "Ion't know. The type who has a man and needs some privacy."

"No man will ever come before you. Know and believe that."

Catching the seriousness of her tone, Shanae smiled. "Thank you, Ma. I love you so much."

Leaning over, Sharee squeezed her daughter tightly in her arms. She'd go to hell and back for her baby and she'd better know it. "I love you more. Now, I need you to do me a favor."

Peering at her with a questioning gaze, Shanae asked, "What's that? Take the trash out?"

"Oh, no. Paul will get that later on."

"Paaaul," Shanae cooed with a grin. "So, I get a name too?"

"Will you stop it and focus?" Sharee blushed.

"Okay, okay. What's the favor?"

"Get up, shower, put some clothes on and get out of this house. I know it may seem like a lot but staying ducked off in here isn't healthy. Hiding from the world isn't going to erase the problems. I know you're still mourning, but a night out won't hurt."

Pondering over her words, Shanae immediately

wanted to disagree. The thought of being around people especially when she didn't have to, caused a fleet of anxiety to sore through body. It wasn't that she couldn't stand being around people, it was the fact that every time she ran into someone who knew she and Isaiah both asked that dreaded question; how are you?

Shanae would lightly smile and give them a generic answer, not wanting to divulge her true emotions. But, how was she really? She was making it. Taking it one day at a time. In all honesty, it's all she could do. Isaiah was never coming back. There'd be no other opportunity to question his love for her, or lack thereof. She'd never be able to ask about the child he'd created with another woman, leaving her yet again in the dark and humiliated. Isaiah would no longer have the power or hold on her heart that he'd held captive for far too long. With that one detail in mind, Shanae perked up at the idea of getting cute and stepping out.

"You might be right. Let me call Bia and Kali and see what they're up to."

Sharee smiled. "I think that'll be good. Go have some fun. Let your hair down. You're young and have an entire life ahead of you to find love again. It may not seem like it, but the man for you will be just that; yours."

For a brief second, Shanae's mind drifted to Levi and her heart warmed and stomach churned. She didn't want to tell her mother that she thought he *may* be her person to love on again, but it wouldn't hurt. Their chemistry was undeniable and he'd been nothing short of amazing while she grieved.

"And, when I meet him I'm gonna lock him down."

"Or he'll lock you down," Sharee smiled and stood from the bed. "A man who knows what he wants stops at nothing to make it evident to his woman. Trust me on that honey."

Leaving her gems sprinkled across Shanae's mind, Sharee left out of her room. Her male friend Paul had her in high spirits these days and she was almost certain he was the one. Until she spoke to the Man above more in depth though, she was holding out on letting Shanae meet him. It was a protective tactic Sharee had to put in place for them.

Gliding her hand across the cool sheets, Shanae located her phone and blinked a few times, blinded by the brightness of her screen. After adjusting it, she group FaceTimed Kali and Bia.

"She's risen," Bia joked.

"Whatever. What're y'all doing?"

Giggling into the screen, Kali pushed Rondo's hand away from the middle of her legs. "Nothing. Chilling with bae and Khyri."

"What Khy doing?" Shanae asked.

Flipping the camera around, Kali placed it on a knocked out Khyri who was sprawled out on the living room floor. They were supposed to be having movie night, watching Black Panther for the millionth time, and little baby couldn't hang.

"Knocked out. We were supposed to be binge-watching movies, but he tapped out on us."

"Y'all are so cute," Bia squeaked.

"I'm 'bout to run to the store right quick," Rondo told her climbing from the couch.

Kali cut her eyes at him. "Right now?"

"Yeah, I need some shells and I thought you wanted some ice cream."

"Look at you," Shanae snickered. "About to go off for nothing."

Kali flipped her off. "Whatever. And, okay. Be safe."

"I will." Leaning over, Rondo smooched her lips before snatching his keys up.

Kali's eyes stayed on him until he was locking the door and pulling it shut behind him. Relaxing back on the couch, she smiled into the screen.

"Whaaat?" she whined.

"Hoe, you in love," Shanae laughed. "You see the way she was looking at that man, Bia?"

"Mhm. I sure did. Ready to attack his ass. Khyri gon' have another sibling real soon watch."

"Hell no," Kali cleared up right away. "I'm trying to wait until he's at least five or six, but by then I would want to be married. I'm not popping out no more babies unless they're for my husband."

Shanae's brows furrowed. "That's in three to four years?"

"Exactly. My husband better come along before then," Kali snickered. "But, anyway. What's up. What you doing?"

"Nothing. I was trying to see if y'all wanted to go out, but you're in the house for the night."

"I'm not," Bia said. "Where you trying to go?"

"I don't know. Get some fresh air or something. It's the weekend and all I've been doing is sleeping and studying."

Shanae wasn't sure how time had flown by so quickly, but her final semester of college was coming to an end. In less than three months. The idea of sitting a semester out because of Isaiah's death had almost happened, but at the last minute she pulled herself together and enrolled after speaking to her college advisor. She'd made it this far and knew that one semester off could possibly lead to two and then she'd be complaining about never finishing. Toughing it out was the best option.

"I feel you. I'm so tired of classes. It's like I never got a real summer break," Kali agreed.

"Glad I don't have to deal with those struggles," Bia chimed.

College had never been on her radar. Even if it had been, she was sure she would've dropped out. Aside from her job at the call center with Shanae, Bia modeled. She had partnered with some of the best in the industry and was quickly making a name for herself. College would just slow her down.

"Lucky you," Kali said in jest. College wasn't for everybody, that she knew.

"Right. So anyway. I'ma get up and put some clothes on. Try to make myself look somewhat presentable."

"Okay. Want me to drive?" Bia asked.

"Yeah, that's cool. I feel like tonight's gonna be one of those nights where I don't need to drive. I'll gladly be a rider."

"Well, you know I got you. Be ready in an hour?"

Shanae nodded. "Yep. That's plenty of time."

"You hoes have fun and be safe. I'ma be laid up for the night," Kali offered.

"We will. Love you," Shanae told her.

"Love you too cousin."

The trio hung up and Shanae exhaled and stood from the bed. She'd literally just agreed to get dressed so there was no backing out now. Heading to the bathroom connected to her room, she started the shower before going back inside her room to the closet. Not wanting to get too comfortable in her mom's crib, Shanae only hung up the things that needed to be hung. Everything else was folded neatly in totes she picked up from Wal-Mart.

Deciding to keep it simple, she pulled out a pair of distressed jeans, a money green off the shoulder crop top that tied at the front, and a pair of black sandals. Staring at the outfit after tossing it on the bed, Shanae twisted her mouth from side to side... pondering. Stalling. She was so indecisive sometimes, it sickened her. Huffing, she headed to the shower before she spent an hour trying on everything in her bin only to wear the first outfit.

After showering, rubbing down in shea butter, brushing her teeth and cleansing her face Shanae felt like a brand-new person. The music blasting from her Beats speaker only enhanced the carefree mood she was now in. Singing, she got dressed and prepared to tackle her hair. Thankfully, it wasn't the tangled mess it'd been in weeks ago. It definitely wasn't fitting into a ponytail; not a neat one anyway.

Grabbing her pick, Shanae commenced to adding volume to her already massive 'fro. When it was to her liking, she put on some eye shadow, mascara, and glossed her lips to finish her look off. Swiveling her head, she realized she was missing something. Snapping her finger, she went back inside her room and grabbed her gold hoop earrings and put them on. Popping her lips, she smiled. "That's it. You clean up nice, girl," she complimented.

When Bia's call came through telling her she was outside, Shanae rushed to exchange her over the shoulder purse for her clutch. Slipping her sandals on a spritzing herself with some perfume, she made sure she had everything before heading toward the front door.

"You look cute," Sharee smiled from the couch.

"Thank you. I'm heading out with Bia. I'll be back at a decent hour."

Sharee waved her off. "You mind staying at her place for the night? I know it's last minute, but Paul had a death in the family and..."

"Ma, it's fine. I'm sure she won't mind. Let Paul know he and his family are in my prayers."

Sharee's heart expanded, in awe of the woman she raised. Shanae had one of the biggest hearts and was more understanding than lots of people. It was unfortunate that her kindness had gotten taken for granted for so many years by Isaiah, but she was still young and had time to bounce back. Sharee knew the real would come along and show her what it felt like to be truly appreciated and handled with care. First, she had to grow some tougher skin and she was hoping this healing journey was providing just that, while shedding her old layers.

"I will. Have fun, baby. Tell Bia I said hi. Let me know when y'all make it in."

Shuffling over to her mother, Shanae kissed her cheek. "I will. Bye!"

With a pep in her step, Shanae strutted to Bia's car and slid into the passenger seat.

"Oooh! Who is she?" Bia beamed, hyping her up.

Blushing, Shanae waved her off. She was so modest about her looks. "Stop. You look cute too. Look at your boobs in that shirt," she laughed.

"Girl, these things would not stay hidden. Plus, a little cleavage never hurt nobody."

"Right. Have you ate?" Shanae asked as she pulled off down the street.

"Nope. Not since earlier. I hope you're not about to say let's go out to eat."

Bia cut her eyes her way and Shanae shook her head no. "I was just asking."

"Oh, okay. Well let me drive and you sit back and enjoy the ride. I know the perfect place for food and drinks," she grinned.

"Oh, goodness," Shanae sighed with a smirk teasing her lips. Knowing Bia, she was going to have them bar hopping and tossing back shots like they were celebrating. And in a sense, they were. Shanae was finally free of Isaiah's hold. Shit, that was damn sure something to celebrate. She'd gotten her life back and Bia wanted to show her girl what the taste of freedom tasted like and she had the perfect spot in mind for the experience.

"I can't believe you brought me here," Shanae whispered for the hundredth time in Bia's ear.

Giggling, Bia just shoved her drink in front of her. "Will you hush. *Shottas* is the perfect place for food and drinks."

Shanae knew she had a point, but still. Levi owned the place, and she was doing everything in her power to act normal just in case he was there somewhere watching her. The one shot she'd been forced to take upon entering had her body heated, and she couldn't wait until the order of wings and mozzarella sticks came out. Drinking on an empty stomach wasn't in the plans for the night. She didn't care how much fun Bia tried to make it sound; Shanae knew her limits.

"What if he's here?" she said, glancing around the place.

"It's his business Shanae," Bia huffed. "Stop being annoying and have fun. Isn't that what you wanted to come out for? You got all cute just to sit here and act like a paranoid little girl. If you want to know if he's here, text him. Otherwise, shut up."

Taken aback by Bia's words, Shanae gasped and giggled. "The disrespect."

Bia chuckled. "Whatever. You know it's all said out of love. Drink your drink and chill. Want to order a hookah?"

Shanae nodded and decided to take her advice. Sipping her drink, she smiled at everyone on the dance floor enjoying themselves. It was slightly packed with people, but not to the point where it was overbearing and uncomfortable. They'd even gotten a booth. The DJ had the place rocking and when he began to play No Guidance by Chris Brown feat. Drake, Shanae stood from the booth.

"I haven't heard this song since the summer," she grinned snapping her fingers.

Swaying her hips with her drink in hand, Bia smiled at her girl. It was good to see her having fun. When she belted out Chris Brown's verse, Bia cracked up and sang with her. Men and women were singing the late summer jam, not caring one bit. It was a banger for sure.

"You got it girl, you got it girrrl!" Shanae sang.

Holding her drink like it was a mic, she sang and rolled her hips. She'd lost some weight while slipping into a slight depression, but it looked good on her. While she was busy dancing, she had an admirer. He'd spotted her from afar but was now up close and personal in her space. Protectively, wrapping a hand around her waist letting it be known she was off limits.

They ain't really love you, runnin' game, usin'
All your stupid exes, they gon' call again
Tell 'em that a real nigga's steppin' in
Don't let them niggas try you, test your patience
Tell 'em that it's over, ain't no debating
All you need is me playing on your playlist
You ain't gotta be frustrated

Shanae blushed and easily fell into Levi's hold. She rotated her hips, making sure to brush her ass up against his crotch. The feel of his hand gliding smoothly across her pudgy stomach made her grin like a school girl as a surge of arousal flowed through her veins. Turning around to face him, she inhaled deeply. His masculine scent had already formed a bubble around Shanae and trapped her, but now her eyes were transfixed on the breathtaking view before her.

A wave of heat bolted through her body at the sight of him. Levi was simply gorgeous. He was a manly man; very well-kept together. She never knew a plain black shirt with a few gold chains hanging around his neck could look so delicious. Even the gold watch on his wrist was turning her to putty. Levi was a walking wet dream and Shanae was ready to submerge herself in all of him.

His beard had been trimmed some. Locs twisted neatly in a design and pulled to the back. Mustache flawlessly trimmed, enclosing lips Shanae couldn't wait to taste on hers again. She'd long ago tuned the music and people around her out. When he smirked, she'd finally come to her senses.

"I see you enjoying yourself," he said, his voice deep and smooth.

Shanae swallowed hard and returned the gesture,

making Levi's heart skip a beat when she smiled. "I am. I was just about to text you to see if you were here."

"Was in the back handling some business. What's up Bia," he spoke.

"Hey!" she waved, grooving in her seat.

Levi focused his attention back on Shanae. Her beauty and aura from afar turned heads, up close and personal it snatched breaths. Shanae possessed the type of beauty that made you take a second look. Having niggas tapping their homeboys on the arm to sneak a glance as she walked by. From her massive afro, to the rich color of her mocha brown skin and infectious smile, Levi would be damned if another man in his establishment pushed up on her. He'd peeped the lustful gazes from almost every man in the spot and he wasn't going for it. Looking was one thing, but approaching her was out of line.

"You look so damn good," he damn near growled.

Shying away, Shanae turned her face out of his direct eyesight. He was one to talk. Gently, he grabbed her chin making her look up at him.

"What? I can't compliment you?"

"Yes. It's just... everything with you is so intense," she admitted shamefaced.

His words. His voice. His smell. His look. His stance. The placement of his hand on the small of her back. It was all so electrifying and terrifying to her in the same breath.

Levi, enamored by her honesty, licked his lips. "As it should be. When it's not, that's when we'll have a problem. You want a problem with me?" he teased, a hint of caution laced through his words.

Hovering over her, Levi's honey golden eyes commanded every inch of Shanae's being. Entranced, she bit her bottom lip and nodded sheepishly.

"Maybe."

He gave her a panty-drenching smirk and whispered closely to her ear. "Problems with me get you punished. That's what you want?"

She couldn't reply. Verbally, her words were clogged in the back of her throat. Her limbs trembled as she nodded, not quite sure what she was getting herself into, but willing to go along for the ride. Placing a kiss in the spot right below her ear lobe, Shanae's knees weakened and his hold on her tightened.

"Don't get weak on me now. I need you to save all your strength for later," he told her, before pulling away.

Later? Shanae thought. *I need to gather all of my strength right now. I about passed out.*

Lost in his lustful gaze, Levi tugged at one of her curly tendrils. "You hear me?"

"Y-Yeah. I hear you. I'm proud of you," she said,

changing the subject before their conversation could go any further.

"Thank you. Y'all want some food or something? I can call an order back."

"I think that's our food right there," Shanae acknowledged as a waitress walked their way.

Baskets of wings, waffle fries, mozzarella sticks, and tacos were placed on the table. "Can I get you ladies anything else?"

Chewing on one of the fries Bia said, "Yes. Some ranch, honey mustard, and sour cream please."

"Gotcha. Any refills on drinks?"

"Yes. For both of us." Shanae cut her eyes Bia's way and she shrugged with a smirk. "What? You said you wanted to go out and have drinks, so that's what we're going to do."

"Drink and eat up," Levi told them. "Everything's on me for the night and whenever y'all come in here."

"Don't be trying to butter us up. It's not working," Shanae told him.

Levi smirked. "It's not? That blush on your face could've fooled me."

Swatting at his arm, Shanae took her seat. "Whatever. Thank you for the hospitality. I'll be sure to give you a 5-star rating on Yelp."

"A'ight. You got jokes I see," he chuckled. "Let me go holla at some people, and I'll be back to check on y'all."

Shanae nodded, biting into a taco. Covering her mouth with her hand she said, "Okay. We'll be here."

Her eyes had a mind of their own as she watched him walk away. His strides were confident, mixed with that bit of gangster Shanae had fallen in love with years ago. Had she not known he owned the place, it wouldn't be hard to tell who did. Levi couldn't make it through the crowd without being stopped every ten seconds. He was well respected in the streets and now as a business owner of one the most talked about and visited bars, Levi's name would be mentioned amongst the greats when it was his time to leave this Earth.

"He is in love with you," Bia tossed out of the blue.

Mid-bite, Shanae placed her taco down. "Why you say that?"

"You can't tell me you didn't see the way he was gawking at you. He wasn't looking anywhere near me and I felt the intensity. I'm telling you," she chewed and swallowed. "He's either in love or damn near close to it."

Shanae wasn't paying Bia any mind. There was no way Levi could be in love with her. That was such a sacred word in her opinion and didn't need to be thrown out there for the hell of it.

"I doubt it. We don't even know each other like that anymore."

"So, because he doesn't know you like that means he can't love you? That's a weird logic, but okay. I'll drop it for now, but only because I'm going to love seeing the look on your face when my observation is right."

"Yes, let's drop it. No one wants to talk about love and all that other mess while we're trying to get drunk and have fun."

Bia looked up at her from her plate and smiled. "Alright. Let's make a toast," she said grabbing ahold of her fresh drink. Shanae did the same.

"A toast to what?"

"A fresh start, fun night, and no talking about love and all that other mess," Bia mocked.

"Now that I can agree on," Shanae said holding her drink in the air as they clinked glasses.

"Cheers!"

Shanae wasn't sure how many shots they'd taken, but it was hours later and she and Bia had shouted cheers more times than she could recall. It was closing time and only a handful of people were left mingling. She and Bia being a part of the crowd. While Shanae sat in the booth trying to get her bearings together and sobering up, Bia was at the DJ's booth harassing him to play her song. The same song he'd already played on repeat thrice.

"If she doesn't leave him alone," Shanae giggled to herself.

Behind the bar, Levi shook his head. Giving out orders to the shift manager on duty, he made sure his staff was good for the night. Though the beachside establishment had been passed down to him, he cherished it as if it were his own from jump. His cousin, Arsenio, had laced him with so much game about the streets and to see him be able to do the same with a legitimate business caused a surge of pride to shoot through his core.

He'd barely made it out of the streets and hadn't it not been for his Godfearing grandmother, he'd probably be dead or in jail. The fact that he was alive and still had his freedom meant more to him that anyone would know. To go legit, make damn good money by doing so and still receive the love and respect from the streets years later? Levi was mad he'd doubted Arsenio and his cousins for so long.

"Y'all gon' be straight for the night?" He asked his crew.

"Yeah. We got it," the manager, Sully spoke. "Go ahead and get your woman. You've been trying to get back to her all night."

Levi smirked. *Damn. Was I that obvious?* "A'ight. Don't forget to check the locks. Can't have no mothafuckas running up in here."

"Run up in here and get shot," Sully spoke evenly. They kept a gun on standby just in case.

After bagging up the money he planned to deposit in the morning, he made his was over to Shanae. Feeling his presence, she slowly turned to face him. A lazy grin covered her face.

"Hey," she spoke softly, licking her lips.

"Y'all about ready to go?"

Shanae glanced toward the dancefloor. "Um, I've been ready."

"Your girl having the time of her life," he chuckled.

"I see. She drove, but I know she won't be able to drive back."

"I know you don't think you about to drive," Levi stated.

"I'm not drunk and she doesn't live *that* far from here.

Levi shook his head. "Nah. Don't matter. You been tossing back shots all night. You never know how drunk you are until you get behind the wheel. I'm not letting you kill yourself or somebody else."

His concern for her made Shanae smile. "Okay," she agreed with ease. "Let me get her phone to call her boyfriend. He'll come and get us."

"He'll come and get her. You coming with me."

Shanae's left brow elevated. "Are you asking or telling?"

"You already know the answer to that. Call her nigga up. I'm ready to relax."

Just as Shanae was getting ready to fetch Bia, she bounced over to the booth with a grin on her face.

"Aww, it's time to go?" she whined. "I was just getting started."

Shanae snickered and held her hand out. "Hand me your phone so I can call Mitch."

"Call him for what? We're having a girls night and he does not need to interrupt us."

"Bia, the bar is closing and you're drunk. Who's going to drive you home?"

Bia frowned and chuckled when she said, "You, silly. Who else?"

A silence formed around them and Bia glanced back and forth between the two. "Oh," she quipped. "I see what this is. Your man won't let you drive me home? I thought you were staying with me tonight," she fake pouted.

Ignoring her first comment about Levi being her man, Shanae outstretched her hand further. "I can another time. Plus, all you're going to do is whine about missing Mitch. Knowing once he comes and picks you up, you won't care nothing about me ditching you."

Bia tooted her lips out in a smirk. "You shol' right," she giggled. "I'll call him."

Dialing up her man's number, Shanae couldn't do anything but shake her head at her friend. Bia loved to kick it and stayed coming through in the clutch if they were going out but make no mistake; if Mitch called or she began to miss him, she was going home. Bia was that friend in the crew who dropped whatever for her man and instead of being annoyed about it, Shanae wished she had a person she could do the same for. That person used to be Isaiah, but at some point in their situationship, she stopped caring about what he wanted.

No more than thirty minutes later, Mitch was pulling up outside and helping Bia into the passenger seat. That liquor had snuck up on her and baby girl could hardly walk.

"Shanae," she sang, holding her arms out. "I'm a bad friend?"

"No, boo. You're such a good friend. We had fun tonight."

"You're a good friend too. And a good woman. Levi, you better treat my friend right. I know you love her, so don't play with her heart. I know where you work at and will fuck you up," she said pointing her wobbly finger at him.

"A'ight," Mitch said, pushing her head inside the car and closing the door. "I'ma get her home. Thanks for having her call me."

Shanae smiled. "No problem. See y'all later."

Mitch gave her a head nod, hopped in his ride and pulled off. Shanae turned to Levi who was waiting for her to make the next move.

"You ready?" she asked yawning.

"Yeah. I'm parked on the other side of the building."

Nodding, Shanae walked ahead of him. Levi's eyes wandered from the top of her curly mane, to the curve of her waist, and stopped at her short legs that seemed to be a mile long in those particular jeans. He wondered if she'd gotten dressed with him in mind tonight. Green was his favorite color, and she was wearing the hell out of it.

When they reached his car, Levi opened her door, and she grinned while lowering herself into the seat. "Ah, a gentleman. I'll have to thank Ms. Gene when I see her."

"Yeah, you do that. She'll be glad to know she raised at least one of her grandkids to still model chivalry."

On the drive to his place, Shanae found herself somewhat anxious. She'd known Levi for majority of her life, but they were grown now. His actions at her crib and tonight let her know she wasn't getting caught up with some young nigga who just wanted to fill her head up. Levi was intrigued and to be honest wanted to see where this thing with them could go.

"You party like that all the time?" he asked her.

Shanae shook her head no. "Hardly ever. Between

work and school, I'm minding my business or in the bed. Clubbing isn't really my thing. Why? You got a problem with that?"

Levi glanced her way and smirked at her defensive tone. "Nah, baby. I ain't got a problem at all. I'm just trying to figure out what I'm getting myself into. The old Shanae was a shy tomboy, who stayed ducked in the house or hugging the block with the boys. So seeing you dressed all fly got a nigga feeling some type of way."

Shanae squeezed her legs tightly together and crossed her arms over her chest. His words were stimulating every inch of her body.

"Well, people do grow up you know."

"Yeah... I know," he spoke lowly, trying to keep his eyes on the road and not the set of thick thighs in his passenger seat.

Pulling up to his place, he pulled into the driveway and parked. Hopping out, Levi closed the gate and walked over to assist Shanae. It was dark outside, but the street lights lit the block up enough for her to peep her surroundings.

"This sure isn't the hood," she murmured as they stepped onto his porch.

"Nah. Far from it."

Levi had no problem with the hood; it raised him. But he knew as soon as he planned to move back home that living in the hood wasn't an option. Regardless of how respected he knew he was, there would always be an envious person lurking and waiting to earn some stripes. As much dirt as he'd done, Levi wasn't taking any chances no matter how many years it'd been since he was in the streets. A peace of mind when he laid his head down at night was all he ever wanted. That couldn't happen if the sound of gunshots and the thought of someone running up in his spot was on his mind.

Stepping inside, he turned off his alarm and locked his doors. As they maneuvered to the living room, Shanae smiled at the family photo he had on his TV stand. Picking it up, she pulled her phone out and snapped a picture.

"Look how young we were," she beamed.

In the photo, she was doing a jail pose while Levi, Arsenio, their cousin Flex, and his brother Coop threw up their set behind her. Shanae couldn't have been any older than fourteen at the time. All she did was hang with the boys every day after school. It didn't help that Ms. Gene's house was right across the street either. Shanae practically lived with her grandma during the summer months and cried when it was time for her to go home.

"Yo' head was big as hell," Levi joked leaning over her shoulder.

Shanae pushed him back some. "I know you not talking. Look at this baggy ass white tee you were wearing, and those baby dreads in your head."

"Maaan," he dragged laughing. "They were hella ugly, but I ain't care. My shit cool now."

She placed the picture down and looked up at him. "Yeah, they are. They look good on you."

Levi stared at her for a second and licked his lips. "Thank you. You want something to drink?"

Shanae released a heavy breath and clasped a hand around her neck when he walked away. He had better get her something to drink because her ass was about to pass out. Being in his presence, in his home had her tripping.

"Yeah. Water is fine."

Shanae took a seat on the couch and told herself to calm down. *It's just Levi. You've known him all your life. Just relax.* When he walked back in with a bottle of water for her and him both, she twisted the cap and chugged it down with ease. Between all the alcohol she'd consumed and her nerves getting the best of her, the thirst was real.

"All that liquor got you dehydrated," Levi noted, coolly drinking from his bottle.

"Yeah. So, um," she began, not quite sure what she wanted to ask him but knowing something needed to be said. "Why'd you want me to come home with you?"

"To chill."

Shanae's brow lifted. "At dang near three in the morning? Be for real."

"Is there a certain time we should chill, I mean let a nigga know. You could've had me drop you off at home, but I ain't see you make no protest about coming here until now."

"I wasn't going home. I was going to Bia's but you see how that turned out. My mama is having company so I was giving her space. You haven't wanted to chill before, but now you do?"

Levi heard the attitude all in her tone and was confused. Shanae was acting like he was some random guy she met at the club.

"You been going through some shit and I have been wanting to chill, but give you space too. You coming at me like I'm some lame ass nigga who just wanted to bring you over here to fuck. You got me fucked up," he spoke calmly, standing to his feet.

"Wait. Where you going?" Shanae slightly panicked.

"To drop you off somewhere else. You don't wanna be here and I ain't 'bout to force you to be."

She stood to her feet and stepped in front of him. With him Shanae was nervous but felt like she could still be vulnerable. It was a crazy feeling, but she didn't want to push him away. He'd been nothing but good to her since he came back into her life and she wanted their relationship to remain that way. Grabbing his hand, she squeezed it softly.

"I'm sorry. It's not that I don't want to be here... I'm just trying to wrap my head around all of this. You were saying all that stuff at the bar and looking at me all weird. You've been here for me ever since Isaiah got killed and I guess I'm just a little lost on where this is going between us. Or what it is you want from me."

Levi captured the innocence and apprehensiveness in her eyes and exhaled. "I only want what you're willing to give me. What I do for you isn't because I want something in return. I never have. Why you always trying to make something so serious? Just let shit flow between us."

Shanae shrugged. Frustration masking her pretty face. "I don't know. I'm so used to everything being forced, this is throwing me off."

Hearing herself admit that aloud made her sick. Everything, down to asking Isaiah a simple question, was forced. Since she was being honest, Shanae never quite felt herself with him after he cheated on her. She'd tiptoe around any problems they had, afraid that anything she said would make him be done with her for good. The only time she did speak her mind was when it came to his child. She hated that he acted like he never cheated, but Jazlynn was a constant reminder of his infidelities.

Shanae was struggling to not compare the two, but

how could she not? Levi was in a league of his own and it terrified Shanae as to how quickly she felt herself falling for him... again. Her teenage crush on him was nothing compared to the feelings brewing inside for him now.

"Tonight, and every other night after this, we not forcing anything a'ight? You can be yourself with me. You know that. Now, what you trying to do? It's three in the morning and I'm wide awake."

Shanae softly smiled. "Can we just talk? I want to know all about your time in LA."

"So you wanna be nosy?"

She shrugged. "Yep. Sure do."

Levi couldn't do anything but chuckle at her honesty. "A'ight. Come in the kitchen and rap with me while I make something to eat."

"I want some of whatever you're making."

He looked over his shoulder at her. "Still spoiled I see."

"And you should already know that."

While he whipped them up some of his infamous grilled turkey and cheese sandwiches, Levi let her in on his life while in LA. She'd visited a few times but hadn't been in a while. She was surprised at how he turned his life around for the better but grateful more than anything. They'd lost so many classmates and friends growing up, Shanae stopped keeping count. Two hours breezed by and

Shanae found herself cracking up at a story he was telling her.

Holding her chest, she wheezed out, "And you made her get out the car?"

"Before she could even close the door on that bitch," Levi laughed. "She catfished me like a hoe. Talking about she was 5'5" and looking for a friend. More like 4'5" and looking up at every friend."

Shanae held her stomach as tears pooled in her eyes. "You got a thing against midgets?"

"Nah. You know my cousin Ju is one, but I ain't fucking one. That shit is weird. She cussed me out so damn bad, I almost ran her little ass over."

"I cannot stand you," Shanae coughed, catching her breath. "You better not let her see you out anywhere. She gon' kick you in the shin."

"And I'm drop kick her ass," he chuckled then yawned. "Damn, it's late. The sun about to come up."

Glancing toward the window, Shanae let out a yawn right after. They were contagious. "We've been in here running our mouths."

"Right. I'ma be knocked out after this shower."

"Could you get me some night clothes to change into?"

Nodded, Levi stood from his seat. When he stretched Shanae's heavy-lidded eyes zoned in on his toned body.

Her mind flashed back to that day in her living room and she shook her head.

"You good?"

She peeled her eyes open. "Yeah. Was just resting my eyes for a second."

"A'ight. Let me grab you some clothes and show you the guest bedroom."

Standing to her feet, she grabbed her sandals from the wood floor and followed him down the hall. When they made it to his bedroom, the scent she'd been inhaling all night engulfed her. It was clouding the atmosphere of his room.

Pulling some briefs and a tank top from his drawer, he handed them to her. "This good? You want some socks?"

"Ew, no. Who sleeps with socks on?" she cringed at the thought.

"Some people," he chuckled. "Had you said yes, I was gon' be side-eyeing you."

"Well, I don't. Never have. Can I have some towels so I can shower."

He hated she mentioned showering because the visions in his head wouldn't leave now. Nodding, he walked out of the bedroom and went to a closet in the hallway. Pulling out two small towels and a bigger one, he handed them to her.

"There should be soap and some other shit you might need under the sink."

"Thank you."

"No problem. Let me show you the room right quick before you get in the shower."

Following his lead, Shanae enjoyed the view of him from the back. The way his muscles flexed with each step he took was the sexiest thing to her. *Who knew back muscles could turn me on?* She giggled to herself and gasped when she accidentally ran face first into him when he stopped at the bedroom door. Before she could blink, Levi had swiftly turned around and secured an arm on her waist.

"Ooh, sorry," she chuckled looking up into those mesmerizing honey colored eyes of his.

"Clumsy. If you wanted to touch me, just ask girl."

Shanae pushed him away from her. "Shut up," she smirked, stepping around him and into the spare bedroom. "What company you be having over here? This room is set up nice."

"None for real. I had it like an office space at first but added a bed for when my little cousins come over."

"Oh, okay."

"Yeah... you need anything else?"

Shanae glanced around the room and sat her sandals

down by the bed. "Nope. I think I should be good. If I think of anything, I'll come bother you."

Levi told her okay and headed back to his room. Taking a seat on the bed, Shanae squinted her eyes in deep thought. *I wonder why he gave me the guest bedroom.* She didn't want to sound unappreciative by his offer, but it puzzled her for a beat.

Shaking the thought off, she grabbed her things and headed to the shower. Locating everything she needed, she locked the door and stripped from her clothes. When she was done twenty minutes later, she peeked her head out of the door to make sure the coast was clear before scurrying back down the hallway. She hated getting dressed in a steamy bathroom; it only made her sweat and that was not what she was trying to do.

Neatly folding her dirty clothes, she lay them on the dresser, dressed in the briefs and tank top Levi gave her and climbed in the bed. She didn't bother twisting or tying up her hair, knowing she'd more than likely wash it tomorrow. Rubbing her legs back and forth over the cool sheets, Shanae lay there staring at the ceiling. Something about being in Levi's house, but not near him felt weird to her. She was yearning for his closeness and struggled for over an hour to fall asleep.

"I could just go in his room," she thought aloud, before

smacking her lips. "No, that's stupid. He would've invited me to sleep in his bed if that's what he wanted."

Rolling over, she groaned and closed her eyes. A good night's sleep hadn't come easy in months. It most definitely wouldn't tonight with her being in a new place. Shanae tossed and turned for the next fifteen minutes before tossing the covers off her.

"The worst thing he could do is tell me to get out," she said to herself, before opening the door.

Like a thief in the night, she crept down the hall, balling her face up every time the wooden floor creaked. If she was trying to sneak out, she'd surely get caught. Creeping up to Levi's cracked bedroom door, she gently pushed it open and stepped inside. He was laying on his side, positioned on the right side of his bed. Tip-toeing to the opposite side, Shanae slid into the bed with ease and exhaled once her head finally touched the pillow. Scooting close to his back, she inhaled his fresh shower scent and her eyes rolled to the back of her head.

"Quit smelling me and go to sleep."

Shanae jumped and shoved his back. "I thought you were sleeping."

Rolling over, he yawned. "Nah. Was on my way until you wanted to creep in here. You couldn't sleep?"

"No. Can I sleep in here with you? You know, like old times?"

"Yeah. Don't be snoring all in my ear either. I'ma put your ass right out."

"I do not snore."

Levi mumbled mhm and closed his eyes. Turning her body away from him, Shanae fluffed her pillow to her liking and finally relaxed her body. As soon as she felt herself drifting off to sleep, Levi pulled her body flush against his, draping his arm around her waist. She gasped softly and tensed up.

"Relax," he spoke in a raspy tone against her neck. "I just needed you closer to me."

Shanae exhaled and placed her hand atop his. If being this close was a sure way for them both to get some good sleep, Shanae was all for it. A smile covered her face as her eyes shut, and dreams of spending every night wrapped in his arms entered her mind.

10

S hanae was first to wake up hours later feeling much better than she had in a while. Going to sleep wrapped in strong arms, with no worries whatsoever brought a peace upon her that she missed. It was crazy what some hours of uninterrupted sleep could do. She smiled to herself when she felt Levi beside her. He'd been the perfect gentleman last night and for the past few months. He'd matured into the type of man she could see herself settling down with when it was that time.

Yawning, Shanae tried to stretch as well and froze up. The grip Levi had on her tightened and the tent in the shorts he was wearing lifted. *Oh, damn. His morning erection is all up on me.* Shanae tried not to panic. But let's be honest... this was Levi she was talking about. The same man who taught her how to kiss. Doctored and kissed the scar on her knee when she tried jumping the fence with the boys and fell. Stayed by her side through two of the toughest times in her life. Eased her worries just by a simple text or phone call. And more than anything, let Shanae be herself with him. How could she not panic?

She lay still, hoping he'd yawn, roll over, or do something besides cause the beat of her heart to thump simultaneously with the one now between her legs. When she felt the rise and fall of his chest steady, she tried scooting out the bed but was pulled back.

"'Chu running for," Levi spoke against her ear.

Sliding his nose up and down her neck, he inhaled the aroma from her body, before suffocating himself in the scent of her hair. It was his favorite part of her. Her crown. Shanae's heart rate increased as his hand glided up her smooth thigh. His briefs fit a little snug around her thickness, but Levi didn't mind. He'd wished the lights were on when she walked in last night so he could see them. When his warm hand trailed up her belly and underneath the tank top, Shanae grabbed his forearm.

"Levi," she breathed, eyes squeezed tightly together.

"Hmm," he hummed, kissing down her neck to her collarbone and repeating the action.

Shanae moaned softly and pouted. "Why you kissing all on me like this?"

"Because," he dragged his tongue up her neck, sucking

her earlobe into his warm mouth. "I love the way you taste."

Her entire body shuddered at his admission. His tongue slithered down her neck once more, and his hand gently stroked her belly. Shanae could hear the breaths she was exhaling. Levi was hardening even more behind her, not giving her much wiggle room to escape him either.

"Levi," she called out again. His hand now toying with the band of his briefs she now deemed hers. He wasn't getting them back even if he asked for them. The tank top either.

Switching positions, Levi was now hovering over her. His face inches from hers, taking in her morning beauty. Her hair wild and turning him on even more. Running her hands up his defined chest, she placed them on the sides of his face and exhaled.

"Tell me what you want," he spoke lowly.

"I want you."

"I want you too."

Her eyes glimmered with need and admiration.

"All of you. I want to value you, understand you, appreciate and cherish you for the woman you are. Learn the ways to your heart and secure it. The mothafucka always belonged to me anyway."

Shanae blinked slow and swallowed hard. She knew

he was right. Her heart... her poor misused heart had belonged to Levi and had he not left, she was sure he would've taken care of it. Taken care of her and showed her how it felt to really give her all to someone and not feel drained because they replenished her. Refilled her cup with the love, attention, affection, and the loyalty she dished out.

"It did?" she questioned.

Levi nodded and commenced to acquainting his lips with her buttery soft skin. "It did. You knew it too. Why you give what belonged to me away?"

How he wanted her to answer him while his lips danced across her body, Shanae had no clue. His manhood poked at her thigh as he continued his exploration down her body. Reaching for the hem of the tank top, he pulled it over her head. Leaving kisses on her perky breasts and taut nipples, Levi traveled lower. Shanae's chest heaved up and down as he kissed her quivering stomach.

His hands glided everywhere his lips touched and tweaked at her nipples. Levi nestled his face in the crotch of her legs. His mouth watered at the scent of her arousal. Grabbing ahold of the band of her briefs, he tugged them over her ass, down her hips and tossed them to the side. Exposed to him, Shanae gasped at the first swipe of his long tongue dangerously close to her sex.

Grabbing his head, she forced him to look up at her. "Wait," she breathed. "Is this right?"

"It will be if you let me finish. Yo gon' let me taste this pussy?"

Shanae's stomach quaked. Her bottom lip tucked between her teeth as she nodded. Smirking, Levi lowered his head, spread her legs and placed kisses over her glistening pussy lips. With her legs cocked back, he peeled her puffy lips apart and dragged his tongue around the edges of her clit.

Shanae's body jerked with need. "Oooh."

Flickering his tongue across her pearl, Shanae's body sank into the bed. Overdosing in her chocolate center, Levi expertly slurped on her pussy like an oyster. He didn't want to waste a drop or let a single swipe of his tongue miss a drop of her juices. Pushing one of her thighs back, Levi was relentless on devouring her. He'd been starved of her presence for so long, he was eating her pussy for lost time. If he never saw her again, he wanted the taste, feel, smell, and sound of her to be embedded in his memory forever.

"Oh, shit."

Cupping her ass in both hands, Levi shoved his entire face in her pussy. Drowning in her overflow, marking his territory with each flicker of his tongue. Levi brought Shanae to her first orgasm, but he didn't let up.

"L-Leeviii," she cried, pulling on his locs. "Wait! Wait! I c-can't... I can't breathe. Oooooh fuuuck!"

As her legs quivered around his head, Levi held onto her tightly and loudly slurped from her pussy like a faucet. The kind you placed your hand under and drank from. That's how thirsty he was for her. His dick strained against his shorts and only when he was satisfied, did he come up for air. Face soaked, beard dripping, and lips glossy, Levi moved upward to see her face. It was flushed but content. She was frowning and smiling at the same time. When her eyes peeled open, she was greeted by his handsome face and a smirk so sexy, she had to kiss him. Lifting her head from the pillow, she smashed her lips into his.

"Mmmm," she moaned tonguing him down.

Tugging his shorts down, Levi played in her wetness with his hand, before smearing it over his rock-solid pole. Shanae continued to kiss him like her life depended on it. And it did. When the tip of his dick slid inside her, she felt like she'd died and gone somewhere. She wasn't quite sure where, but her soul was floating away with each stroke. Helping him out, Shanae spread her legs more, opening up to him more than she already was. A second try and Levi glided inside her and lost his breath.

"Goddamn," Levi hissed breaking their kiss.

Staring down at her, Levi stroked her deeply, giving

her every inch of him. And Shanae took it. He was well-endowed; much larger than her ex. Pushing her legs back near her ears, Levi sank deeper into her.

"Ahhh," she moaned loudly, the whites of her eyes on display.

Levi tossed his head back as her back arched, sending him deeper inside her oasis. "This shit is insane," he muttered to himself.

Lowering himself, Levi came chest to chest with her. Deep slow strokes were delivered as he kissed and bit on her neck. Shanae scratched at his wide back, marking him up. The more she moaned, the harder it was for Levi to think. She sounded so sexy moaning in his ear. Her fuck faces made him wish he were recording just so he could show her how good he did her body.

"Huuu, bae," she whined, feeling another orgasm creep up her spine.

Levi couldn't speak. Stroke after stroke, her body was opening up for him. Inviting him in, holding him hostage. Making Levi crazier about her. Making him fall in love with her.

"Damn, I love you," he spoke honestly, not giving a fuck about the consequences of his words. That's how he felt.

Shanae's heart exploded the second she climaxed. Her legs stiffened and body trembled as she came... hard.

Lifting away from her neck, Levi pounded into her, chasing after his release. He stared down at her the same time she stared up at him. There were tears in her eyes and he didn't know if it was from what he'd just said or the pleasure and pain he was giving her body

On the brink of exploding, Levi's hand sank into her curls and gripped them tightly. The sounds of her wetness and skin slapping made him reach his peak that much quicker.

"Uuugggh," he groaned, and at the last second came to his senses and pulled out of her; leaving a trail of his seeds from her mound.

Stroking his nut out, he coated Shanae's glistening stomach. Breathing hard, he released the grip on her hair and grinned with utter satisfaction. Falling damn near on top of her, Shanae giggled and kissed his cheek.

"You are not light," she told him.

"Shit, I can't move. That pussy got my body weak."

Shaking her head, Shanae stroked his sweaty back, not caring that he was on top of her. Their slick bodies intertwined couldn't have been a better way to start her day. Once they caught their breaths, Shanae couldn't help but ask. If she didn't now, she never would.

"Levi."

"What's up, baby?" He yawned, ready to go back to sleep.

"You love me?"

He lifted up so he could look at her. Her skin was glowing, adding to the natural glow it already had. Her baby hairs sweated out across her forehead and eyes low. She was in her purest, rawest form, asking a question she knew her heart wasn't ready for had he not given the right answer.

"I've loved your pumpkin head ass since I was seventeen-years-old. So, the answer to your question is yes."

Shanae's heart swelled and eyes misted. "How'd you know you loved me back then?"

"You wanna have this conversation right now?"

She nodded and grinned. "Yes, now tell me."

"Fucking spoiled," he shook his head but did as he was told. "The day I was leaving for LA and you were calling my phone, I couldn't answer. Telling you face to face or hearing your voice would've made me stay. Had I stayed, we probably wouldn't be here right now."

She stroked his face. "Don't say that. You never know what could've happened."

"Nah. I know me, and back then nobody was safe. Not even you. I'm back now though and I'm not leaving your pretty ass ever again."

Shanae pecked his lips. "You promise?"

Rolling on top of her, Levi lifted her leg and sank

inside her. "I promise. Now, let me see you really take this dick. We got some making up to do."

"Okay," she moaned breathlessly.

Hours later, much later than either of them knew it was, Levi was pulling up to Ms. Sharee's house. They'd lounged around his crib all day sleeping, talking, fucking, and watching movies. She opened up to him more than she had with any man; even Isaiah. Levi was just so easy to talk to and she never felt like he was judging or belittling her. His reappearance in her life was more welcoming than she thought it'd ever be.

It was going on seven in the evening and Shanae was still about to go in the house and catch some much-needed sleep. Thankfully, her mama's car wasn't outside. She did not feel like doing the walk of shame.

"Look at you," Levi chuckled. "Can't stop yawning for shit."

"Thanks to you. My body is so sore. I'm going to sleep good tonight."

Levi scratched at his scalp and cleared his throat. "You wanna stay the night with me?"

"Um, I have class early tomorrow. I don't want you having to wake up all early when I leave."

He wasn't worried about none of that. "I'd prefer waking up to you; Ion't care how early it is. I ain't ready for you to leave me yet."

"Awww," she cooed, leaning over the console to kiss his lips. "You're so mushy."

Levi smirked. "Go pack a bag and quit playin' with me."

"Ooooh, yas. Saying it like that with all that bass in your voice. What else you want me to do?"

"Sit that pussy on my face again if you hurry up."

Shanae damn near tumbled out the car the way she hopped out. Levi shook his head with a grin on his face as she rushed inside the house. Before she closed the door all the way, she stepped back outside and told him to come in.

"I need to shower and stuff. You can chill while I get dressed," she said, walking around her bedroom, tidying up some. She'd left it a complete mess while getting ready the night before.

Levi stretched out on her bed, and Shanae tossed him the remote to watch TV. He was mad comfortable around her and for good reason. They had chemistry; the type that even after years of being apart from one another they still connected. He didn't have to bullshit with her and fake like he was feeling her just because. Not many men at his age could say the same.

Watching her swoop her hair into a ponytail high on her head, he bit his bottom lip. In the mirror, Shanae caught his gaze and blushed.

"Why're you looking at me like that?"

"Just appreciating my view." His gaze dropped to her hips and ass, and Levi shook his head. The things he'd done to her body in the last six hours were unlawful, and he still hadn't had enough.

"Un, un," she grumbled, watching him lift from the bed. "We are not doing that in my mama's house."

Levi gave her a puzzled look. "Doing what? I was about to use the bathroom."

"Oh. Okay."

Shanae's belly clenched and heart skipped a beat as he walked by her. She thought he'd surely just make his way to the bathroom and leave her be, but she should've known better. Placing a hand on her waist, Levi kissed her cheek before gentle smacking her ass.

"Scary self," he kidded and headed to the bathroom.

Smiling, Shanae shook her head and took a seat on her bed.

Inside the bathroom, Levi couldn't help but wonder what she was thinking. He knew telling her he loved her was probably a lot for her to handle, but he would forever keep it one hundred with her. Shanae didn't have to tell him she loved him back; Levi knew she did. He was going to make it his duty from this day forward to ensure she never had to search for or go without the loving he had to give her anywhere else. He was going to be all she needed... all she was missing.

When she was done showering, Shanae moisturized her body all while trying to pretend that Levi wasn't sitting on her bed. He made her so nervous but in a good way. He let her get dressed in peace, thankfully. Had he touched her while she was in the process, they'd be there all day. After gathering her bag for class and an overnight one, she slipped on a pair of leggings, a shirt that read 'No, you can't touch my hair,' and a pair of sandals.

"You got everything?" Levi questioned.

"Yeah. I think so. Wait. You are taking me to class in the morning, right?"

Levi just stared at her and blinked slowly. "Nah. I was going to make you catch an Uber."

"Oh, okay. That's fine too. My school isn't that—"

"Shanae. Why would I tell you to stay with me then make you catch an Uber to class?" he tapped her forehead with his index finger then placed a kiss there. "Use that big head of yours, ma. Let's go. I need to stop somewhere before we head to the crib.

"Okay."

Levi grabbed her bags while she locked up the house. Inside the car, she wondered where they were headed, and instead of holding back like she'd normally do, she asked.

"Where do you need to stop at?"

"Why? You afraid of being spotted out with me?" Levi asked the question jokingly, but when Shanae didn't reply, he glanced her way.

She was twirling her phone in her hand, biting the corner of her lip and bouncing her right leg. She wasn't afraid, but more like nervous. Being spotted out with Levi would give people something to talk about. Something to gossip and be all in her business about. The thought hadn't crossed her mind until now, and she couldn't help but wonder what the perfect timing to start dating again was? Granted, she and Isaiah were broken up and had been for a while when he passed, but in a way, Shanae still felt like she had to show some sort of respect.

"Damn," he chuckled somewhat in disbelief. "You still caught up on your ex, huh?"

"No, I just..." she sighed and decided to tell the truth. "I'm not caught up on him, but he hasn't even been gone a year and I'm already messing around with you. Is that wrong?"

"Was it wrong when you were riding my dick this morning?" Levi said flippantly.

Shanae's head jerked in his direction. "What! Don't talk to me like that."

"Nah. You obviously need me to talk some sense into your ass. You worried about a dead nigga's opinion when he never gave a fuck about yours. Never gave a fuck about you, but you wanna act like he treated you like a Queen," he scoffed. "If it's gon' be an issue with me trying to love you and show you the real, let me know now. I'm not competing with no nigga. Dead or alive. You can bet money on that."

His hand tightened around the steering wheel, and eyes stayed on the road. Had he looked over at Shanae with how pissed he was, she'd burst into tears. Her emotions were all over the place and out of whack. She wasn't trying to piss him off, but he's the one who asked.

"You're the one who asked me a question. Don't get mad because I told the truth," she grumbled, blinking back angry tears.

Levi nodded and bent the block. "You right. I did ask, but you sitting there like you cheating on the nigga or something. I ain't never threw salt on another nigga's game and I won't start now. I'ma tell you this though... if you keep letting people dictate how you live your life just to please them, you'll be left empty inside. If you think fucking with me is so wrong, then I don't know what to tell you 'cause I'm not gon' stop fucking with you. So, you better get them emotions in check and let this be the last time we have a conversation about your ex. You ain't his anymore."

Without letting her get a word in, Levi hopped out his

car, shut the door, and walked inside a building. Jaw damn near to the ground, Shanae watched him waltzed inside before she looked up at the sign on the building. *The Market.* She grinned despite how she was feeling.

"When did we even stop driving?" she mumbled.

The Market belonged to Mr. Wallace and his wife, Georgette. It'd been in the neighborhood for over four decades and was one of the most visited convenient stores in the neighborhood. Whenever lunchtime came around in high school and Shanae didn't want to eat what they had, she'd sneak out of school and cross the field to the store. A swarm of nostalgia filled her being as memories from back then flooded her mind. They didn't last long though. A knock to her window made her jump, stopping the trip down memory lane.

She smiled, rolling the window down. "Hey, Gwoup."

"What up. I knew that was you in here with all that damn hair," he chuckled. "How you been?"

"I should be asking you that. How's everyone?"

Shanae hadn't seen Isaiah's brother since the funeral and she wasn't complaining about it either. Finding out their brother had yet another child on the way at his funeral and not by them still rubbed her the wrong way. There weren't any hard feelings, but Shanae figured the less she saw, spoke or dealt with any of Isaiah's people, the better off she'd be. The quicker she'd forget about his dishonesty and betrayal. It was sad to imagine, but one of these days would be the last day she thought of him.

"Keeping together as best as we can. Especially for his kids," Gwuop said and shook his head. "Damn. You ain't know, huh?"

"No, but it wasn't my place to know. We weren't together."

"But still. Ion't want you thinking he was out here moving foul."

Shanae couldn't help but laugh. "There's no need for me to think; I know he was. That's why we weren't together."

Gwuop scratched at his head and smirked. "Yeah... I guess you right. But it's all good. You know we gon' show you love regardless. You still my sis."

"Mhm. I hear you."

"Who you out in the hood with?" He asked, and Shanae then remembered whose car she was in and having a conversation with.

On cue, Levi walked out of the store eating a bag of chips. Tossing a couple in his mouth, he glanced to his left where a few of Isaiah's friends were posted up on Gwoup's truck. Shanae's eyes darted from Levi to Lance, Isaiah's best friend, who was gripping the handle of his gun. She felt like she was watching one of those horror movies he used to pick out for them and was holding her breath. When Levi smirked and kept it moving to his ride, she exhaled.

Looking over his shoulder, Gwoup mugged Levi and stepped away from his car and chuckled. "Ah, yeah... that's what you on? Bro ain't even been gon' that long."

"My life doesn't end just because his did, Gwoup. I'm sure I'd be the least of his concerns with a new baby and all, so let's not play."

Back peddling, he gave her a nod and a look she couldn't quite read. "A'ight, you got it. You be safe out here. Never know who you really out riding around with."

Unbothered like a mothafucka, Levi polished off his bag of chips and tossed the bag in the trash nearby. His eyes stayed on Gwoup's truck until it was off the block. Dusting his hands off, he hopped inside and shifted gears. Shanae sat silent, trying to dissect what Gwoup's parting words meant. She knew Levi... for the most part anyway. His words had an underlying message and Levi was just waiting for her to question him because he knew she was.

Trying to see where his head was at Shanae asked, "Are you still upset?"

"Nah. I'm good now. You upset? Wanna get something off yo' chest?" he looked her way and smirked. She smiled back.

"No. I'm not upset. I understand what you were saying. It's not a good feeling when you're giving your all to someone, but it's still not good enough because of someone else. I don't want you to ever feel like that or think I don't love you enough to put you in that type of head space. I'ma get my emotions in check. I promise."

"Don't do it for me, do it for you. I'm glad you heard a nigga though, 'cause I would've been messed up having to fake cut you off," he chuckled, grabbing her left hand. Placing a kiss to the back of it, Shanae exhaled.

"You and Gwoup have beef with each other?"

"It's some old shit, but I guess he and his niggas still feel a way," Levi shrugged. "Ion't give a fuck, though."

"Why though? You're not even banging like that anymore. Are you?"

Her voice went up an octave when she asked that. He'd told her he turned his life around for the better and went legit, but Shanae wasn't so sure he was telling the complete truth now. Levi had no reason to lie to her though. So, to appease her worried thoughts he answered her question the best way he knew how.

"Nah, and if I was them niggas would've been laid out before I could step foot out the store. The streets will forever be in me, but I'm all about my business now. I'm too old to still be in the streets shooting at niggas over some petty shit. That life ain't for me anymore, I told you that."

"You're not that old."

"Don't matter. My mindset is on a different level. I could've been dead at fifteen, even nineteen before my grandma shipped my ass away. When you get to a level in life where you just want to live and not worry about someone taking that option away from you, there's no turning back. Every move you make from then on out has to be strategic and for the betterment of your livelihood. Fuck what the streets think; they ain't never loved nobody anyway."

Truer words had never been spoken and Shanae fell deeper in love with him. Instead of brushing her question off, he broke it down to her in a way she could understand and appreciate. Levi valued his life. He may have not at one point in his life and was moving recklessly in the streets, but that was little boy behavior. He was a grown man now and had to move as such.

"Okay," she giggled. "One more question and I'm done,"

"I'm listening."

"What old beef did you have with Gwoup? Maybe I was out the loop back then, but I don't remember y'all having an issue. Isaiah's his brother, so I would've known."

Levi glanced her way at a red light. "'Cause you just know everything, huh?"

She smiled. "No, but I think I know enough about you to know that type of information."

When the light changed, Levi battled on whether or not he wanted to let her in on one of the biggest secrets he'd been keeping from her for years. His guilt had eaten him up already when he moved and he dealt with it, but he never thought he'd have to bring it up again. Plus, his feelings for her were stronger. Realer. The type of shit he could tell her would break her down and he'd already seen her at her lowest. Levi would leave her alone before hurting her with the news he had. So, he kept it to himself.

"It was just some street shit. Nothing you need to worry your pretty little head about."

"You sure? I can handle it."

He looked her way and the softness of her eyes almost broke him. Turning away he nodded. "I'm sure. Now sit back and ride. We almost home."

Shanae looked at him a second more, leaned over and kissed the side of his mouth and sat back. "Okay. I hope you don't mind me staying up late. I have a test to take on blackboard and some other work for these classes. I'll be glad when I walk that stage in a few months."

While she rambled on about her studies, Levi's mind was on the secret he was keeping from her. The real beef with Gwoup was because a crew of his niggas had been the ones to run up in Shanae's grandma's house looking for him, thinking it was his grandma's, and killed her. After he laid down multiple bodies from their crew and other lives were lost, Levi was sent to LA. What fucked him up was when he found out Shanae was in a relationship with Isaiah.

His own brother had orchestrated the hit on her grandma's house, Isaiah played along like he had no clue who the niggas were behind it and consoled her the entire time she grieved for Ms. Sheryl. It was one of the grimiest moves Levi had witnessed be done, but he didn't say anything. Regardless of how close they had been, he felt like it wasn't his place anymore and that Shanae wouldn't believe him. Or worse, blame him. The detectives ruled the case as a home invasion gone wrong when really, had they came to the opposite side of the street, he'd be dead right now.

With Isaiah now dead, Levi felt there was no need to dig up old wounds. Shanae would never forget her grandma, but Isaiah's death was still fresh. Knowing she had been indeed sleeping with the enemy all this time wouldn't matter because he was gone. Levi was going to put her up on game to stop speaking to Gwoup though. The nigga was just as guilty as the shooter, if you asked him.

"Levi," Shanae whined.

"Yeah, baby?"

"You're not even listening to me."

He smirked. "I am. I heard what you said."

"Yeah? What did I just say then? If you can tell me, I'll fix dinner so we won't have to order anything."

"You was doing that anyway," he laughed and she punched his arm. "A'ight, a'ight. With yo' little ass fist."

"What did I just say?"

"You said you love a nigga." He glanced her way and smirked. "Yeah, you thought I wasn't listening. I heard you loud and clear, Pumpkin."

Shanae blushed at the pet name he'd given her. "I do though. For real."

"I believe you. I love you too, girl."

"You better. Now what you want me to cook?"

"Nothing. I'll cook while you do your homework. I'ma need you to walk that stage in a few months and I don't want no excuses."

Turned completely on by his dominance and authority, Shanae couldn't help but lean toward him. Placing her hand in his lap, she stroked his dick and kissed on his neck.

"I just love it when you boss up on me. That shit is so sexy."

"Yeah? How much you love that shit?"

Shanae licked his neck. "Enough to suck all on this when we get home," she moaned, squeezing his erection in her hand.

"Shiiiit. Let me hurry up then. I need to get your ass in check more often."

Laughing, Shanae sat back in her seat with a content smile on her face. Their relationship may not have started off the best or on the most ideal manner, but Shanae didn't care. Starting today, she was going to live for herself and no one else. Not even Levi. Yes, she loved him and appreciated him more than he probably knew, but Shanae wanted to get back to the old her before she could completely give herself to someone else. Isaiah may have thought he'd damaged her for the next man, but all he did was set the blueprint for what not to accept; a fuckboy.

11

Adrenaline pumped through Kali's veins as she moved around her kitchen preparing dinner. She'd just picked Khyri up from daycare not to long ago and as soon as she got in the car, Ms. Rhonda called. Thinking she was calling for her grandson, Kali answered and now she was mad she had. *Why did I even answer her call?* She thought. Ms. Rhonda was the perfect grandmother and Kali loved her dearly, but if she didn't stop calling her phone about her nutcase of a son, she was going to lose it. Ms. Rhonda didn't deserve that, but what she was saying to Kali was literally going in one ear and out of the other. Ms. Rhonda was better off talking to herself.

"He's getting better. Said you won't even reply to his text messages."

"I don't have to. That's something he and I have both discussed. If he calls and Khyri is with him, I'll answer. If he wants to call Khyri, he has an iPad he can reach his son on."

Nine times out of ten, Khyri's iPad was glued to his hand so if Erik did call, they could talk. Calling her phone had become a nuisance and he knew it but didn't care. Or was trying to show patience with the entire situation. Erik knew he fucked up putting his hands on Kali and since, she'd done everything in her power to make it known that she was not going to traumatize Khyri because he couldn't keep his hands to himself.

He'd just started back getting him on his own, without the supervision of someone in his family around and hated it. It wasn't a court order, but it was Kali's and had she found out he hadn't abided by her rules, she was going to get the law involved. She didn't care how much history they had or that he was her baby daddy. When it came to Khyri, all bets were off and she meant that.

Ms. Rhonda sighed into the phone. When she heard of how her son had been wilding out and abusing Kali, she was pissed off. He wasn't raised that way and when she questioned him about the situation, he tried playing the victim... like always.

"I understand that you don't want anything to do with him, but I can't keep playing mediator."

"And I'm not asking you to. He's your son, so of course you're going to have his back. My thing is, I don't need anyone trying to convince or persuade me to move differently with him. I know Erik. I know him on a level that you or anyone else doesn't. Unfortunately, I have no choice but to deal with him for more than the next eighteen years and I hope by then, he's come to his senses. Until then, I don't have much to say to him. Especially if he's not coming to me with an apology, his act right, and changed behavior. 'Cause at the end of the day talking about what he's going to do means or proves nothing to me. Nothing at all."

Kali stopped pacing her kitchen floor and exhaled. She hated to get all riled up with Ms. Rhonda, but damn. She could only deal with so much. Between her family and his, she was about ready to call all of their asses off. She knew they were just looking out, but the moment she popped Khyri out, Kali knew she couldn't go running to everyone for help. Some situations she had to go and grow through on her own. This was one of them.

"Alright. Well, I guess I don't have anything to say to that other than you're right. I'll stop hounding you," she chuckled, lightening the mood. "Where's Khyri?"

"In his room. Hold on," she said before hollering Khyri's name. His little feet pitter-pattered as he ran toward the kitchen.

"Yes, Mama?"

"Hey baby."

His smile stretched across his face, making Kali smile. "Hi Maw Maw."

"What you doing?"

"Playing with my toys," he answered in a soft tone, holding his Black Panther action figure in the air.

"I need to buy you some more toys, huh?" Ms. Rhonda suggested and Kali shook her head no but knew there was no use in doing that. Whatever they wanted Khyri to have, he got.

"Yes!" he cheered.

"Alrighty then. I'll come by next week so we can go to Target."

"Okay!" He took off toward his room.

Turning her oven on, Kali placed her phone on the counter. "What day next week? I have three classes on Wednesday and have to go to work right after."

"I can pick him up from daycare that day and let him spend the night."

Kali went over her work schedule for that day. Wednesdays were her long days and by the time she got Khyri from either her mama's or Ms. Rhonda's she was exhausted.

"That should be fine. Thank you so much."

"You're welcome sweetie. Go ahead and finish cooking dinner and I'll talk to y'all later."

"Okay. Talk to you later."

Sliding the pan of macaroni she'd whipped up into the oven, Kali checked to see if her oil was ready yet. Khyri wanted chicken for dinner, like always, so that's what her baby was going to get. Connecting her phone to her wireless speaker, Kali turned the music up and dropped her first batch of chicken into the pot. Her broccoli and cut up red potatoes were boiling on the stove and since she didn't feel like cooking any cornbread, they were eating Hawaiian rolls instead.

When her doorbell rang, Kali frowned and turned her music down some. She wasn't expecting company and whoever it was damn sure hadn't called before just popping up. Turning the fire down on her broccoli, she walked to the door and checked the peephole. An annoyed smirk covered her face at the two faces on the other end. Pulling the door open, she propped a hand on her hip.

"Who y'all think y'all are just popping up over here?" she asked her siblings.

Kamilla's head was in her phone and Kross grinned. "When have I ever needed an invite? Where nephew at?" he asked, kissing her cheek. "Damn! We pulled up on the right day, Milla."

"What's up sister," Kamilla grinned walking inside.

"Nothing. What's up with you? Where you been ducked off at?"

Closing her door, Kali headed back inside the kitchen where Kamilla followed her. Kross had made his way to Khyri's room. Checking the food, Kali then grabbed two wine glasses from her cabinet.

"You know I stay at work," Kamilla told her, slipping her jacket off and hanging it over the chair.

"Besides being at work. I see you posted your boo on Instagram."

Smirking, Kamilla rolled her eyes. "I sure did and covered his face right on up with an emoji."

They laughed and Kali poured her some wine. "As you should. These hoes be trying to find any reason to not like you. Especially over a nigga."

"Men too. Ain't that what Erik was mad about?"

Kali rolled her eyes hard and frowned. "Please don't bring him up. His mama just talked my damn ear off about him and ain't changed my mind one bit."

"Did you tell Kross what happened?" Kamilla whispered and Kali shook her head no.

"Nah. He'd lose his shit if he knew that nigga touched me. Erik's lucky I didn't. Things could have been much worse, for real. He just don't know."

Sipping her peach Moscato, Kamilla nodded. "Right. Anyway... Jyro flying me out of town next week."

Kali did a little twerk while moving her chicken around. "Okay! That's what I'm talking about. Where y'all going?"

"He won't tell me. Said it's a surprise or whatever. You know I don't do well with surprises."

"Shoot, I do," Kali laughed. "Tell him to fly me out somewhere."

"Him and Rondo are boys. Mention something to him about going with us."

Kali shook her head no. "Can't go. I have class and who gon' watch Kyri?"

"You act like we don't have two parents who will willingly keep him and he has a whole daddy. Just say you don't want to ask him."

"I have class and work Kamilla. Everyone isn't their own boss like you."

"You will be, just wait. Running a business isn't easy, so don't think I have it good. I mean, I'm blessed that I was placed in this position, but you know I started from the ground up too."

"I do. You motivated me to finish school too. You and Khyri."

Kamilla smiled. She and Kali were super close, the way their parents had raised them to be. Around the time

Kali found out she was pregnant, Kamilla was opening her first beauty salon. For years she saw how scarce their city was with beauticians with quality work. She'd always done their hair growing up and her friends' hair throughout high school, so when it came time to really put some muscles behind her passion, she found her purpose.

Milla's Touch had now been open and thriving for two and a half years. She had four other stylists who worked there and they all specialized in different services. Her next step within the next year was to expand to a larger building. People from out of town had started to book her and travel, so it was only right.

"And I'm glad you are. I'm super proud of you. You can take a break sometimes. Use some PTO, have someone take notes from class and enjoy a few days away to yourself. Trust me, you'll enjoy it more than you think."

Kali thought about what her sister was saying while the food finished cooking. It sounded good, but Kali knew she wouldn't be taking a break soon. Taking a break to her meant she was celebrating something and so far, there wasn't anything to be taking days off for. If there wasn't anything she learned from her parents she'd always remember to hustle and get yours first, celebrate the fruits of your labor later. Yes, she'd been busting her ass like crazy but she had a little further to go and she was going to do it big.

"I hear you. Maybe I'll take a trip around Christmas break. I'll be out of school for a whole month."

"That's a long time," Kamilla chuckled. "You could take two trips."

"Maybe I will. Kross, Khyri... come eat!" she yelled.

Kross jogged in the kitchen with Khyri high in the air like an airplane. He laughed and begged to be put down when he saw Kamilla. Rushing toward her, Kamilla swooped him up and kissed all over his face."

"TeTe," he squealed, loving the attention he was giving her.

"Don't be kissing all on him. I don't know where your lips been," Kali kidded.

"Same place yours been, hoe."

Kali laughed. "Nowhere."

"That's what your ass better have said," Kross grumbled. "I ain't trying to hear that shit."

"Boy whatever," they said in unison, waving him off.

Taking their seats around the table, Kali fixed Khyri's plate and he dug straight in. Kamilla watched for a second as he used his little spoon to scoop the macaroni. He was so focused on getting it on there. It was the cutest thing. Kross piled his plate high, while Kamilla went light. Kali sat back sipping on her wine.

"You not eating?" Kamilla asked taking her seat.

"In a little bit. You know once you finish cooking you don't be hungry for real."

"Shit. Who said that? I be as hungry as when I started," Kross laughed.

"That's because you eat like no one feeds you," Kamilla told him.

He shrugged, said a quick prayer and dug in. Growing up, Ada, their mother, made it a habit of them all sitting down and eating as a family. Regardless of what they had going on, dinner was the time they all came together and discussed everything under the sun. Rich could've been out hustling for days at a time, but he made sure his ass was at that table with his wife and kids.

It was the small things like that that made Kali envious of some women who worked it out with their child's father. She wanted that special bonding time. For Khyri to be tucked in at night by his father and wake up to them both. She hated having to explain why he couldn't stay with him some days or why he had to spend the night with him while she worked. It was wishful thinking and as bad as she yearned for that type of family dynamic, she knew a loving environment was much better than a toxic one.

"What you looking all sad for?" Kross asked, shoving potatoes in his mouth.

Kali cleared her throat just as a FaceTime call from Rondo came through. "I'm not."

Swiping the screen, her bright skinned turned a shade darker at the sight of Rondo's face on her screen. His eyes were sitting low. Lips looking luscious as hell as he blew smoke from the blunt and licked them after. The crisp line up in his head made her mouth water. There was nothing like your man getting a fresh cut and looking all extra fine afterward.

"What up, baby," he spoke, voice thick and laced with need. He missed his girl.

"You. You look good."

"Aye," Kross said getting her attention. "Whoever that is, tell 'em we eating so call back."

Rondo's upper lip lifted as a deep scowl settled on his handsome face. He sat up some on his bed. "Who the fuck is that talking to you like that?"

"That's my br—"

Kross snatched the phone out her hand. "Nigga, who you?"

Rondo was ready to pull up until he saw who it was. "Aye," he scoffed with a slight chuckle. "You was about to make a nigga slide through there."

"This nigga," Kross dismissed. "What up fool. You mess with my baby sis?"

"Yeah. That's all me right there."

Kali's clit thumped. Rondo was making shit clear from jump that she was his woman. Had he said something other than that, she was gon' be the one pulling up on him.

"I feel it. I shouldn't even have to tell you to do right by her," Kross said in a warning manner.

"Nah. No need for the silent threats. We good this way."

"Right," Kali said, snatching her phone back. "Now what if that was my daddy?"

"Shit. I was gon' let that nigga know who I was. What else you think I was gon' do, hang up?" he laughed, hitting the blunt.

"I would have been mad embarrassed had you hung up like some punk."

"Nah," he shook his head. "Ain't no hoe in my blood. Hit me later though. I see you cooked."

"Yeah. Want me to save you a plate?"

Rondo nodded. "Yeah. Gon' do that. I'll come by once these people get up out my crib."

"What people?"

"It ain't no hoes, why you looking like you ready to pop off."

Kali sucked her teeth. "Oh, I know it ain't. But okay. Text me when you on the way."

"A'ight. Don't fall your ass to sleep either or I'ma wake

you right up. I'm hungry."

When he licked his lips, Kali knew that double innuendo meant he was coming to get more than some food. Hopefully, she could get Khyri in the tub and in bed before he showed up.

"Mhm. I hear you. Call when you're on the way."

Rondo let her know he would and she hung up the phone. Picking up her glass, Kali gulped down the rest and smiled. When she felt her siblings staring at her, she snaked her neck like only a black woman could do when someone was staring too damn hard.

"What? Can I help y'all with something?" she sassed.

"Don't make me fuck you up," Kross mumbled. "When you start messing with him?"

"A while back. How you know him is the question."

"On some money shit. And he from Highland Park."

Kali stood to fix her a plate and grab some water. "He is."

Kamilla ate in silence, not wanting the spotlight to be on her next. Her nigga was a boss for real and the last thing she needed was Kross putting her in the hot seat. He peeped her already though.

"And what'chu all quiet for? You mess with somebody I need to know about too?"

She shook her head from side to side and chuckled.

"Nope. I'm grown. You'll meet my nigga when you settle down with someone."

"Shit, I ain't gon' never meet him then."

They all laughed, but knew he was dead serious. Settling down was nowhere in Kross' past, present, or future. If you showed him a woman who could make him change his ways, he'd think the world was ending. Even though he had the perfect example, these women out here weren't built like his mama. She was solid and held their father down and learned so much from him. Nowadays broads just wanted to fuck on him, eyeball his funds, and see how much stress they could put him under. Before he let a broad think she had the upper hand, Kross cut them off. There was this one chick who almost changed his mind though. One out of the handful he'd ran through.

"He a real one though so I ain't gon' be on you like that," he told Kali. "He met Khyri?"

Kali nodded. "Yeah. The reason I'm into it with his daddy now."

"Aye, that's on that nigga. He couldn't take care of his responsibilities like a man, so he can't say shit about the next nigga stepping in. He better keep it cool."

When Kross stood to dump his plate, Kali and Kamilla made eye contact. If only he knew how uncool Erik had kept it, this conversation would've gone completely different. Kross may have joked and gave his sisters the third degree sometimes, but he'd lay anybody out behind them. He'd done it before and would again if he had to. Erik had better get his shit all the way together, and not just for himself this time.

———

K ali knew it was too good to be true. Nothing in her life ever went right for this long and she had been waiting for Rondo to slip up. It was sad, but the truth. She was so used to being disappointed, him fucking around on her didn't even come as a surprise. Kali had kept her cool the entire day. They'd gone out to eat, to the mall and had plans to catch a movie later on. There wasn't going to be any of that now though.

While they were at the mall, every store they went in Kali felt like somebody was watching them. It was an eerie feeling she couldn't shake, but every time she looked around for the person, no one was there. It was weird, but her intuition and gut were right. When they got back to her place, Kali played nice and sucked Rondo to sleep. He was lying next to her on the bed at one point, stealing all the cover, but as soon as she knew he was in a deep sleep she got up and took his phone with her into the living room.

"I'ma smack this nigga out of his sleep if he fucking

around on me," she mumbled, scrolling through his text messages.

Unlike almost everyone she knew who had facial recognition on their phone, Rondo didn't. He swore the shit was the feds and he wasn't fucking with. As if they didn't have his picture already. Kali didn't care one way or another. She stored his passcode to memory and it came in handy today.

She scrolled by a few names, none of the messages standing out to her. She stopped and tapped on a number that wasn't saved. The last text sent from it read: *You looked real good at the mall earlier.* Kali frowned. She knew she hadn't been tripping.

Scrolling upward in the thread, she went until she couldn't anymore. Starting from the beginning, which had a date stamped on it from a month after they started talking, Kali silently read their conversation. It was a whole bunch of nothing for a while. Her giving him money. Rondo flaking on her. Her begging to see him. Videos and pics of her in the nude. Kali gave the girl her props, she was pretty but so fucking what. Rondo was her nigga; period.

One message made her sit up straight on the couch. Her jaw clenched and stomach dropped at the exchange.

Stalker: So you still ignoring me? I tell you I'm preg-

nant and this how you act? You a fraud ass nigga, Rondo. I promise.

Rondo: *Man, leave me alone with that shit. I ain't ever in life ran up in you raw.*

Stalker: *Oh how quickly we forget, huh? You don't remember the night of my birthday?*

Rondo: *Fuck you and your birthday. Stop texting me with yo' weird ass.*

His texts to her stopped there, but ol' girl kept going. She was threatening him, promising to give him hell for the rest of his life and even said some slick shit about Kali. Kali wasn't nearly worried about a broad popping slick at the mouth. She was raised by some straight savages and her hands were certified. They had to be because bitches were haters and stayed trying to mark up her face. If ol' girl wanted to catch a round, it was going to be from a gun. Bitches didn't play fair and she had a son to live for.

"So he wanna play with me, huh?" she gritted, standing from the couch.

Walking into her bedroom, she stood at the side of her bed where Rondo was knocked out. His mouth was hanging open and arms tossed behind is head. The same position he'd been in when she topped him off. Eyeing his ripped body, a thought came to Kali's mind. Smirking, she eased on top, straddling him. Groaning, Rondo slipped his hands from behind his head and held her waist. When he turned his head, Kali reared back and slapped him so fast. Before he could register what was happening, she had a grip around his neck. Rondo popped up, damn near tossing her from his lap.

"What the fuck wrong with you," he seethed, pulling on her wrists.

"You got some bitch pregnant?"

He frowned. "Man, what? You tripping."

"No the fuck I'm not. You got a baby on the way and wanna be laid up with me," she hissed, tightening the grip around his neck.

Seeing the crazed look in her eyes, Rondo flipped them over in the bed and pinned her arms above her head. "Aye. Chill your ass out. I ain't got nobody pregnant."

"So, who was that bitch stalking us at the mall? I already went through your phone, so lie if you want to."

She jerked against him trying to get free, but it was no use. Rondo's hold on her was too strong. When she tried kneeing him, he put all his weight on her, trapping her little ass.

"Stay your ass still," he growled slamming her against the bed.

"I can't believe you."

When her voice cracked, Rondo knew shit was real. As angry as she was, Kali was going to be super hurt if he did indeed have a child on the way. Yes, she had Khyri, but that was different. She came into the relationship with a baby; not one on the way while they were dating.

"Man. What you about to cry for? I don't have no baby on the way, Kali."

"Well who is that girl texting you then?"

"Some broad me and one of my niggas fucked. Not at the same time, so stop looking like that. I smashed and passed her to him."

"Ugh!" she groaned trying to get loose. "You niggas are trifling."

Rondo couldn't help but smirk. "Nah. These hoes are trifling and that's exactly what she is. A hoe I knocked down, and my nigga fell in love with her. She trying to pin a baby on me. For what? I don't know, but I promise you it's not mine. I don't fuck with that girl at all."

"Well, let me ask her," she breathed out, trying to sit up.

Rondo chuckled nervously. "Now why you wanna go and do all that dumb shit, huh? You don't trust me?" Leaning over, he kissed along her neck.

"Nooo. Mooove. Don't be kissing on me with that nasty mouth."

"Shut up. My shit wasn't nasty a few hours ago when it was slurping all on that pussy."

Her clit thumped at the reminder. He'd placed them in a 69 position and went crazy on her ass. Kali wiggled but got nowhere. She was still in her panties and a big t-shirt from earlier, so when Rondo pushed them to the side and toyed with her clit, she almost gave in.

"Nun, un," she huffed, pushing him off her and sitting up. "This not how that's about to go down. Why I can't ask her if you don't fuck with her. She ain't sending them texts back to back like that for no reason."

"'Cause," he sighed, rubbing a hand down his waves. "I think y'all friends."

"What!" Kali screeched trying to hop up.

Laughing, Rondo tackled her and wrapped his arms around her. "Yo, chill."

"Nah. I'm 'bout to fuck you up for real now."

"I'm playing, I'm playing. It's a girl from our summer classes though. Y'all not friends."

Kali squinted, trying to jog her memory of the girls in their class over the summer. None stood out. "Who?"

"The intern."

She sucked her teeth. "Are you serious right now? Don't play with me."

He nodded, nestling his face in the crook of her neck from behind. "Yeah. That bitch crazy. I had her sneak me some answers one time, gave her some dick, sent her on her way and now she on some psycho shit."

Kali couldn't help but laugh and relax in his embrace.

"That's what you get. You better tell her to quit speaking on my name."

"I ain't tell her stalking ass nothing. You better keep yo' hands to yourself, that's what you better do," he said, biting her neck and slipping his hand inside her panties.

Snatching her panties off, Rondo lifted her leg, freed his erection from his boxers and slid into her gushy walls from the side. The angle he was in had him deep, causing Kali to struggle breathing.

"You gon' keep yo' hands to yoself?" he gritted, strumming her clit.

"Oooh, yes. I'm sorry."

"What'chu sorry for huh? Apologize louder." He lifted her leg higher, going deeper.

"Rondell!" she screamed, calling out his government.

Rondo smirked and shifted them so she was on all fours. Smacking her ass, he made her arch her back and toot that ass up high in the air just how he liked it.

"What you sorry for?" he said, throwing his back into it and hammering her pussy.

Kali was face down in the pillows, struggling to breathe. She still threw that ass back though. Yanking her by her hair, she gasped and moaned while cumming all over his dick.

"I'ma keep my hands to myself," she wheezed out as he clasped a hand around the front of her neck. Applying just the perfect amount of pressure to have her trembling against him.

"You better or I'ma punish this pussy every... single... time."

With each word he spoke against her ear, Rondo plunged deeper, repeatedly hitting her spot. Turning her head some, Kali captured his lips and tongued him down. She didn't remember what makeup sex was like at all, but Rondo quickly reminded her. Squeezing her muscles, she moaned inside his mouth and giggled when his grip on her neck tightened.

"D-Don't do that," he groaned. "I'm not trying to nut yet."

"So what. This my dick and I make it do what I want," she talked back, bending over on the bed.

Bouncing her ass up and down on his pole, Kali tossed her hair over her shoulder and looked back at him. The desire in her eyes and the wetness in between her legs had Rondo in a trance. Smacking her ass, his head fell back.

"Fuuuck," he hissed lowly. His own release so close.

When Kali contracted her muscles again, Rondo quickly withdrew himself from her, and in four long spurts, released over her backside. Some shot in her hair, but he didn't even notice. His eyes were squeezed shut and breaths ragged. She'd literally fucked the breath out of him. Kali chuckled to herself, kissed his lips, and climbed from the bed to shower.

"Where you going?" he rasped, barely able to keep his eyes open.

"To shower. You wanna join me?"

Rondo yawned and shook his head no. "Nah. Go ahead. Wake me up in a few hours though. I got a meeting to go to."

Kali walked back over to the bed. "You must think I'm crazy."

He looked at her like she was. "Ion't think that. Not even after that shit you just pulled," he smirked.

"Who you got a business meeting with all of a sudden?"

"With this cat named Lano. I'm trying to open up that smoke shop I was telling you about."

She nodded. "Oh. That's right. I do remember you telling me that. Well, that's good right?"

"Yeah. All that school work gon' pay off."

Flouncing over to him, Kali ran her hand over his waves and smooched his lips. "Don't forget about me when you get all well-known and famous," she joked.

"Never that. I got you always. You gon' be right by a nigga side. You and my lil' partna Khyri."

Kali smiled, loving how he always included her baby. "And, I got you too."

"That's all that matters then."

Hours later after a much-needed second wind, Rondo was up getting dressed. Fastening his watch, he brushed a hand down his multi-colored *Grind Addict* tee. He copped him, Kali and Khyri some cool little fits from the clothing company based out of Kansas City and planned to make a trip soon to rack up in person. The young dudes behind the brand were really making a name for themselves and Rondo couldn't do nothing but respect it.

"Why didn't you get me a shirt like that?" Kali asked from the bed. She had her laptop open, books scattered about and notebook ready to study.

"Didn't think you'd want this one. I'll cop you one though. You still trying to go to the movies or you studying for the night?"

Kali glanced at everything on her bed and yawned. "We can go another day. I need to study a little bit."

Leaning across the bed, Rondo gave her a kiss. "A'ight. That's cool. I'ma make some moves and call you on my way back. You need anything while I'm out?"

"Nope. Just for you to make it back safely to me. Hope your meeting goes good."

"Me too. I'll lock the door so you won't have to get up," he told her.

Kali mumbled an okay and listened for the door to close. She stared at the bright screen of her MacBook and shook her head. She had some blackboard assignments due tomorrow that she planned on knocking out today. The thought of doing them sounded good, but somehow, she'd drifted off to sleep. Knocks from the front door jerk her from her slumber, scaring her half to death. She hadn't been sleep but all of ten minutes.

Hopping up, she scratched at her damp hair and unlocked the door. Figuring Rondo had left something, she didn't bother to check if it was him or not... but she should've. Her eyes bucked when her sights settled on Erik instead of her boo.

"Is something wrong with Khyri?" she asked, trying not to panic. He'd be the only logical reason Erik had for popping up at her crib.

He shook his head no. "Nah. He good. I wanted to holla at you for a minute."

"If you didn't come to apologize and prove to me that you can be a better man for our son, we don't have shit to talk about."

She wasn't about to play these games with him. It was bad enough he popped up as soon as Rondo left. If Kali didn't know any better, she'd think his ass had been posted up outside waiting for him to leave.

"That's what I'm here for. I didn't come to argue or none of that."

Kali gave him the side eye. "And you better keep your

hands to yourself."

He lifted his right hand in the air. "I will."

Slowly, Kali eased her door open and let him step inside. She was glad she'd dressed in a pair of leggings and a tank top, so she didn't have to go change. Regardless of the fact that they had a child together, she wasn't going to disrespect Rondo like that. Walking to the living room, she sat down first and he sat across from her in the chair.

"So, what's up? What'd you need to tell me that had you thinking it was okay to pop up over here?"

Kali wasn't beating around the bush. The quicker their visit came to an end, the quicker her nerves could settle. She was playing it cool on the outside, but deep down was a bit nervous about them being alone. Erik was unpredictable and she didn't want to do anything to set him off.

"My fault. I guess I should've called first, but I knew you would've cussed me out."

"Glad you know."

Erik chuckled. "On the real, I came to let you know that I'm sorry for putting my hands on you. Not just this last time, but all the other times as well. You ain't deserve none of that."

Kali's throat began to ache. The feeling of tears coming on was super strong, but she held it together. She had to. One moment of weakness in front of him and she'd never forgive herself. He'd seen enough of her tears. Erik continued when she didn't say anything.

"I love you and Khyri. Y'all was the family I always wanted, but I fucked that up. I gotta live with that. My anger was never supposed to ruin things and it had me tripping out, doing shit I know I shouldn't be doing. And then I had my mama 'nem in my ear and was trying to figure out what was up with us. It was just a lot going on and then you never wanted to hear a nigga out."

"Erik," Kali spoke calmly. *Why the hell is he talking in circles? And so fast?*

He chuckled and scratched his neck. "My bad. My thoughts are all over the place. I um, I went to the doctor some weeks back."

Kali's heart dropped. "I know you didn't come over here to tell me you're dying."

"What?" he chuckled heartily. "Nah. I bet you'd like that though. Then you wouldn't have to deal with me ever again."

"Don't say that," she said, voice barely above a whisper.

They stared at one another. Trying to search each other's eyes for where they went wrong. Kali knew the exact moment. The minute she let him semi-control her day-to-day life is when he thought he had total control over her. When she never left after he abused her loving the first couple of times, Erik thought she surely was there to stay. Their issues surpassed what either of them were ready to face. Not knowing the problem was deeply-rooted in Erik. Which was no excuse for his behaviors but could shed some light on why he acted a certain way sometimes.

"So, yeah. I went to the doctor and let them run some tests and shit. They told me I'm bi-polar. That's crazy ain't it?"

Kali didn't mean to, but she sniggered. "Actually, it makes a lot of sense."

"Man, fuck you."

They shared a laugh. Something they hadn't done in months. It sounded foreign to them both, but they welcomed it. This conversation between them was long overdue. If they weren't arguing, they were ignoring one another.

"Are they having you take medication or anything?"

He nodded. "Yeah. That's what I wanted to tell you. Gotta get my mental together. I'm trying to do right by Khyri. Not by you anymore 'cause I clearly don't have access to you like that, and I'm cool with that. That last blowup had fucked me up."

Kali swallowed, choking back on her tears. Her feelings were hurt more for Khyri than her own.

"Yeah," she cleared her throat. "You really spazzed on

me. Khyri doesn't ever need to see us like that again. I won't let him and I won't let you do that to me."

"And I won't. On my life, from this day forward I'ma show you nothing but respect. I can't have you trying to take Khyri away from me. I'd lose my mind."

"And we don't want that. You just got the mothafucka back," she laughed, breaking the tension in the room.

"See," he grinned, waving her off and standing to his feet. "There you go talking shit. That ain't gon' change, huh?"

Kali stood up. "Now you know it's not."

"So, you accept my apology? I know you want me to prove myself to you and I plan to do that, but I just had to catch you up to speed with what I had going on."

"Yeah. I accept. Just keep your word and we'll be good."

Erik held his hand out with a grin on his face. Placing her hand in his, Kali shook it, and gasped when Erik pulled her in for a hug. Her body tensed up but relaxed when he squeezed her tight. Wrapping her arms around him, she exhaled.

"Thank you. I swear a nigga can never repay you for all the pain I caused, but I hope this eases it some."

Kali just nodded. If she spoke, she'd break down in tears. This side of Erik was the one she'd missed for so long. The gentle side. The part of him that cared for her well-being before his own. Pulling away from his embrace, Kali cleared her throat and gave him a smile.

"I know that was probably hard for you, so thank you. I'm not brushing what you did under the rug, but I won't keep holding it over your head either. Today is a clean slate. From here on out our only concerns should be the upbringing and well-being of Khyri. Deal?"

"That's a bet," he said as they slapped hands like they were homeboys.

"Good. Whew," Kali huffed. "I thought I'd never see the day when we could actually be cordial and co-parent."

They shared another laugh, finally happy to be out of the dark place they'd fallen into with one another. Kali wasn't perfect by far and she knew she had some things of her own to work on. What she appreciated was Erik taking the blame for his actions and not placing them on someone else. Even when he went off on a tangent, he came back and took ownership for his wrongs. Kali could appreciate that.

Now, she needed to try and convince him to meet Rondo. Kali didn't see him not being in her life, so that meant he'd be in Khyri's as well. To keep everyone at peace, she promised to set that meeting up sooner than later. Right now, she was thanking God for giving she and Erik peace within their relationship. Lord knows it'd been a long time coming and Kali was so grateful.

12

"Alright y'all. I'm gone," Layla announced heading to the door.

Her shift at *Shottas* just ended and she was ready to get out of there. Before heading home, she had one stop to make. Even at two in the morning, Layla had somehow fallen into a routine on most days of the week. One she wasn't sure she'd get accustomed to but surprised herself when it happened.

"'Preciate you tonight," Levi told her from behind the bar.

"You know it's all love. Don't ask me to come in tomorrow," she joked. "That's my official off day now."

"I'ma call just to fuck with you."

Layla waved him off, tossing her purse higher up on her shoulder. "And watch me ignore it."

Joking around with the crew for a few more minutes, she was walked to her car by one of their security guards. Levi didn't play when it came to his business or his employees. Their safety meant just as much to him as his own.

"Thank you Block," Layla told him.

"No problem. Get home safely."

Layla gave him a smile and closed her door. Hitting the locks, she cranked up her ride and buckled her seatbelt. Glancing at the clock on the dash, she released a sigh. She had enough time to hit up this food spot Brody got her hip to and make it to his job just when he went on break for lunch. It'd been their routine for a few nights a week since she offered months back.

When she got off work, she'd take him lunch if he hadn't prepared his own. Sometimes she just went to visit. In the mornings when he got off, he'd bring them breakfast or cook. What started off as Brody feeding her that one time, turned into a pattern. One they both appreciated. It wasn't just about the food, though that shit was hitting every time, Brody and Layla could both agree that the quality time spent was a bonus.

Glad that she didn't have to get out of the car, Layla went through *Moe's* drive-thru and picked up their order. The other reason she liked the spot was because she could pre-order and still receive the food hot and fresh once she got there. It was businesses like Moe's that would forever make Layla support her own. Some black owned business had work to do as far as customer service was concerned, but what business didn't. Well, besides. Chick-fil-A? Their employees were top tier and deserved tips for their work ethic. It was out of this world.

Stuffing her change back inside her purse, she pulled out of the parking lot and turned her music up. Most days after work she'd be dog tired with aching feet, but the mere thought of Brody's handsome face gave her a boost of energy. As much as she'd avoided him months leading up to actually realizing how cool he was, Layla felt like she'd played herself. He'd come into her life and brought some positive energy with him. Leaving his aura and good vibes all up in Layla's place and bubble she tried staying ducked inside of.

Layla chuckled at how immature she'd been with Brody and how it didn't faze him a bit. He was comfortable with checking her and that loneliness she once felt no longer resided. She went from not wanting to be bothered by him to missing him whenever he was away. That desire hadn't been present since her ex and instead of shying away from the possibilities of them being more than friends, Layla was leaning all into it.

Pulling onto the premises, Layla whipped around the roundabouts and drove a little ways before she saw his booth. Parking next to the security car Brody drove while at work, Layla started to get out but stopped when her phone rang. Her brows furrowed but for good reason. It was damn near three in the morning and no one called her this late except Brody, Amelia or... Tatum. The mere thought of her mother had Layla hesitantly reaching inside her purse in search for her phone. Peeping the unknown number she started not to answer but did anyway. *Maybe it's an emergency,* she thought not wanting to be insensitive.

Her eyes bounced back and forth between the red decline button and the green answer one. Shifting her thumb to the right she tapped the green circle and exhaled.

"Hello?" she spoke slowly.

The person cleared their throat and Layla frowned. "Yo, what up?"

Snatching the phone from her ear, Layla stared at her screen and shook her head.

"What the fuck do you want?" she spoke harshly in disbelief.

The sound of him chuckling made her nose flare. "Damn. Like that Lay? You don't miss a nigga?"

"Miss you? Liam please get the fuck over yourself. Quickly. There ain't shit to miss, but I'm assuming that's why you're calling. How did you even get my number?"

"Don't worry about all that. I see you answered," he tittered, trying to get under her skin.

"I'll be sure not to next time and block you."

"Don't sound so bitter."

It was Layla's turn to laugh. *The fucking audacity.* "Far from bitter. I just have much better people and things to give my time to besides a fuckboy of an ex. It's kind of sad that you can't let go, honestly."

"I've tried," Liam confessed, voice low losing its steely edge. Layla tooted her lips out. *I bet.* Isn't that how it always goes though?

"I fucked up doing what I did to you. I been out here dating these airhead ass broads and keep comparing 'em to you... to what we had. They ain't shit compared to you. You actually gave a fuck about me."

Layla remained quiet, unmoved by his lame speech. Confessing what the next bitch wasn't didn't matter one way or another to her. She was confident in herself. A trait she'd struggle to obtain after his shady moves in the past. It was comical that he was calling to clearly get this off his chest, when she was the one who'd cheated. Yes, her decisions had been fueled by his ill intent and no she was never apologizing either. She hoped that's not what he called for. He'd be better off calling on God; he forgave those who sinned, not her.

"I'm trying to figure out why you care to share all of this with me right now?" She asked, tone dry as ever.

"I want you to forgive me, man. Try giving us another chance. You're a good woman Layla and I failed to realize that then, but I know now. I know you was a little insecure back then and I probably played a part in that, but I can help build you up now. I wanna be a better man for you."

Confusion like none other settled across Layla's face. *This nigga has to be smoking crack. Yeah, that's it 'cause ain't no way he think he makes sense.* Chuckling, Layla shook her head. Liam was being a real live comedian right now.

"You know, forgiving you would bring you some type of satisfaction, so I won't do that. You don't deserve the privilege to ever have access to me again. Period. Everything I needed to know about how you felt for me was expressed that night and I'm good with that. We never have to speak again and when you see me out keep it pushing. I'm not sure if you've caught a case of amnesia or what, but there will never be nothing between us again. A nigga like you could *never* help me with a thing. You can't even help yourself." Layla talked her shit with ease. He'd gotten her riled up now.

Liam sucked his teeth, pissed off. "A'ight man. You ain't gotta say all that."

"Nah," Layla dismissed him and continued.

"I'ma say what needs to be heard, so listen up. I get it. You're butt hurt behind my actions, but the root of it all started with your mama. You see, she cheated on your daddy, a nigga who clearly didn't care enough about his offspring to hold his house down otherwise his woman wouldn't have strayed and been out hoeing. Ain't that what you called it when I cheated? Poor Liam, traumatized by his parents' fuckups so he tried to ruin someone else's life and make them carry his burdens while playing victim. The thing is, you can't and never will be able to ruin a Queen like me. Had you been given the love from the woman who birthed you and hurt you first, you'd know how to treat a woman. Know that no matter what you say or do, you can no longer faze me. So stop wishing upon a star for us to get back together, 'cause it's never happening homeboy. Fix that pride and ego of yours; that bitch karma likes to feed off of that negative energy. Now, sleep on that and don't ever call my phone again."

Not caring to let him get a word or breath in, Layla hung up in his face. Tapping on the unsaved number, she blocked it before putting her phone on do not disturb. She couldn't believe Liam had the nerve to call her on that type of bullshit. On another day, Layla would've been in her feelings, angry by how she'd allowed him in her space and fucked it up. Not tonight though. Brody had been watching her the entire time she was on the phone and knew her having an attitude behind some other nigga wasn't going to fly on his watch.

Stepping out the car with their food in hand, Brody pulled the office door open for her. Layla went to speak but lost her train of thought that quickly at the sight of him. She'd forever be grateful for a husky built man in a uniform. The way the material of his security vest stretched across his wide chest and broad shoulders made her stomach churn.

When he grinned, giving her that alluring stare that bored into her soul, Layla saw her future. Their future. A couple babies. A nice 4-bedroom home where he'd walk in the door and be greeted by the aroma of her cooking. A mix of Ari Lennox, Reyna Biddy, H.E.R., Jhene, and Summer Walker on the speaker system while she met him at the door with a kiss to those lips that whispered sweet nothings in her ear. Lips that assisted in speaking positivity and love into her life. Brody was a man. A grown man who Layla would gladly accept his hand in marriage. The thought should've spooked her, but it eased her once worried thoughts.

"I got something on my face?" Brody joked, walking up on her.

Layla smiled. "Hey. I was just looking at you in that uniform. You sure you can't arrest people?"

Brody's brow arched and he smirked. "Nah. But if you want me to throw some cuffs on you, it's gon' cost you."

"Hmm. What's the price?"

"My food, woman," he laughed, grabbing the bag from her hand and smooching her lips.

He lingered in her face a bit, letting her wrap her arms around him. Their platonic friendship had quickly transformed to something more. Layla wanted to steer from making it sexual, loving how sex hadn't played a factor in their connection, but goodness. Brody was relentless with the affection and attention he gave her.

"You got on that perfume that I like," he told her once they sat down.

"Do I?"

He nodded and popped the lid to his food. "Yeah. That shit smells good on you. Or it might just be you." Layla crossed her legs and he looked her way. She blushed and rolled her eyes. He smirked, knowing he'd gotten her all worked up with his words. "How was work?"

"Oh my gosh," she groaned. "Long as ever. Levi better not ask me to cover another Thursday night shift for a while. I'm exhausted."

"That's what you was in the car fussing about just now?"

Layla scratched her brow. "Nun, un. I was cussing my ex out."

"That nigga still calling?" Brody chuckled, taking a bite of his food. "What you do to that man?"

"Cheat on him."

He stopped chewing and damn near choked. Coughing he said, "Nah. You serious?"

Layla nodded. "Mhm. But it's not what you think. He basically paid someone, his homeboy, to see if he could sleep with me. At the time when we got together I told him I wasn't ready to be in a relationship, that I had some issues of my own but he didn't believe me. I was faithful to him up until that point. Like he had tested me just to see if I'd fail and I did."

"That's some hoe shit," Brody grumbled. "He paid his homeboy to hit and blowing your line down? What part of the game is that?"

"I have no clue, but I'm so over him. Been over him."

Brody couldn't even say anything. He just shook his head. Niggas were out here getting lamer by the day and he hated to see it. Liam was the worst type of nigga to be involved with. He acted like a woman scorned. When they fell into a comfortable silence, a gnawing pressure built in her stomach, traveling upward and settling in her chest. Taking an inhale Layla cleared her throat.

"Don't think I'm some type of hoe," she told him.

"Why would I think that? You think you a hoe?"

Layla shook her head no. "No, but what I just told you

345

would normally have people thinking that I was. Having their face all frowned up at me and stuff."

"Why you care what people think? Fuck them."

"I don't. I care what you think."

Brody finally made eye contact with her. Wiping his mouth, he pushed his almost empty container away and turned his chair so he was facing her. Stretching his hand to her, Layla took the notion and stepped over to him. Sitting in his lap, Brody draped an arm around her waist. Just months ago Layla claimed to not want to prove herself to anyone, letting Brody know that there was no need to. That quickly changed when it came to him though. She cared what he thought. Seeing her as some type of hoe because of her past wasn't a good look for them in her eyes.

"Can you do something for me?" he asked and she nodded. "Start putting you first. I appreciate you for keeping it a buck with me, that's solid. You a real one for that 'cause most females would've lied. You ain't most females though and to be straight up, you a gem in a world full of fake shit. Women doing whatever to get, keep, and lose a nigga. If you ain't tripping about your past, neither am I. So what you fucked ol' boy's friend, that was on him."

Layla laughed, her body slightly bouncing in his lap. "You're crazy."

"Nah, I'm for real. That shit don't move me. Everybody done cheated or got cheated on in their life. It ain't cool, but that's the reality of the world we live in. Mothafuckas are ruthless. I used to be on the same wave, but that's the past. Even if you was a hoe, you my hoe now so it don't matter," he said making Layla smile and shake her head.

Turning some in his lap, she admired his new cut. Gone were the sponge curls and in their place was a set of wavy black hair. Layla knew his birthday was approaching soon and she wondered what to get him. It was a random thought, but that seemed to be happening more than often since they'd connected. As happy as he made her, she wanted to provide the same emotion for him if not more.

"I can't stand you," she laughed.

"I know. Could barely look my way when I used to speak to you. Now look at you... all on my dick," he joked and she licked her lips.

"Not really. I could really be on it if you want me to."

Feeling frisky, Layla ran her hand across the bulge in his polyester pants. Brody grabbed her wrist and shook his head no. Layla pouted.

"You don't find me attractive? Is that why you haven't tried to fuck me?" she blurted, feelings in shambles.

"You hear yourself?" Brody actually laughed pissing her off more.

With a mug on her face, Layla tried getting up but he pulled her back onto his lap. He squeezed her thigh and kissed her cheek.

"Chill out. You already know you fine as hell to me. I tell you that all the time. Show you that all the time. I stay in your face," he laughed and she playfully rolled her eyes.

"Then what is it then? Is sex not something you want to share with me?"

"Nah. It's not that. I will fuck the shit out of you and have you acting a fucking fool behind me, but that's not what we on. As fire as I'm sure that pussy is, this," he said tapping on her head, "is what I'm more interested in. I gotta see where ya head is at before I connect with you on that next level."

"But you know where my head is at," she whined, tugging at his beard. "Just let me touch it."

Brody laughed loud. "Layla, quit playing with me. You heard what I said."

"That's not fair. You treat me all good, feed me, make sure I have good days, rub my feet and all but won't give me no dick. That's selfish. Hell, you could at least give me some head. Stingy ass."

"A'ight bet. You answer this next question truthfully

and I'll suck on that pussy until I get tired. And I can go all night. If you die, you die, so be prepared."

Layla trembled in his embrace. "O-Okay. What's the question?"

"Did you go visit your mama?"

"Awwww, that's not right," she groaned, crossing her arms over her chest.

Brody was truly spoiling her and he loved it. He made her okay with being soft around him as all women should be able to with a man they trust. She loved it too, but not right now. Layla was so fine to Brody with that frown on her face, gold septum piercing sparkling in her flared nose, intriguing brown eyes and locs hanging loosely around her shoulders.

"How it ain't right? You the one promised you were going to visit, so what happened?"

"I just haven't yet. Been kind of nervous about it and I want to talk to my therapist first."

"She's not gon' talk you out of it or into it. You gotta do it for you."

"And you! I want some head, shit. You be stressing me out," she fussed mushing his forehead.

Brody grinned and eased a hand between her legs. Layla sighed as he cuffed her mound and massaged it in the palm of his large hand.

"I ain't giving you nothing until you face this fear.

She's your mother. It don't matter if you never speak to her again, but you made a promise to yourself. That gotta amount to something. Hold yourself accountable, love."

Though she hated to admit it, Brody was right. The thought of sitting down and speaking to Tatum sounded good, probably because she was high when she mentioned it, but the truth was that it frightened her. Layla didn't want to be told even more lies and add on to her resentment. Especially if Tatum was going to give her the run around about her actions. But, she knew she had to do this. Not just for her, but for them. Layla was willing to take this risk for the sake of them building a relationship on trust, communication, honesty and commitment.

"Okay," she sighed relaxing in his embrace. "I'll do it next week."

"A'ight. Don't trip, it'll be all good. Have a little faith."

Having faith wasn't the issue. It was her temper she was worried about. Let Tatum say the wrong thing and Layla was calling it a wrap on it all. Hopefully she didn't have to take it there because deep down, the little girl in her wanted a relationship with her mother. A real one this time and not the ones she used to make up in her head when she was seven.

Sitting quietly inside of Dr. Rush's office, Layla looked straight ahead. As promised, she kept her word and reached out to Tatum. Her first thought was to meet her somewhere public but knew that'd give her free reign to run out if things went left. In here, closed in by four walls and a professional who knew Layla's past hurts, she felt safe.

"Layla," Dr. Rush called out. "Could you tell your mom why you brought her here today."

The request made her stomach flip and hands jitter. Layla was trying to muster up the words but couldn't. Not right now. Tatum gauged her mood and decided to speak first. Seeing as though they were there because of her poor decisions.

"Layla," Tatum said, facing her. The sound of her name coming from her lips made Layla swallow the lump in her throat. Over the phone it sounded desperate and much worse in person. She was pleading to be heard.

"I know why we're here. She wants answers to why I left her."

"Speak to her," Dr. Rush suggested. "Speak to her as if I'm not in the room."

Tatum nodded and reached for Layla's hand. She snatched it away and finally looked her way. The hurt that was rippled across her striking features crushed Tatum's heart. Quickly, Layla checked her emotions. She had to remember that this wasn't about Tatum, this was for her healing journey to continue. Tatum was simply a roadblock.

"Is that why we're here?" she asked.

"What do you think?"

"I think that I made the worse choice in my life, but it was the only one I had at the time."

Layla scoffed in disbelief at how easily she just lied. "The only choice? Really?"

"No, not the only one but the safest. You have to believe I didn't want to just give you up. I had to. Had I not, neither one of us would be here today."

Really focusing on her mother, Layla couldn't deny her beauty. It was somewhat shadowed by her dark past, but Tatum still had a youthfulness to her face. Her eyes were soulless though. Completely rid of the life she saw in her daughter's. They shared the same russet reddish-brown skin, mysterious eyes, slim frame and striking facial features. The only difference was their height. Tatum was much shorter, but the two could pass as sisters without a doubt. Even at forty-six, she'd aged beautifully, giving young girls a run for their money. Sad thing was, she felt much older than she looked.

"Okay," Layla sighed ready to get to it. "Why? Why'd

you abandon your only child and leave her in front of a fire station and not tell anyone?"

The icy tone in her words, words Tatum cringed at hearing, made this all so surreal. She'd gone over how she and Layla's first face to face conversation would be and this wasn't what she had in mind.

"I wasn't ready," she said before delving deeper. Deeper than Layla was prepared to hear. "At the time when I got pregnant with you, I was only nineteen. I wouldn't say it was young, but it was young enough to a girl like me who was getting pimped out by her boyfriend's dad. We'll just call him J."

Layla gulped. The action seeming as if it echoed in her ears.

"I had only been with my boyfriend for six months maybe, when he introduced me to his dad... my pimp. At that age I considered myself grown and listened to nobody. Not even Missy who was only trying to look out for me. I'd always been rebellious as a child, and worse as a teenager. Our parents couldn't tell me a thing without me mouthing off and running away.

I ran right to my boyfriend's house and into a predator that I couldn't escape for the next fifteen years. When my boyfriend went away to school I was still close with J, not realizing he was setting up the plot to get me exactly where he wanted me. No matter the amount of attention and love I got at home, it was something about it all coming from him that swayed me. I know now it was manipulation and mind games. It went from nice compliments, expensive gifts, trips out of state, shopping sprees, and so much I thought I could only get from him.

That all quickly changed though. It went from good to worse before I knew what was even happening. The sex, abuse, drugs," she trembled with tears in her eyes. "There was so many drugs. So many men. Women too. He'd dope me up, get me all dolled up and sell me to the highest bidder. Men of all calibers paid too. People in high places and even the lowest at one point as well. I was his top money maker."

Layla gasped. "There were more girls getting pimped?"

"Of course. How do you think he made all his money? I brought in all the money though. I was fresh and young, hadn't been touched by anyone but him. I hadn't even given myself to his son yet. Everything happened so fast. Literally, in the span of some months my entire world flipped upside down. I went from planning to enroll into college to being J's whore."

Grabbing a few tissues from the table, Tatum wiped the tears from her face. Reliving it all wasn't the hard part. She'd done that for years. Telling Layla it all hurt her the most but it had to be done.

"One night, I got really bad stomach pains and told J about them. He waved me off, not caring. As long as I could still work, he didn't care about how much pain I was in. One of the older woman he pimped out took it amongst herself to buy me a pregnancy test. My worst fear came to life after I peed on that stick. I was pregnant and had no idea who the father was.

When J found out, he tried making me get an abortion but I refused. Even though I didn't know who I was pregnant by, I wasn't killing my child. I just couldn't. J beat my ass so bad, I couldn't work or do anything for months. I begged him to let me keep you. Damn near on my death bed because he couldn't make any money off me and that some other man besides him had gotten me knocked up. It wasn't until my seventh month when he finally came around and started being nice again.

By that time I hadn't seen any of my family in months. I hadn't reached out to any of them and couldn't if I wanted to. I had no phone, no car, and he had people watching every move I made. When I was seven months I ran into my mama's best friend, Quita. She went on and on about how happy she was to see me, and how she couldn't wait to tell my mama. Guilt ate me up inside because I knew there was no way I'd be able to come home and explain to my parents that I'd been pimped out and gotten pregnant. I faked like I was happy with J,

355

making every excuse as to why I'd been missing and since I was over eighteen, there was nothing they could do about. Not even when I gave birth.

J didn't even rush me to the hospital when my water broke. He had a doctor come to the house and had me deliver you there. I had no family, no friends, nobody I loved there with me. Just a bunch of strangers. You were the cutest baby too. Never cried much either. J seemed to be okay with you staying at the house with all of us, until one day he wasn't. He'd stare at you for a long time, with this look in his eyes that made me so uncomfortable. One day, I was fixing you a bottle because you would not latch on for anything. I had you in your car seat in the kitchen near me and he walked in a kicked it so hard you flew out of it."

Tatum broke down crying, not understanding how J could've done that to her baby. At that moment she knew it was time to make a change. Sniffling, Tatum got herself together and continued. Layla set there in utter shock with goosebumps covering her arms. She kept having to swallow so she wouldn't throw up. The story she was telling her was so vivid, she could hardly believe it but she knew it was the truth. She felt it in her soul.

"Of course, he apologized claiming he didn't see you but I knew better. He'd done that on purpose and from then on you were attached to my hip. It wasn't until he began to threaten to kill you and me that I knew I had to get you away from him. He'd act like what he was saying was in a joking manner, but you don't joke about killing a baby. Or anyone for that matter. The last straw was when he beat me so bad, I couldn't open my left eye, my jaw was broken and he left you in the room by yourself for twenty-four hours straight. He didn't let me feed you, change your diaper or anything.

One of the girls somehow convinced him to let her watch after you and he agreed. I guess as long as it wasn't me, he didn't mind. He wanted me nowhere near you and knew not having you was punishment for something I didn't even do. His excuse for beating me and locking you in the room was because I smiled at his male company. Which was a lie because I had nothing to smile about besides you and you weren't even in the room at the time. Anyway, I tip-toed around him for the next week, trying to come up with a plan to leave. He realized what I was doing and promised to kill us again if I didn't get rid of you. Said you were slowing his money down and a distraction. Said if I – if I didn't want him to p-pimp you out to get rid of you or he would."

Dr. Rush drew in a quick breath, outraged by what she was hearing. Layla couldn't breathe. She struggled to catch her breath as tears streamed down her face. Her frame quaked with as soft whimpers and loud sniffles became the only sound in the room. She was crying for more reasons than one, but the main one being the suffering Tatum went through. First from the hands of her abuser, then her own daughter. All this time, Layla had been blaming her, not understanding that Tatum was sincerely sorry. She just needed to hear her truth.

On wobbly legs, Layla stood from her seat and eliminated the space between them. Falling into her mother's small frame, she hugged her tight. Trying to erase all the heartache she endured. All the scars she was left with. The PTSD she suffered from for so long. Layla wanted to hug it all away.

"I'm so sorry," she sobbed, breaking Tatum's heart even more.

"Sssh. It's okay. Don't be sorry for me. I'm going to be okay," Tatum soothed, rubbing her back. Remembering how she'd rock her to sleep the same way. She blinked out her own tears this time. "I need you to be okay. Don't apologize for the way you felt."

Layla pulled away but held her hands. "But I am. I've been treating you like shit and you saved me from a life I probably wouldn't have been able to survive in. All those times you tried to reach out and I just brushed you off. I feel sooo bad."

"It's not your fault. I knew you'd come around. I didn't care how long it took; we were going to hash this thing out. I love you with all my heart, Layla Marie Love. Nothing in this world was going to ever make me give up on you."

Rushing her again, Layla squeezed her tight. Gratitude soared through Tatum's chest and ran through her veins like blood. She'd waited so long for this opportunity and thanked God all morning for it.

Sniffling, Layla nodded and took a deep breath. "Why didn't you just take me to Missy's or to Grandma and Pop's?"

"I was embarrassed, but more afraid than anything. I didn't want J to find out and hurt not only you but anyone in our family as well. I know now that I probably could have, but back then the thought terrified me."

Taking a seat, Layla swiped a few tissues and blew her nose. She hadn't cried in so long, everything she'd been holding in came pouring out. All the years of the unknown, trying to figure out why Tatum wasn't around. Going through her teenaged years wanted to just feel like she belonged. Becoming a young woman and giving her body to any man who showed her a bit of attention. Getting her heart broken by Liam, the first guy she actually cared about. When her thoughts got to Brody, Layla really broke down. He was so good to her and she had no idea what she did to deserve him. Overwhelmed with emotions, she took in a deep breath and smiled before laughing.

"Whew," she huffed. "I'm sorry. All these emotions are taking over me right now."

Dr. Rush patted underneath her eyes, trying to keep it professional. "There's nothing wrong with that. Nothing at all. Crying cleanses the soul."

"Really?" Tatum questioned. "As much as I've cried, I still feel troubled. A little less now that my baby knows the truth, but still. It's been years and I don't feel healed at all."

"Healing starts with letting go. Let go of who you used to be. The person before and after the traumas. You don't need her to exist anymore. Layla doesn't need her to exist anymore. Breathe life into the new you that's trying to be born. Starting over doesn't always have to be a bad thing. It means you're willing to create a life that works for you. One that feeds your soul positivity and not the negativity from the past. You have to let it go. Both of you."

Layla stared at her mother and smiled. She was more than ready to start fresh. She'd already went into the session with an open mind and now that she felt more of a connection with Tatum, she wanted to see where their relationship would go.

"Could you forgive me for the way I've treated you?" Layla asked her.

"I never held it against you. You were never in the wrong, no matter what anyone said."

"I know but I still could've went about things differently. One of the things I'm learning through therapy and just in life is owning up to my own mistakes and bad judgment in situations. I take fault for our disconnect too Ma, it's not just all on you."

Tatum smiled and her heart softened at the word Ma. She hadn't heard it in years. "And I do too. But that's all in the past now. We have some making up to do and I don't want to spend it being sad or angry anymore. Deal?"

Layla nodded and smiled. "Deal."

Outside in the parking lot when their therapy session ended, the mother daughter duo made plans to have lunch together. Layla didn't want their day to end, plus she was starving and had a slight headache thanks to all that crying she'd done. When they got to her car, she couldn't help but ask Tatum the question she'd been dying to know.

"So, what happened to J?"

"I killed him."

The seriousness in her tone made Layla's eyes damn near pop out of her head. When Tatum smiled, Layla relaxed some but the smile didn't seem genuine. It never met her eyes.

"I'm joking," Tatum laughed. "He is dead though. I

guess all that bad he released into the world caught up with him. You know that bitch Karma doesn't play. She gets hers regardless."

Listening to her mama get kind of hood on her made Layla chuckle. They were more alike than she thought.

"You're right. What do you have a taste for?"

"I feel like pigging out on some pizza, honestly. I would offer to cook for you, but I don't even feel like it right now," Tatum chuckled. "I do cook every Sunday though. You're more than welcome to stop by."

"I will. I'll be there every week from now on. I don't eat meat though."

"Oh, that's fine. No wonder you look so healthy and thick. You're still so pretty," she said tearing up again.

"Ma, please."

Layla couldn't shed another tear. Tatum waved her off. "Okay, okay. I'm just so happy. You don't understand. I've waited years for this moment."

"Me too. But, I'ma disappear if I don't eat." They shared a laugh. "We can go to Round Table. I haven't had their pizza in a while."

"That's fine with me. Lead the way."

She told her okay but stopped when Tatum called her name. "Yes?"

"I love you. I just want you to know that. Thank you for this chance."

Layla choked back on her tears and softly smiled. "I love you too."

Tatum nodded, her heart on full. Inside her car, Layla sucked in some deep breaths, trying to get her emotions in check before she called Brody. She knew she'd start bawling all over again hearing his encouraging voice. When the phone rang for the fourth time she almost hung up, but he picked it at the last second.

"What's up love. How'd it go?"

"It was everything you told me it would be plus more. Thank you," she uttered.

"See, baby! I told you. I'm proud of you, Layla. Real shit."

She could hear the smile in his voice and that made her smile. Having a man who supported you through whatever and wanted to see you win, was the type of man you didn't take for granted. Brody had given her that extra push when she needed it, helping break the generational curse before it could manifest. Layla didn't even know it was brewing.

"Thank you, babe. I owe you so much. Want me to bring you something to eat back?"

"Nah. I owe you. I'm not really in the mood for no food. My appetite seems to have this intense craving for a fine, brown skin, poetic baddie, who I'd like to feed me something else. You think I can get that?"

The underlying sensuality of his words caused a ripple of excitement to shoot from her toes to her clit. His invitation was a passionate challenge, testing her willpower, and had she not been heading to grab food with her mama, Layla would've failed. Terribly. She was going to break every traffic rule trying to get to his place.

"Can you give me like an hour?" she asked, voice low, so damn turned on.

"An hour?" he hummed. "I think that'll work. How about you take your time and spend it with ya mama. I ain't going anywhere."

After being abandoned and placed on the backburner more than once, Layla normally hated hearing those words. With Brody she knew he meant them. She'd never get tired of hearing him say it.

"Okay. We're compromising," she chuckled. "I like that."

"I heard it's one of the keys to a healthy relationship. How you feeling though? Was it awkward?"

"At first, yes. But it got better. I feel," she paused just as a bird randomly landed on her driver's side mirror. Smiling, she watched as it flew away just as quickly as it landed. "I feel free. Like nothing is holding me back anymore."

Thinking back to the poem she wrote in her journal at seven years old, Layla knew it'd have much more meaning one day. Regardless of it being twenty-years later, those same words that saddened her before, were now uplifting her spirits and had come to fruition. She could hardly believe it, but today had changed her life for the better. It was only up from here.

EPILOGUE

Epilogue

"Rondo, Rondo," Khyri yelled from the backseat of his truck, holding his iPad in the air. "Look!"

"He can't look right now, baby. He's driving," Kali explained turning around some. "Let me see."

Khyri shook his head no. "No, no, no," he chanted, frantically waving his little hand. Shooing Kali away.

Shaking her head, she sat back in her seat and rolled her eyes. "What you do to my baby?"

Rondo chuckled. "Aye, if my mans say he don't want you to see what he got going on, then you can't see it."

"Whatever. Y'all be trying to team up on me 'cause I'm the only girl, but that's okay. Wait until my little baby gets here."

"We need to have a little baby of our own," Rondo put out there and she looked him upside the head.

"And do what with it? I'm not popping out any more kids unless it's for my husband."

"Word?" Rondo smirked.

"Word is bond, my nigga," she said in jest, making them laugh.

"A'ight. Well I know what I need to do then. Ring first, bust all in that pussy second," he said the last part in a whisper near her ear.

"Why you have to talk so nasty all the time?" she huffed, mad 'cause she couldn't do anything about it.

They were headed to Erik's house to drop Khyri off, and then to the grand opening of Levi's new bar. Over the last six months, Kali and Erik's relationship had done a complete 360. Ms. Rhonda was no longer trying to play mediator between the two. Erik's attitude and behavior toward everyone, not just Kali, had improved. She and Rondo were still going strong and Kali was in a good space in her life.

Rondo graduated back in December with Shanae and was in the process of opening his smoke shop. It'd be ready within the next few months and Kali was so happy for him. Though hood as could be, he didn't choose the route this world set up for him to take. He'd beat the odds and was securing his future like a real businessman. His big homie/mentor Lano had put him up on game to last him a lifetime and he was applying it to every aspect of his life.

"My daddy," Khyri yelled as they pulled up to Erik's place.

"Mhm. You look just like him too," Kali mumbled watching Erik walk over to the back-passenger door behind her.

"What up son," Erik beamed, unbuckling his booster seat. "What's up y'all?"

Rondo gave him a head nod. "What up."

"Did that package come to your mama's house?" Kali asked.

"With the shoes?" She nodded. "Yeah. They in the house."

"Oh okay. It should be another one coming next week."

"Why you buying him all these shoes?" Erik asked only because he told her he wanted to start doing more for him. Leaving her to not have to worry about paying out so much money a month. He'd gotten a better job and was kicking her money every week, sometimes twice.

"That's Rondo ordering all that. Talk to him."

Rondo shrugged. "A man can never have too many pairs of shoes. Ain't that right, Khyri."

"Right!" he shouted, looking up from his iPad.

Erik chuckled at how hype he was. "Exactly. Let ya

mama know. I'ma catch y'all later though. When you want me to drop him off?"

"When you're ready. He's supposed to be going to a birthday party next weekend, so I guess before that is cool."

"A'ight. I'll have him call you later."

"Okay. See you later, Khy. Can Mommy have a hug and a kiss?"

Leaning inside the window, he smooched her cheek and hugged her neck. "Bye!"

"Peace out Khy," Rondo said tossing him the deuces and he did the same.

Backing out of the driveway, Rondo couldn't make it down the street before Kali's hand was unbuckling his jeans. He looked down and smirked.

"Like that?" he asked, licking those perfect lips of his that she loved.

"Mhm. The way you carry yourself is so sexy. Make me just wanna touch all on you."

"Shiiit," he dragged adjusting his seat some. "Go ahead, ma. We got a minute before we get to the bar anyway."

Not needing to be told twice, Kali got to work. Sliding his warm dick into her mouth, she hummed in satisfaction. The fact that Rondo handled any issues when it came to Erik and Khyri like an adult had her falling deeper in love. She hadn't told him she was yet, but she was sure he knew. Though her fairytale of raising Khyri under one roof with Erik was a fluke, it didn't mean it still couldn't happen with Rondo. He was truly her knight in hood armor and she wanted to properly show her appreciation.

Across town at *Bottom's Up*, Levi's new bar, Shanae tugged at the dress she was wearing. Everything she tried on that day had annoyed her and she cried trying on every outfit. At seven months pregnant, the thought of putting on clothes, let alone having to actually do it frustrated her. Nothing fit right and she just wanted to stay home. But today she couldn't. It was a celebration and regardless of her discomfort, she was supporting her man.

"Stop," Levi spoke in a hushed, authoritative tone against her ear. Wrapping his arm around her neck, he kissed her cheek and rubbed her belly. "You look good."

"I feel so fat. Does my booty look too big in this dress?"

"Lemme see. Turn around."

Levi glanced down at her ass and discreet but soothingly rubbed on it like she loved. "Nah, baby. It's fine. You fine and my daughter got you glowing like a mothafucka. Chocolate skin just glistening and shit. Let's go to my office for a minute," he said, kissing on her neck and running his fingers through her scalp.

"Baaabe," Shanae groaned. "Stop. Your grandma is walking over here."

"She know what time it is. Me and you wasn't having movie night for no reason."

Shanae pinched his arm. "Let me find out that's the real reason you had me over there."

"Why else?" he joked. "I'm playing. I really had you over so I could stay out of trouble. Had you not wanted to hang with me all them times and just chill, we wouldn't be standing here."

Shanae poked her lip out. "Don't say that. You know I'm emotional. I can't imagine my life without you."

"I can't either," he said lowering himself to the ground.

Shanae gasped, slapping a hand over her mouth. Tears sprang to her eyes as Levi held onto her hand and kissed her protruding. Bending over, she held him close around the neck.

"Babe," she cried, soaking shoulder of his shirt.

"Yes? What'chu crying for, Pumpkin? Stand up 'fore you hurt Sage."

Hearing their daughter's name, Shanae lifted from his shoulder and shook her head. A silly grin was on her face as she looked down at the true love of her life. He didn't look a lick of nervous on one knee ready to profess his love to and for her. His locs were neatly twisted to the back and Shanae couldn't help but run a hand over them, staring him in his eyes. Those eyes that snatched her heart at fourteen and ran with it.

"You serious right now?" she whispered and he laughed.

"Yeah. You gon' let me do this?" When she nodded, he proceeded. "I could say so much Shanae. Whenever I thought about marriage and the possibilities, you were the only person that ever came to mind. The only person I wanted to share my last name, raise my kids with, build with. Shanae, you saved my life, baby. Shit, you are my life. My damn backbone, you hear me?"

Shanae was a hot mess. She nodded and placed her hand on his cheek.

"I don't want to spend another six years without you. I want to raise our daughter together and she grows up knowing that her mama was loved by her daddy. That he cherishes the fucking ground she walks on."

"You better say that!" someone shouted nearby.

"On the real, you're my best friend and I'll never leave you again. I'll never let anybody hurt you again. Let me love all that pain away and make you my wife. Can I do that?"

Shanae nodded.

"You sure?"

"Yes, Levi," she breathed out, tears steady falling.

He smiled. "That's what I needed to hear. Shanae Milan Peterson, will you marry me?"

"Yes," she said just above a whisper, wanting only him to hear her.

Her answer was good enough for him. His baby was shy sometimes and Levi knew it. Sliding the ring on her finger, he stood to his feet palming her belly with one hand and wrapping the other around her waist before kissing her so deeply it made her shudder in his embrace.

"That's right son," Ms. Gene, his grandmother said clapping. "You better had put a ring on that girl's hand."

Breaking their kiss, Shanae looked up at him and smiled so wide. Levi made her feel like fairytales were real. That all those daydreams of them really meant something. Levi loved her, flaws and all, and would spend the rest of his life letting her know that. His proposal hadn't been planned, but he felt like there was no better time than now to do it.

"You really love me, huh? This day was supposed to be about you."

"I do. And you're a part of me so, we can share it together. We share everything else."

"You think we have time to sneak away to your office?" she asked seriously.

Levi tossed his head back and laughed. "You something else, man."

"I'm serious right now."

"Let's greet some people and sneak away in an hour. That sound good to you?"

"Make it thirty minutes and it'll sound even better."

Levi kissed her lips and grabbed her hand. He was game. Across the room, Kali was calling Layla on Face-Time trying to see where her and Brody were. She and Rondo had gotten there just in time to see Levi propose and she couldn't believe it. She and Layla had grown close over the months with Rondo being her cousin and all, so she invited them to the grand opening.

"Call her later. She probably forgot," Rondo told her.

That was going to be her best bet because Layla was out of commission at the moment. Laying across Brody's bed in all of her naked glory, Layla could hardly keep her eyes open. Brody had just given her the most superb dick in her life. It was superior. Top tier. Had no competition. The head honcho.

They'd waited as long as they could to have sex, an agreement they both decided on, for as long as they could. Layla realized that over the years she wasn't just having casual sex with people. She was sharing their demons, their issues, their worries, their negative energy and all. Whenever she was done, she'd always feel worse than before. She didn't want to feel that way with Brody. She wanted them to be aligned and on the same wave and was glad they did wait.

"Kali calling you," Brody told her walking out the bathroom drying off.

"Oh shoot," she hopped up. "We were supposed to go to Levi's grand opening."

"What time it start?"

She picked up her phone. "I think five. It's only five-thirty. We can still go."

"You sure? You walking with a limp it look like." When she looked down at her legs, Brody cracked up.

"Don't try to play me," she said trying to walk by him and go into the bathroom.

Brody grabbed her around her slim waist. "Awww, you mad 'cause I put it down on your ass?"

"Nope. I'm glad actually. Now I know that we're really meant to be."

"How you figure that?"

"The vibes are still good. And, I don't have the urge to run out on you."

Brody scratched at his beard. "Is that what you used to do?"

"Yep. Run out 'cause I knew the feelings they had for me, weren't ever going to be reciprocated. Plus, it was only sexually satisfying if that. My mental was still messed up, so it put me in a bad head space."

"How you feel now?"

That's why Layla appreciated Brody. He cared about her wellbeing almost more than she did. A regular nigga wouldn't be standing here having this conversation with her.

"I feel like we should get another round in before we leave. You don't feel all this positive energy between us?" she chuckled, pecking his lips. "No, for real. I'm good. I feel like writing a poem about it."

His brow arched and he smirked. "Aww, shit. My dick gets its own poem? That's love right there, ma."

Layla slapped his arm and went inside the bathroom. "You play too much."

"What? I'm serious? How it's gon' go?"

"Step in the shower with me and I'll tell you."

Brody dropped his towel and rushed behind her, making Layla crack up. Not only could he make her laugh, but he brought her peace. Something that had been hard to come by. Not just for Layla, but for Shanae and Kali as well.

The last couple of years of their lives had tested them like no other. They stood strong and held themselves together like they knew they could. Like only a black woman could. The love they put out into the universe had taken a minute to come back around but when it did, they were blessed tenfold.

Things only happen in life for a reason, and people who aren't meant to be in your life only last for some seasons. Most come to teach you a lesson and once their assignment is done, so is the relationship. Most people never experience love. Only broken fragments of what it should be. Once Shanae, Kali and Layla realized that and glued those pieces back together, there wasn't a word their exes could tell them.

In the beginning, they didn't understand why they were going through so much. Especially behind a man. Once they reclaimed their time and remembered what they deserved, blessings began to pour in. It may have hurt at first to lose the men they thought they loved... but was it really a loss? In the end, they all won and would continue winning. Deciding to love and put themselves first, letting their past go, had been the best decision they'd ever made.

The End

ACKNOWLEDGMENTS

To the readers, thanks so much for your support! If you're a new reader of mine, welcome! So glad you took this journey with me.

I hope you took from this book what was intended just for *you*. Not everyone deserves *your* love and loyalty. As women, we have to take care of *our* hearts. We have to know when enough is enough. We have to know that it's okay not to be okay sometimes. We aren't perfect. We love hard. We shed tears no one sees. We want to give up. We start over so many times, but more than anything we pull through and make it look easy!

I pray that if you're going through anything similar to Shanae, Kali, and Layla, that the Lord sees you through. Only you know what's best for your heart and who deserves your love.

If you enjoyed this stand alone, please leave a review. Tell another reader about this book if you'd like and send me messages if you feel the need. I evoked a lot of emotions while writing this book, so I know you may want to get some things off your chest. Lol! That's perfectly fine. My inbox is always open.

Again, thank you for the support!
Love,

Bri-Ann Danae

AUTHOR

ABOUT THE AUTHOR

A lover of everything romance and what it entails, BriAnn beautifully merges complex urban socio-economic realities into her writing, and presents her novels in a way her readers can relate. Though fictional, she grasps the attention of her audience, snatches their breath away with each page, and leaves them yearning for more by the end of the book.

A lasting impression of her work, is what BriAnn strives to leave behind once the readers close out the pages. The Urban Romance genre - as she calls it - isn't just butterflies in your stomach, or dark and gritty, as describe by the internet. She classifies her writing as soul snatching, heart yearning, chest throbbing, and downright some of the most exhilarating literature one could grace their eyes upon.

OTHER BOOKS BY ME

Speechless When Love Hurts 1-3

I Was Never Supposed To Love You 1-3

She Used to be The Sweetest Girl

He Want That Old Thang Back 1-2

Juvie & Solai: A Hood Love Story 1-4

Feenin' For A G 1-2

The D-Boy Type Is What She Likes 1-2

Sen & Neicey: Life After Love

A Senful Holiday

My Heart Is A Fool 1-2

My Heart Was A Fool

The Love

Am I Good Enough To Love?

In No Need For Love 1-2

She From The Gutta 1-2

Phresh & Nykee 1-3

When She's Broken

The Story of DeLano Trevino

A Senful Wedding

Girls Just Wanna Have Fund$

Stay For A While

NEXT UP

Coming Soon

Made in United States
Orlando, FL
20 February 2024

43899082R00215